Praise for the Sophie Ka

Sex, Murder An
"Packs a bigger jolt than a venti latte at Starbucks."
—*Cosmopolitan*

"A terrific mystery. Kyra Davis comes up with the right mix of
snappy and spine-tingling."
—*The Detroit Free Press*

Passion, Betrayal & Killer Highlights
"(A) high-octane hookup."
—*Cosmopolitan (A Red Hot Read)*

"Davis spins a tale full of unexpected turns and fun humor."
—*Romantic Times*

Obsession, Deceit And Really Dark Chocolate
"Wry sociopolitical commentary, the playful romantic negotiations
between Anatoly and Sophie and plenty of Starbucks coffee keep
this steamy series chugging along."
—*Publisher's Weekly*

"The tensions between Sophie and Anatoly is thick right from the
beginning and paired with the mystery it kept me turning pages to
see if and when it would explode."
—*Romance Junkies*

Lust, Loathing And A Little Lip Gloss
"A cast of quirky, wonderful characters, a well-crafted plot and a
generous helping of snarky humor make this one a winner. Sophie's sassy first-person narration is a bonus—she's one of a kind."
—*Romantic Times*

"Humor, romance and an appealing, spirited protagonist"
—*Publisher's Weekly*

Vows, Vendettas & A Little Black Dress
"There's not a "normal" (read boring) character in the bunch,
which is what makes this series so much fun."
—*Booklist*

"If you enjoy an amusing and colorful story, this is the book for
you. The read is fast with gripping but funny suspense. I loved
Sophie's devious little mind."
—*Freshfiction.com*

Praise for Davis' Other Books

Just One Night series
"...crackling with intensity. Davis...skillfully creates an uplifting story in which sex is presented both a freedom and as a metaphor for power, and where raw chemistry is the clear winner over bland complacency."
—*Publishers Weekly (starred review)*

So Much For My Happy Ending
"Davis' tragicomic tale is both entertaining and horrifying at once....harrowing...hopeful and even wildly funny at times."
—*Romantic Times*

Pure Sin Series
"I'm absolutely in love with this series...so much passion, so much intrigue"
—*Jessys Book Club*

A Sophie Katz Novel

VANITY, VENGEANCE & A WEEKEND IN VEGAS

NEW YORK TIMES BESTSELLING AUTHOR

KYRA DAVIS

 TABLE OF CONTENTS

I dedicate this book to my son whose curiosity about the world has fueled my own. Isaac, you are a constant source of inspiration, motivation, and pride. Thank you.

 # ACKNOWLEDGMENTS

I want to thank my son, Isaac, who helped me come up with the title of this book and my mother, Gail Davis, whose input is always invaluable. I especially need to thank all of my readers on Facebook and Twitter who have done so much to promote this book, particularly Christina Makar who founded and runs both the Kyra Davis Fans and Group page on Facebook.

PROLOGUE

People who really hate you don't usually call you up for a chat, particularly if they know their animosity is mutual. Sure, an enemy might gossip about you behind your back or, if you're an author like me, they'll probably give you a one-star review on Amazon (if you're a business owner with enemies it might not hurt to check your Yelp page). But it's rare that someone will pull out their smartphone and waste their breath and battery power on private insults. Not if they have a Twitter account.

So when Fawn called, I knew something big was up. There are few people who I hate more than Fawn. For one thing, she slept with my friend Mary Ann's boyfriend, Rick. Of course Rick is what the British would call a wanker, and Mary Ann has now moved on to Monty, a better and slightly less annoying guy who has offered her love, fidelity, an engagement ring, and a very generous prenup. So under different circumstances, I would have considered Fawn's affair with Rick something to be grateful for.

But sadly it's not that simple. Fawn is one of those people who goes out of their way to make others miserable.

She's vengeful, catty, jealous, and to use Mary Ann's words, "just ewwy."

She is also in prison. She and Rick got into a lovers' spat, which ended in an attempted murder conviction. Karma's a bitch, but apparently not as big of a bitch as Fawn.

Which means that this woman wasn't using up minutes on her cell phone plan to talk to me. She was using up her week's worth of phone time allotted to her by the California State penitentiary system. You didn't do that just to be a pest.

"Hello Sophie, did you miss me?" That's how the conversation started, with her caressing my name with a soft and zealous malice.

As it turns out, Fawn had learned of a secret my live-in boyfriend, Anatoly, had been keeping from me.

Anatoly is the first man I have ever truly loved. I love his hands, I love his little half smile, I love the way his Russian accent gets a little heavier after I've kissed him a few times.

I love the way he argues with me when I'm feeling quarrelsome and the way he comforts me when I'm feeling lost. I love that after six years together the passion and tenderness has only grown.

Fawn called to tell me Anatoly had a secret or, to be more specific, she called to tell me Anatoly had a wife.

I knew when I heard those words that she wasn't lying. It would be too easy to disprove. Of course the marriage had to have ended before we met, that much seemed obvious. But why hadn't he ever told me about this? After all, I had been divorced too so I wouldn't have judged him. What kind of person keeps a failed marriage secret from the woman he shares a home and a bed with? A man who can't be trusted, that's who. A man who is incapable of letting anyone in. Ever.

It didn't feel like Fawn was torturing me with her horrid little phone call. It felt like she was destroying me.

This information was going to cost me both my relationship and the happiness I had been cultivating for years.

What I didn't understand at the time was that the information also had the potential to cost me my life.

CHAPTER
ONE

"If we can legally spank our disobedient children why can't we smack our philandering men? It's not like one group is more mature than the other."
—*Death Of The Party*

My anger was blurring my vision. I could feel its vibrating pulse as it filled me up and then oozed out, consuming the room. I know my boyfriend, Anatoly, felt it too. Or perhaps I should say my soon to be ex-boyfriend. It was all a bit surreal. This was me, Sophie Katz, breaking up with the man who I had whispered words of love to only hours ago. Well, at least I planned to break up with him. There was a small chance that I might actually kill him before I got around to making the break-up official.

"I was going to talk to you about this," he said. His dark brown hair was a tiny bit longer than he normally wore it and was slightly ruffled giving him a roughish appearance. He leaned back against the leather cushions of our couch—my couch, not ours anymore. I couldn't share anything with him now. Not my furniture, not my beautiful San Franciscan Victorian—not my life.

"You were going to talk to me about this?" I repeated, my voice was so low it sounded like a purr. Mr. Katz, my feline pet, stirred from his position on the window seat. "Did I not give you enough time?"

"Sophie—"

"After all, we've only known each other... how long has it been now, six years? Was that not enough time, Anatoly?"

"I know this sounds like an excuse," he said slowly, his gaze locked with mine, "but this wasn't a typical situation. Your safety was an issue."

"Ah, so you had to lie to protect me. You're right, that's not typical at all." I walked away from the edge of the couch and over to the built-in mahogany bookcases. They were so solid and steady... unlike anything else in my life, really. In front of me, the titles of my own published novels were lined up like oversized dominos. Words to Die By, C'est La Mort, *Fatally Yours* and my most recent release Death of the Party, and so many more. Proof that all my professional accomplishments had done nothing to make my personal life any easier.

"I never loved her, Sophie."

I exhaled loudly, observing how my breath unsettled thousands of dust particles from the shelves. "So you were married to a woman you didn't love. And I found out about it from a sociopath." I turned around. "A convicted felon who happens to be a hell of a lot more honest than the man I've been fucking for the last six years."

"We may have known each other for six years but to be fair, we didn't actually start sleeping together until—"

"Shut up!" *There's a racquetball game going on in my head. I can feel the ball being slammed against the inside of my temples again and again and again.* "When did you get divorced?"

There was a long pause. His dark brown eyes stayed on mine, but I saw something in them that I had never seen before... was he afraid? Anatoly, the man who had served first in the Russian army, then the Israeli army, only to then come to the States to become a private detective... *he* was afraid?

"Oh my God," I whispered.

"Sophie," now rising to his feet, "it's not as bad as it appears."

"No!" I raised my hands as if to ward him off. "You're still married?"

"I married for citizenship. I wanted to come to America. That was all. And the woman I married knew that."

"So you got married in order to break our immigration laws?"

Anatoly's mouth curved into a humorless smile. "You're not upset about my breaking the immigration laws."

"No, I'm upset because you're a liar! How many times have you accused me of holding back on you? How many times have you berated me for not telling you about every detail of my life? And all this time—"

"I've never asked for all the details of your past." His voice was steady and patient. I wanted to reach down his throat and tear out his vocal cords. "I've only asked you to share the present and I've done that for you. You know who I am *now*. Who I was and what I did before I met you is not relevant."

"Yeah? Well, I hate to point out the obvious, but you are *presently* married!" I broke eye contact and stared angrily at the wall behind him. There were pictures of my friends and family—my Eastern European, Jewish mother kissing my African American father on their tenth anniversary. I had expected to eventually have a ten-year anniversary with Anatoly with or without a wedding ring. I had expected a twentieth and thirtieth too. But now? What on earth was I allowed to expect now?

"So that also means that I am *presently* your mistress," I pressed on, "and in case you haven't heard, mistresses are not en vogue on this side of the Atlantic! So in the *present,* you suck!"

Anatoly sighed and turned toward the window giving me a perfect view of his profile. The illumination of the floor lamp cast a glow against his fair skin. He was beautiful and suddenly I hated him for it. Hated him for all the times I had told him I loved him, all the times I had touched his face, ran my fingers through his dark hair and asked him to make love to me.

This morning when I had woken up everything had been different. I had been tucked into the crook of his arm, my hand, light brown and in perfect contrast to his lighter complexion, had been resting on his chest. This morning the world had been exactly how I wanted it to be, and now everything was a mess, destroyed by one little revelation that was snowballing into an avalanche of revealed betrayals.

"Have you heard of the Bratva? Otherwise known as just the Russian Mafia?"

"I can't even begin to imagine how that's pertinent and I'm not at all sure I want to find out," I said. "You're married to somebody else. Perhaps we should just leave it at that and call it a day."

"Sophie, the woman I married—"

"Your wife," I snapped. "That's her proper title so you might as well use it." Mr. Katz shifted his position so as to better observe the fireworks.

"The woman I married," Anatoly repeated, stubbornly, "is the daughter of someone who is very high up in that particular crime organization."

"Your wife's a mafia princess," I said flatly. I had never known Anatoly to make up elaborate stories, but then again he had never had to. This was clearly new territory for him. My ex-husband, Scott, used to make up elaborate lies all the time. He was much better at it. For instance the first time I caught Scott in the hands of another woman he told me she was his chiropractor and was simply giving him an adjustment. Even then I knew it was bullshit, but I appreciated his creativity. But the daughter of a mob boss? Please. The man could at least respect my intelligence enough to come up with a story better than *that*.

"I told you before that I had gotten involved in some criminal activity while living in Russia. Nothing big. I didn't threaten merchants or kill the family members of people who were being uncooperative."

"Oh, so you're not a homicidal extortionist? Well, that's reassuring. I guess there's not a problem then, huh?"

"Sophie, just listen to me. The things I did—arranging for the sale of certain items on the black market, surveillance, gathering information on rival criminal organizations, acting as a bodyguard—I was good at it. And so once they found out that I wanted to go further than Israel, that I wanted to come to the States, they made me a deal. I had to do one job. That's all. In exchange, I would be allowed to marry Natasha."

"You married Natasha, the Russian criminal mastermind?" I sneered. "Don't tell me she ditched Boris after he failed to blow up moose and squirrel."

"In addition to getting citizenship," he went on, ignoring my sarcastic interruption, "there was also the promise that upon my completion of this job she would be allowed to be free of the criminal world of her family. I wanted to do that for her almost as much as I wanted citizenship here."

"Why?" I snapped. "You just told me you never loved her."

"I don't have to love someone to want to help them. My motives weren't entirely selfish."

"Just mostly selfish."

"Exactly, " he said with wry smile. "I was young, and I had been through a lot and... and America is the land of opportunity," he noted quietly. "I've always been opportunistic. And I did *like* Natasha. Our relationship wasn't entirely platonic. But our sexual chemistry aside—"

"Oh for God's sake you really stink at this, you know that?" I slammed my hand against the bookshelf for emphasis. "When you make up a lie to cover up a betrayal you're supposed to do two things, make the person you're lying to feel better about everything and give them a story believable enough to latch onto!"

"Sophie—"

"No one can do denial like me, Anatoly," I said, cutting him off. "I'm the girl who chooses to believe that I need ice cream for calcium and nightly cocktails to channel the genius of Hemingway. But even *I* can't buy this bullshit. And just so you know, imagining you having sexual chemistry with a woman you've been hiding from me *does not make me feel better about things!*"

In the silence that followed I could feel the tears threatening to come, but I managed to push them back. I wouldn't cry in front of a stranger.

And that's what this man was. This man who I thought I was going to spend the rest of my life with. When I had married Scott, I had been so young, only nineteen. In the two brief years we had been married, Scott had screwed me over big time, but it hadn't really come as a shock. Scott had been fun, and he distracted me from what had been a truly difficult period. He showed me a good time, and our impromptu Vegas wedding had seemed wild, impulsive and romantic. But did I ever think he was an upright, loyal and dependable guy? Even at nineteen, I hadn't been *that* naive.

But Anatoly—he was a different story. It's true that I hadn't trusted him when we first met. In fact, I had thought that he was a serial killer and he had suspected the same of me. Not an auspicious beginning. But eventually it became clear that neither of us were the Jeffrey Dahmer type and Anatoly and I had started to get to know each other... intimately. It took a while for us to move from casual fling to life partners. There had been breakups and arguments aplenty, but in the end, we had found each other irresistible. I learned to trust him. I didn't think he would ever hurt me... not like this. Not by lying about who he *was*.

But that's exactly what he had done. The man before me wasn't just a Russian-immigrant bachelor who made his living as a PI. According to him, he was a married mafia thug who had more secrets than I could ever guess at. It didn't matter so much what part of the story was a lie and what was the truth. What mattered was that the man I thought I knew would never have needed to say any of this. That man wouldn't have had anything to lie about! This morning I had kissed a stranger. Hell, last night I had gone down on a stranger. That made him a liar and me a slut, and now I wanted the stranger out of my home so I could stand in the shower until this dirty feeling was washed away.

And maybe I could wash some other feelings away too. Like love, and longing... but mostly pain. I would stand in the shower for ten hours straight if I thought it could make this pain go away.

"I want you to go now."

"Sophie—"

"No. I mean it." My voice was so quiet it was amazing that he could hear me. Then again, maybe he couldn't. Maybe all he had to do was look at my face to understand what I was saying.

"I'm going," he said quietly. "I'll be out of town for a few days taking care of some...some business. But I'll be back. I am going to fix this."

He turned to leave.

"You can come back for your things but not for me," I called after him.

"Ah," he said as he opened the front door, "but you're the only thing I want."

I managed to hold back the tears until the door was closed behind him.

CHAPTER
TWO

"Hooking up with one man just to get over another is kinda like kicking an alcohol addiction by picking up meth."
—Death Of The Party

"He told you he married into the mob?" Dena asked as she stared at me from the other end of the couch, her thick Sicilian eyebrows raising almost to her hairline. I had called her and Marcus two hours after Anatoly left. For those hundred and twenty minutes I had thought I needed to be alone. But the silence of the house, which had always been a comfort to me before, suddenly felt oppressive. I tried to fill the void by talking to Mr. Katz, but while my cat was a great listener, he consistently refused to add his voice to our conversations. Dena and Marcus had responded immediately to my summons, arriving within ten minutes of one another. Dena looked fierce as always. Marcus had given her a new haircut only last week and it was even shorter and more stylish than normal. Like a tattooless Ruby Rose. And her black cane with the silver jaguar-shaped handle added rather than detracted from her sex appeal. Marcus was looking rather yummy too in his cashmere, camel-colored blazer worn over strategically faded blue jeans. His mocha skin was glowing, hinting at the possibility of a recent facial. They were both making me look bad.

But then perhaps anyone could have made me look bad at that moment. I had immediately lain down on my bed after taking a shower so now my hair was not only frizzy but also shaped in a rather lopsided manner. I had no makeup on, my eyes were puffy and red, and I was wearing biker-shorts and a T-shirt with a big bleach stain on the front of it. If it had been Halloween, people would have assumed I was dressed up like a clinically depressed hobo.

"Married to the mob. It all seems so needlessly dramatic," Marcus mused. He crossed over from my fireplace and found a spot in the leather armchair nearest me. "And so dated. Wasn't there an '80s movie titled *Married To The Mob*? I'm sure that's what it was called. It starred Michelle Pfeifer. You're dating a 1980s version of Michelle Pfeifer."

"Um, not quite," I said dully as I tucked my legs underneath me and leaned back against my sofa cushions

"Well no, not quite," Marcus agreed wryly. "Anatoly's considerably more butch. You have to give him that."

"No, I meant that Michele Pfeifer was the victim in that movie. Anatoly's not a victim. He chose to marry this woman, and he chose to make up this stupid story about the mob!"

"Are we sure he's making it up?" Dena asked.

I gave her a sharp look. "You think Anatoly used to work for the mob."

"Well stranger things have happened," Dena pointed out.

"In a million years I never would have thought some psycho would try to copycat the murders in your first book, but there it is. It happened."

"OK, I'm having a hard enough time dealing with what's going on right now. Can we not revisit the ugliest part of my past?"

"You're right." She glanced out toward the street as a truck rumbled by the house. "There's no need for me to go that dark, not if all I'm trying to prove is that strange things happen. For instance, you remember when that weirdo tried to convince you that your house was haunted? That was pretty out there."

"Or the time your late brother-in-law's family went on the news and claimed your Brooks-Brothers wearing sister was a gangsta from the hood!" Marcus chimed in. "Oh, or how about that politician who was sexually attracted to stuffed animals? Anatoly having mob connections wouldn't be half as strange as that."

"No, no," Dena corrected, "that politician liked to have sex while dressed up *as* a stuffed animal. In the world of sexual fetishes that's a huge difference."

"Um, guys?" I said meekly.

Both Dena and Marcus turned to me as if suddenly remembering I was there.

"If you don't mind, I'd like to *stick to the crisis at hand!*" I yelled. "No one is currently trying to gaslight me or do a smear campaign on one of my relatives, and I'm not sitting here crying my eyes out because Anatoly tried to get it on with Scooby Doo! I'm crying because he *got* it on with a wife I didn't know about! He didn't even take the time to come up with a good lie to help me get over it!"

There was a long pause as Marcus and Dena considered this. Mr. Katz removed himself from his spot under the coffee table and left the room. My cat only enjoyed watching substantive arguments.

"Maybe we're not looking at this the right way." Dena tapped the top of her cane with deep purple painted nails. "Anatoly didn't tell you he was married and that's bullshit no matter how you spin it. But if you haven't seen or even spoken to your spouse in over six years I think it's fair to say the relationship is over, even if there is a piece of paper somewhere saying otherwise. So in every way that counts, he's single."

"Dena! He's been lying to me for years!"

Dena nodded and then fixed me with a stare. "Like I said, it's bullshit. But Sophie, you haven't always been honest with him either."

Her words hit a little harder than I think she intended them to. I wasn't near ready for her to look at this from both sides. I was so angry, and although I really wanted to deny it, some of my anger was directed inward. How could I have missed this? I pressed my fingers to my temples. It still felt like a racquetball was ricocheting around in there and I was moving past dizzy and into serious nausea.

From the corner of my eye, I caught Marcus shooting Dena a quick warning look which Dena acknowledged with a shrug and a sigh. "I'm not taking his side," she said carefully, "but maybe we should consider the possibility that Anatoly left his wife without taking the time to fill out any divorce papers was because he just needed to bounce without pissing off the in-laws. If I was married to someone who had mob connections, I wouldn't be pushing for alimony when things went south."

"You *really* think Anatoly married into the mob... that he would actually do something that stupid?"

"Well he's a man, so yes, I think he's capable of doing incredibly stupid things."

"I'm sitting right here, Dena," Marcus said dryly.

"A straight man," Dena corrected herself, but her tone implied that the caveat was only added to placate him. "Anyway, I think marriage, in general, is rather stupid. I'd rather get it on with a fat Marlon Brando than let someone rope me into domestic servitude."

Underneath the flood of turbulent emotion was a nagging feeling. Had Fawn told me that Anatoly had married into... into something? I had been so shocked by the call I hadn't been able to absorb every word. "If he was really on the run from the mob shouldn't he be running?" I asked. "He's been in San Francisco for—"

"Six years," Dena finished for me. "Yeah, but maybe he settled here because it's the last place the mob would look."

"Why would San Francisco be the last place the mob would look?" Marcus asked.

"I don't know, but in New York, Chicago and Vegas you occasionally hear about some sort of mafia something. But the mafia never makes headlines here in San Francisco. Maybe they don't like our weather."

"Right," Marcus said smoothly, "or maybe they're just rainbow-phobic."

"None of this matters," I moaned. "What matters is that Anatoly's been on my case to be more open with him and all the while he's been hiding a wife. That's why he didn't want to marry me."

"Okay, hold up. You didn't want to marry him either," Dena pointed out. "You said you were done with marriage and that you would rather live with him without a government certificate."

"Would you stop being so damn reasonable and start indulging my righteous indignation?" I cried and then buried my face in my hands and started sobbing in earnest. I heard Marcus get up from his seat and perch himself on the armrest nearest me so he could make soothing little circles on my back.

"Look at me! I'm a mess," I choked when I finally found my voice.

"We're all allowed to be messy every once in a while," Marcus cooed. "There'll be plenty of time to tidy up your life later."

"The thing is," I moaned, "if he had told me right at the get-go that he had an estranged wife who he never planned to reconcile with, I might have found a way to be okay with it because, well, you know," I reached out and took Dena's hand in mine, "you're right, I'm not exactly biting at the bit to get married again. Even if he had told me about all this a year or two into our relationship, we might have found a way to work through it. But he never *did* tell me! He was never going to say a damn word, and so I had to find out about his wife from the person who has caused more pain to those I love than anyone else on earth."

"Yes," Dena said darkly, "that part is seriously inexcusable."

"It's the lying," I insisted again. "The total deceit and the secretiveness. You know he's been getting calls lately, calls that he's been trying to conceal from me. He said it was business, but now I think it was her."

Marcus lifted his eyebrows. "Why would she start calling out of the blue after six or more years?"

"I don't know, maybe she found him on Facebook," I snapped.

"Ah, another good Facebook security tip," Marcus said sagely. "If you're running from the mob set your profile page to private."

I almost smiled. Almost. "I just have this feeling that the calls were coming from her," I continued. "There's a reason this whole thing is coming to a head now. I just know she's not totally out of his life. I know it the way I knew that he was keeping a secret from me. I should have listened to my gut from the start." I shook my head vehemently. "God, I feel like such an idiot! Like I'm one of those women you see on daytime talk shows who needs to learn how to stop being a victim."

"Honey," Marcus said with a sigh, "who in their right mind thinks their live-in-boyfriend is secretly married? And when you *did* find out you kicked his hot ass to the curb."

"That's not being a victim," Dena agreed. "That's taking care of yourself."

"And now I'm alone."

"No," Dena said firmly, squeezing my hand a little tighter. "Never alone."

"I know. I have family, friends, a reasonably affectionate cat… but it's not the same."

"Yeah, I get that," Dena said, then cursed softly under her breath. "This whole thing is so fucked up. How did Anatoly react when you confronted him?"

Immediately the look on his face flashed before my eyes.

There was the façade of cool, but it had been thin this time, even transparent, and behind it, I had seen the pain both pure and intense. These were *his* lies that we were dealing with. *His* manipulations and yet when I had confronted him it was *me* who was causing that pain.

I started crying harder, and Dena and Marcus slipped into silence as they waited for me to get it out of my system.

When the sobs were finally reduced to sniffles, Dena put her cane gently on the redwood coffee table before scooting even closer to me and putting our joined hands in her lap. "You'll get through this."

"You sure?"

"Yes, I'm sure."

I used the back of my free hand to wipe away my slowing tears and stared out the bay window. The street light outside my house flickered and died and suddenly all I could see of the outside world was darkness.

"I'm sorry I defended him," Dena said. "I shouldn't have done that."

"It's okay," I said, quietly.

"No, it's not. It's not what you needed to hear." She paused and then took in a quick, startled breath. "Wait! I know what you *really* need!"

"What?"

"You need a three-day free pass to Vegas' annual sex toy trade show!"

Marcus coughed softly and turned away to hide a smile. From anyone else, this would have sounded insane. But this was Dena. I kept my eyes on the window. "I don't think that's what I need."

"Of course it is. I go every year just so I can keep the

inventory of Guilty Pleasures up to date with the latest and greatest in sexually deviant technology. It's a fantastic show, Sophie, and it starts this Friday!"

"Dena—"

"This is too much all at once," Dena pressed on. "If you don't distract yourself, you're going to sit here and go over it all again and again and again. You'll over-analyze."

"Oh God, I don't even know if it's possible to overthink this thing. It's all so convoluted."

"Please. You can overthink *anything*. But the good news is that it's very hard to think in Vegas. The whole city is designed to encourage people to turn off their brains. Oh, and *Puppetry of the Penis* is going to be in Vegas this weekend!"

"No!" Marcus gasped. "They never perform in Vegas!"

I looked at Marcus in confusion and then back at Dena. "*Puppetry of the Penis*?"

"Yeah, it's a traveling show with a bunch of guys who can tie their dicks into a whole bunch of funky shapes, like origami. I already have two tickets. I was going to take Jason, but you know what? He can play with his own penis. You have to come, Sophie. It'll be better than Zoloft."

"I just broke up with the love of my life! What about this situation makes you think I would want to watch a whole bunch of guys on stage tying their dicks up in knots?"

"Because it looks painful,"

"Really painful," Marcus agreed under his breath.

"—and if you use your imagination," Dena continued, "you can pretend that it's Anatoly's cock being deformed and laughed at on stage."

I hesitated for a moment. "People laugh?"

"That's the whole point. It's a comedy act."

I looked over at my built in bookshelf. Those weren't all my books. Those were Anatoly's Leon Uris' next to my Alice Walker novels. His Faulkner's nestled against my Fitzgerald's. His books on soccer next to my books on art. We had combined our lives and now I was going to have to disassemble all of it. "Maybe a weekend of Vegas-style debauchery isn't such a bad idea," I said, quietly.

Dena grinned. "It's a fantastic idea. We can all go!"

Marcus shook his head making his well-trimmed, short locks swing side to side. "I have clients this weekend. Weaves, cuts, and highlights and that's just Saturday."

"But your clients will understand if you have a family emergency," Dena insisted.

"Honey, women who need a color aren't very under-standing."

"Marcus," Dena said again. "Family. Emergency."

My eyes were still on the bookshelf. What about the books we had bought since we had been together, the ones we had both read? Who would get those?

I was deep in thought over this when I realized that the room had gone silent. Marcus was watching me with a worried expression. "Who will get to keep the new, autographed David Sedaris book?" I asked softly.

Marcus exhaled loudly his eyes moving from my face to my disastrous mess of hair. "All right," he said, "we'll go to Vegas."

"I'm sorry," my sister said, a thin undercurrent of static made her words a little more difficult to hear through my cell, "did you say you're going to *Vegas*? That's a little random even for you!"

I sighed and rested my head on my knees. After Dena and Marcus left I had packed up some of Anatoly's things in boxes, and then when I got to the closet, I had faltered and ended up putting on one of his shirts. I was still wearing it and now I was on the floor surrounded by old pictures of us. Totally pathetic.

"Really? That's the part of the story you find most interesting?" Mr. Katz pressed himself against my leg and looked up at me expectantly. "You did hear the part about the secret wife, right? And his little story about the mob? Shouldn't you be asking me about *that*?"

"Of course that's all horrible," she said slowly, "but yes, Sophie, I find the fact that you're hightailing it to a Vegas sex toy trade show right after walking away from a long-term relationship to be the most interesting part of this story."

I hesitated, a photo booth strip of snapshots in my hand. For once I could actually see my sister's point.

"This is just like the time you went to Vegas after dad died."

And just like that, I thought she was crazy again. "Not even a little bit." I dropped the photo booth shots and picked up a picture of Anatoly and me at the Crissy Fields 4th of July fireworks show. I really needed to stop torturing myself. And I would, right after I went through one more stack of photos.

"Really? If I remember rightly, you couldn't deal with

your emotions then either. So you ran off to Vegas with Scott, got drunk or high or God knows what, and then the two of you enlisted a female Elvis impersonator to marry you in a Denny's parking lot! Do you remember that, Sophie?"

"Of course I remember that," I snapped. "I mean some of it's a little fuzzy, we really did drink a lot that night. But I do remember parts of it."

"Oh dear Lord."

"Come on Leah, I was only nineteen. Ten full years ago!"

"Fifteen years," Leah corrected.

"Okay, I'm having a crisis and you think this is a good time to remind me of my real age? As far as I'm concerned nineteen was and always will be ten years ago." Mr. Katz pressed against me more insistently. I had forgotten to feed him. I groaned and forced myself to my feet.

"Fine, but—"

"But nothing." I carefully stepped over the clutter of memories, left the room and headed down the stairs to the kitchen, Mr. Katz close at my heels. "Yes, I'm upset. But I guarantee you I'm not going to marry anyone this time around. At worst, I'll hook up with the latest waterproof bullet toy in a hotel bathtub."

"You need help."

"Which is why I'm going to a sex toy trade show. That will help." I wasn't at all sure that was true, but I was enjoying shocking Leah enough to pretend.

"Well just so you know, I'm not going to do any drugs."

"What are you talking about?"

"I know what kind of things people do in Vegas. I know

they… drop things—"

"Drop things?" I poured some food into Mr. Katz' bowl. He rushed in to eat before I was done and ended up with a small pile of kibble on the back of his head. "What kind of things do people drop?" I asked as I put the bag away. "Inhibitions? Money? The beat?"

"Acid."

I paused. "I'm not sure more people drop acid in Vegas than they do eight blocks down from here on Haight Street."

"I just want you to know that I won't be doing any of that."

"Okay… wait," I froze, my hand resting on a drying martini glass. "You're not suggesting that you'll be coming, are you?"

"Of course I'm coming."

"You can't!" I stammered. "You're not invited! You hate Vegas! You'd have to find a last minute babysitter for my nephew! You're coordinating Mary Ann's wedding and that's only a month away! You're a social conservative! No social conservatives at sex toy trade shows! It's a law, Leah!"

"Sophie, I am not going to let you go unchaperoned to Vegas when you're upset again! Not after what happened last time!"

"Oh my God, are you listening to me at *all*? I am totally over the lets-have-a-female-Elvis-impersonator-marry-us-in-a-Denny's-parking-lot phase of my life!" I pounded my hand against the kitchen counter for emphasis. "Now I'm in the to-hell-with-men-I'm-buying-a-vibrator phase! Try to keep up."

"And mama will take care of Jack if I tell her where

you're planning to go. She remembers what happened last time too."

"Leah," I said, taking the martini glass in hand and crossing over to the freezer for the vodka, "this is not a good plan."

"Sophie—"

"I'm going with friends this time, not some guy I've been dating. There is no risk of matrimony."

"Humph."

"Did you just humph?" That even got Mr. Katz' attention. He glanced up from his meal with an inquisitive stare. Nobody humphed anymore.

"I really think I should be there."

"It's not necessary," I sighed. I tried to shoot Mr. Katz a look of exasperation, but now that we'd finished humphing, he had returned his focus to his meal. "Both Dena and Marcus will be there to save me from...from the LSD dropping bachelors who will undoubtedly be trying to drag me to the alter."

"I don't like this."

I hopped up on the counter and took a sip of my drink. I knew the sound of victory when I heard it. "It's for the best that you stay here. Mary Ann needs you. You know how brides get in the last thirty days leading up to their wedding."

"True," Leah admitted, reluctantly, "It's just that... oh, hold on a moment." Leah's voice became more distant as she pulled away from the receiver, "Jack, stop that right now. Pancakes do not go into the DVD player!"

There was some more muffled scolding and the protesting cry of my young nephew. "Leah, Leah can you hear me?" I asked. "I have to go. I need to consume a lot of alcohol and all this talking's slowing me down."

"You know better than this, Jack!" Her voice had become even more distant indicating that she was now at least a few feet from the phone. "I simply can't have you trying to feed our appliances anymore!"

"Leah! I'm hanging up now, okay?"

"How would you like it if I tried to put a DVD in *your* mouth! You wouldn't like it, would you, Jack? Would you? No, no! Don't you dare put your tongue on that DVD!"

I hung up the phone. Between letting my sister try to comfort me here in San Francisco and going to Vegas to look at vibrators and origami shaped penises... well, the latter was quite clearly the saner option.

CHAPTER
THREE

"Doing Vegas while sober is like driving into the setting sun without sunglasses. Everything's just a bit too bright and a little irritating; but put on your shades and it's all fabulous."
—Death Of The Party

Dena and I arrived in Vegas at four o'clock on Friday. Marcus had moved his appointments around so that he could meet us later in the evening at the bar of a new hotel named Hotel Noir. He and Dena had decided to share a room and I was to have a room all to myself. Ostensibly this was because they wanted my weekend getaway to be as luxurious as possible. But the truth was that neither of them wanted to listen to me crying into my pillow all night long. As soon as the desert sunshine beat down on me, I knew I had made a mistake in coming. Vegas didn't feel like a town that welcomed depression. Perhaps I should have vacationed in Greece.

But I tried to put on a happy face for Dena as we checked into The Encore and then went to the convention center to scope out the sex toys.

"What are these? Serenity balls?" I asked as I stared down at two small, smooth white balls resting in the velvet interior of a decorative case. Dena and I had been at the sex toy trade show for less than two hours and already I was sex-toyed out. Vibrators, lotions, gels that were supposed to "Increase sensitivity," oh and one couldn't overlook the plethora of pleather. Individually this stuff might be fine but seeing it all thrown together like this was enough to make you want to become a nun. But the serenity balls held promise. I needed some serenity.

Dena shook her head. "They're not serenity balls, they're Kegal balls. You're supposed to hold them in your vagina and squeeze. Like a thigh master but obviously not for your thighs."

"That's just lovely. It took me five years to get comfortable with tampons. I certainly won't be sticking whole balls up there." I quickly moved my eyes away only to have them land on a woman in a bikini in the middle of a sex swing demonstration.

Dena gave the vendor of the balls a tight-lipped smile before pulling me away. "I carry those in my store, but the truth is Kegel exercises will work just as well without them. But *those*," Dena pointed over to a large table filled with what looked like bath toys for children, "those I can sell."

Reluctantly I followed her over to the table as a cheery and surprisingly conservatively dressed woman stepped up to help us.

"Hi, are you familiar with our products?" She asked as Dena picked up a bright pink, plastic anteater with a suspicious looking nose.

"You guys are the ones who make the rubber ducky

vibrator, right?" Dena asked.

"Oh yes, but we have a lot more animals now," The woman pushed her golden brown hair behind her ears and tapped the top of the anteater's nose. "See, this clit massager nose actually vibrates *and* moves back and forth really quickly. You can use it in the bath of course, and when it's wet, it feels more like a tongue."

I tilted my head and tried to imagine getting it on with an anteater. There really was nothing about the thought that was appealing

"And the great thing about our products," the woman continued, "is that they can double as children's toys!"

"I'm sorry, what did you just say?" I asked instantly snapping out of my visualization exercise.

"You see, since they do *look* a little like children's toys and they *are* waterproof, your kids can use them as bath toys. That way if your kids hear the buzzing sound after you've put them to bed they'll simply assume mommy's having her bath! Just a clever use of sound association."

I stared at her as I hovered between horror and amusement. "You do know that children often put bath toys in their mouths, right?"

"Oh, no worries! They can't choke on these."

"Well, okay, maybe not but… you know how moms say, don't put that in your mouth, you don't know where it's been? In this case, the mom will actually *know* where it's been, and that's a big problem."

"Which is why we have this!" the woman crossed to the other end of the table and came back with some kind of spray. "Sterilizer. Spray it with this, wait ten minutes and your toy's ready to go."

"Yeah, I don't think you're getting my point. It's not really a hygiene problem, at least not entirely. Sometimes it really is the thought that counts."

The woman furrowed her brow in confusion as Dena made a note in her iPhone to order the ten-minute sanitizer. "The thought of what?" the woman asked. "The thought of an anteater? Because we have an octopus too—"

"No!" I snapped. "That's. Not. The. Point!"

Dena stuffed her phone back in her handbag. "Actually I'd like to see the octopus. Does each tentacle do its own thing or do they work in unison?"

"Each tentacle has its own function," the saleswoman assured her as she handed over the octopus.

"Dena, this is insane! No one who shops at your store is going to want… wait, *each* tentacle has its own function? What do they do?"

Dena gave me an evil smile. "It gives a whole new twist to The Beatle's Octopus' Garden, doesn't it?"

My phone rang, flashing Marcus' number across the screen. Grudgingly, I stepped away from the table. "Hey Marcus, just in time. I was about to be eaten by an octopus."

There was a long pause before Marcus cleared his throat. "Sweetie, do me a favor and don't tell me what that's a metaphor for. I'm at Hotel Noir now."

"Really? You've already dropped your stuff off at Encore and everything?" I glanced at my watch. "But your flight only landed forty minutes ago."

"We landed early. Hon, I have to tell you something."

Immediately my heart sank as my mind raced through the various possibilities of what else could go wrong in my life. "Should I have a drink before I hear this?"

"Most definitely. Why don't I just circle back to Encore and we'll meet at the bar there."

I pulled the phone away from my ear for a moment. "Dena, it's Marcus. He wants to meet at Encore rather than Hotel Noir."

"Tell him no," Dena said, somewhat distracted by the octopus which was vibrating so hard it was about to launch itself off the table. "I've been wanting to see the Hotel Noir since it opened. You know they have a theater in the hotel, right? They have an eleven o'clock showing of *The Maltese Falcon*. I was thinking we could see it after we have drinks."

"*The Maltese Falcon*," I repeated. Without hesitation, I brought the phone back to my ear. "We're meeting you at the Hotel Noir at... oh, you know, at the bar we originally agreed on... um, Double Indemnity, right?"

"Yes, that's the place but Sophie, I really don't think this is a good—"

"And check the theater in the hotel. See if you can get three tickets for the eleven o'clock showing of *The Maltese Falcon*. I'm coming now."

I hung up and turned to Dena. "Humphrey Bogart and Sam Spade are SO much more uplifting than an oversexed octopus."

Dena shook her head. "Why does it always have to be either or with you." She held up the octopus. "Rent a couple of old movies and multitask."

I laughed and shook my head. "Come on, Marcus is waiting for us."

"Sophie, there's at least ten more booths I need to stop by before I can get out of here for the night."

I glanced around the room. There was a woman in a

black leather catsuit dancing around using nipple clamps as finger cymbals.

"Can *I* go then?" I asked.

Dena sighed. "You have no appreciation for innovation. Fine. Go meet Marcus. I'll be there in an hour."

When I got to Hotel Noir, Marcus was sitting at the bar tapping his fingers nervously against his martini glass. That gave me a moment's pause. Marcus had a thing about martini glasses. You could gesture with one in your hand, but it had to be a smooth, elegant gesture, demonstrating not only your sophistication but also your ability not to spill. Tapping was not allowed. And tapping out of time with the music, which was *exactly* what Marcus was doing, was a major Marcus No-No. Something had him off his game.

Carefully, I weaved my way through the crowd of unsophisticated, spill-prone revelers and made it to his side. When he saw me, his mouth turned up in a small, fleeting smile.

"Don't tell me," I said, slowly. "*The Maltese Falcon* is sold out for the whole weekend. No, worse, *The Maltese Falcon* is sold out *and* you gambled me away in a poker game so now I have to be the beard to some fat, hairy, closet-case with an evangelical family."

Marcus smiled wistfully. "Honey, you're describing a category four hurricane. We're being pummeled by a category six." He signaled to the unusually attentive female bartender that he wanted another drink like the half empty one in his hand. "Did you come in through the main lobby?"

I shook my head. "I came in through the entrance over —"

"Good," Marcus said cutting me off. Our drink arrived, and I could have sworn the bartender's eyes lingered a second longer than necessary on Marcus' Dolce & Gabbana covered shoulders. Someone needed their gaydar checked.

"It's the house specialty," Marcus said as he pushed the drink toward me. "They call it A Touch Of Evil which is apparently just another way of saying Spicy Martini."

"What kind of Vodka do they use?"

"Grey Goose, double shot."

"I love you, Marcus. Of all my friends you're my favorite enabler.'"

"I love you too." He hesitated a moment before adding, "Honey, Anatoly is here."

I choked on my double shot martini.

"*My* Anatoly?"

"How many Anatoly's do you think I know?"

"He followed me here," I said, quietly. He had used his professional sleuthing skills, found out I was coming to Vegas and followed me here! This was bad. It was stalkerish and it infringed on my privacy. Totally inappropriate in every single way.

So why did I feel so giddy?

I took another long sip of my drink, not because I needed to take the edge off but because I needed the glass to hide my smile.

"He came all the way to Vegas for me." I put the glass down and forced my mouth into a frown. "Well he's totally crossed the line. I don't care if he's been crying himself to sleep every night, he can't just follow me around the country. It's pathetic, and I'll tell him—"

"Sophie, if I tell you something... something you won't like, do you promise not to go all Carrie Underwood on me?"

"Carrie Underwood?" I parroted, suddenly feeling lost.

"You know that song where she slashes her cheating boyfriend's tires and carves her name into his leather seats? Don't do that, okay?"

"Why would I want to carve my name into leather seats?"

"Well, you probably wouldn't... but then again you might if I told you that Anatoly was here with another woman."

The frown I had forced my mouth into got heavier and a lot more real. "Another woman?"

"It's possible that she's just a friend but..." His voice trailed off.

"But what?" I asked, softly. When Marcus didn't answer, I raised my voice to a much louder volume. "But what, Marcus? What aren't you telling me?"

"Nothing," He said throwing up his hands as if protesting his innocence. "It's just that they seemed—close."

"How close?"

"Last I saw them they were sitting on a sofa in the main lobby." Marcus paused long enough to down the rest of his drink. "He had his arm around her."

"HE HAD HIS ARM AROUND HER?"

Marcus looked miserable. He flagged down the bartender and ordered another drink, steadfastly refusing to meet my eyes.

"What does she look like?" I asked desperately. "Is she cute? Hot? If you were straight would you do her?"

"I'm not straight."

"No shit, Marcus. If you *were* straight would you want to have sex with this woman?"

Marcus hesitated. The music in the bar seemed to have gotten louder. Or maybe the ringing in my ears was being caused by something else, like the little voice in my head that was screaming.

"I don't think I'd be into her if I were straight." He said slowly as his drink arrived.

I sighed feeling the tiniest bit of relief. "So she's ugly?" I asked.

"No, I just don't think that as a straight man I'd be into the bleach blonde, bunny type. I see myself more with a Rihanna kind of girl."

"Double D?"

"Maybe," Marcus hedged. "Maybe triple, but they have to be fake. There's no way boobs that big could stay up on their own if they were real and there's no way she could have been wearing a bra considering the skimpiness of that top."

"Oh *hell* no." I slammed my drink and got to my feet.

"Where are you going?"

"Where do you think I'm going? I'm going to the lobby, and I'm going to rip Anatoly's balls off!"

"Honey, this is not a good plan."

"This isn't a plan! This is rage that needs an outlet!"

The few patrons who were close enough to hear me over the music threw bemused smiles in our direction.

"Yes," Marcus said, "well that's not so good either."

"Marcus, there's no way any of this can be good!" I heard the faint edge of hysteria in my voice. "At this point, all I can do is aim for bearable! If I can hurt him now and then chill out by watching people being murdered in a film noir, then I might be able to bear this— this mess!"

"Ooh, you still want to see *The Maltese Falcon*? I didn't think you would so—"

"Wait, are you telling me that my ex-boyfriend has moved on in less than a week *and* you didn't get us tickets to *The Maltese Falcon*? Are you serious? Are you trying to make me suicidal?" Yes, I was definitely hysterical. Obviously, the movie wasn't important but *something* had to go according to plan.

"Okay," Marcus put a firm hand on my shoulder. "Tell you what, I'll go get the tickets now and you sit here and have another cocktail. If you still want to castrate Anatoly when I get back, I'll lead you to him."

"The only reason you'd be going with me would be to stop me from actually committing assault."

"There are worse motives to have." He waved at the bartender again who was by his side in lightning speed. "Get my friend another drink, darling. You have my card." Marcus then turned and gave me a light kiss on the cheek before pushing me back down on the barstool. "Stay," he said, sternly before giving me another kiss, this one on the top of my head, and walking away.

I waited for him to be out of sight before finishing off what remained of Marcus' drink, leaping back onto my feet and pushing my way through the crowd toward the lobby. My balance wasn't all that it should have been. I shouldn't have slammed two cocktails in the space of five minutes. I *should* have downed three. Right now I was just drunk enough to be overly emotional but not drunk enough to forget. Not a good place to be.

When I got to the lobby I spotted him immediately. He was still on the sofa, his back toward me and his arm still draped over a blonde woman's shoulders. I took three steps toward them and then lost my nerve. I skirted behind a corner and flattened myself against the wall. I wanted to yell at him, scream at him even, but you can't scream when you can't breath. I opened my mouth hoping the air would just float on in but my throat was completely constricted. I tried again to suck in a steady breath, but I only managed a gasp. When I exhaled, it came out as a moan.

"Are you all right?"

I glanced up to see a man with impossibly green eyes looking down at me. He had strawberry blond hair. I don't like guys with strawberry blond hair but those eyes... they had to be colored contacts, right?

"Are you all right?" he asked again.

I realized then that I was trembling. "No," I whispered. And then a little louder, "No!"

He tilted his head slightly to one side. "Can I help?"

Help me, yes, yes please help me! But how could anyone help me with this? I peeked around the corner. Anatoly still had his back to me, and I watched as he stood up and reached down to pull her to her feet. He didn't let go of her hand once they were standing. Instead, he draped a small duffle bag that I hadn't noticed before over his shoulder and started leading her toward the elevator. I recognized the duffle bag. Anatoly always used it for short trips, so perhaps he had just checked in and was going to his room for the first time—with her. I ducked back behind the wall and grabbed Mr. Green-eyes' arm. "Yes, yes you can help me. Do you see that tall guy in the black T-shirt and dark jeans talking to that bleach-blonde bimbo in the bright red, low-back top?"

The man looked at me quizzically before looking to see if he could spot the couple in question. "Yes," he said, dragging the word out so the *s* turned into a hiss.

"That's my boyfriend, and he's about to go upstairs. I need to know if he takes that... that woman into his room with him. Or her room... maybe it's her room. Anyway, I need you to get on the elevator with them, get off on the same floor as him, give me their room number and tell me if they went in together."

"I think I may be changing my mind about wanting to help you."

"No, you can't change your mind! This is life or death!"

"Someone's going to die if I don't spy on your boyfriend for you?"

"Umm, maybe? I mean yes. Sure, someone will die." *Like Anatoly right after I bludgeon him with a copy of* He's Just Not That Into You.

"I still think I should stay out of it."

Again, I glanced around the corner. The elevator hadn't arrived yet but it would in a moment. "I'll pay you," I said quickly. "I have..." I dug around in my purse and pulled out my wallet, "$185 on me. You can have all of it. All I need is a room number."

"I'll do it for $250."

"But I don't have $250!"

"I take checks."

"What? What! You're *shaking me down*?"

"Not at all. I'd be happy to walk away from this whole thing but if you want me to spy on my fellow man I'm going to require fair payment."

"You're unbelievable!"

The elevator arrived, but now there were too many people waiting for it. Anatoly stepped aside and allowed a woman in a wheelchair to take what would have been his spot.

"Fine!" I hissed. I pulled my checkbook out of my purse and scrawled two- hundred and fifty dollars across it in blue pen. "What's your name?"

"Alex Kinsky."

"Alex Kinky?"

Mr. Green Eyes smiled. "Kinsky."

"Polish?"

"Russian." He took the check from my hand before I had a chance to remark on that. "The elevator's here. Don't move from this spot. I'll be back with a room number."

I nodded and watched the kinky, Russian stride across the room and slip into the elevator with Anatoly and his bimbo just before the door closed. What if he didn't come back? What if I had just paid some guy Two hundred and fifty dollars for nothing?

Well, then I'd cancel the check of course. That was the benefit of not paying cash.

But what if this was some kind of identity theft scheme? Now this guy had my name and account number... what could a really skilled identity thief do with that?

What if Anatoly really was taking that woman up to his hotel room to make love to her?

Breathing was becoming hard again. I closed my eyes.

Everything was going to be fine. Maybe they wouldn't even go into the same hotel room. Maybe they'd get off on different floors. Maybe… maybe…

Maybe my heart was breaking.

CHAPTER FOUR

"The best thing about alcohol is that it makes your bad judgment socially acceptable."
—Death Of The Party

I couldn't have been in that hallway for more than ten minutes—probably considerably less. But that's not what it felt like. All of a sudden nothing seemed to make sense. Why did I need to know Anatoly's room number? Was I really going to go up there and confront him in front of a woman? Perhaps a naked woman *in his bed*? Did I really want to have her lying there smugly listening to my hysterics?

I was acting on instinct and raw emotion, which is exactly what had brought me to Anatoly to begin with. What kind of idiot was I to trust in those things again?

The anger began to slip away, and I started to feel just—empty. I shouldn't have come to Vegas. What was the point? What was the point of doing anything?

I stepped into the lobby just as Kinky stepped off the elevator. He walked over to me, and his eyes were sympathetic. His sympathy made me want to cry.

"Room 608," he said softly.

"Together?" I asked, and he answered me with a nod.

"Right, well now I know, right? I mean I had to know otherwise… otherwise, I wouldn't know and that would be bad." I was babbling, but if I stopped talking I'd have to think and—and *feel* this. "You should cash that check soon," I continued. "Who knows, maybe you can turn that $250 into $2000, right? I mean this is Vegas! Anything can happen in Vegas!"

I could feel the strain of my smile, all big and fake. I could feel Anatoly's arms around me, hear his laughter, feel the way he used to brush my hair from my face.

"Don't use it on the slot machines, worst odds in the casino." *Talk so you don't cry.*

"Can I get you a cup of coffee?" he asked. "A little conversation over mochas? I've been told I'm a good listener."

"Mochas, I don't usually drink mochas." I looked up at the overhead lights. They were too bright for the theme of the hotel and way too bright for my mood. "I don't think I can carry on a coherent conversation right now either."

"I didn't say you had to be coherent," Mr. Green eyes said… what was his real name again? Andy? No Alex. Alex Kinsky. Should be easy to remember—but there was no need to.

I kept my smile plastered across my face but looked away. "Thank you, Alex, but I'm gonna pass. Enjoy the rest of your night and, um, thank you for—for telling me." *Thank you for confirming my worst fears, thank you for letting me know everything I believed in for the last six years was a lie.*

I could feel Alex Kinsky's eyes on me as I wandered back into the bar. I bumped into a tall Latino man sporting a black T-shirt and an arm full of tattoos. Anatoly had been thinking of getting a tattoo… I had been helping him decide on a design. But I wouldn't be helping with those kinds of decisions anymore.

And yes, Alex was still watching me… watching me until I finally managed to lose myself in the crowd of jubilant people, many of whom would spend the weekend gambling everything they had on games of chance that they would almost certainly lose. When I finally got back to the bar, I spotted Marcus looking around for me. By his side was Dena. Dena noticed me first and reached out her hand. The gesture itself almost broke me. But then again this moment felt too big for tears What I really wanted to do was destroy. I imagined myself taking the bottles behind the liquor bar and smashing them against the counter. I visualized what it would be like to knock every single barstool to the ground. I imagined screaming and scaring everyone in this bar to death. Surely it would take something that big to exorcise this feeling. Something that violent.

But I couldn't do that. So I sat on the barstool offered to me and numbly retold the brief story in its entirety, stopping only long enough to consume large gulps of alcohol. And I kept the hurricane of emotion contained inside my heart where it could do the most damage.

Dena and Marcus exchanged looks when I got to the part about the check, but neither of them chastised me for it. Instead, they just bought me another drink. Marcus placated me by noting that the busty-blonde girl looked skanky. He even took it a step further by insisting that Anatoly was an asshole who didn't deserve me. Dena remained noticeably silent.

"If we want good seats we should probably go up to the theater," Marcus said, glancing at his watch.

"I'll meet you there," I mumbled. "I have to go to the ladies room."

"I'll go with you," Dena said as she tried to link her arm through mine.

I jerked away from her. "I don't need your help."

Dena narrowed her eyes. "Excuse me, but did I do something to piss you off?"

"It's what you're thinking right now," I slurred. "Your thoughts are pissing me off."

"So you're a mind reader now?"

"You're thinking that Anatoly didn't do anything wrong this time. You're thinking that I broke it off with him and he's a free agent!" I slammed the rest of my drink before adding, "You're thinking that anything goes in Vegas, especially if you're newly single! Go ahead, tell me where I'm wrong."

Dena's eyes were now so narrow I could barely see them through her lashes. Marcus kept his face as blank as possible as he looked around the room, studying the light fixtures, his glass, and various other inanimate objects.

"I don't think it matters if I was thinking that or not," Dena said coolly, "because clearly, you were."

"I'm going to the ladies room," I growled, "unassisted, thank you. I'll meet you at the theater."

Dena opened her mouth to protest but Marcus, finally bringing his eyes back to his present company, patted her reassuringly on the shoulder.

"Sophie's a high functioning drunk. She'll make it to the bathroom and the theater by herself."

It was a small triumph that Marcus thought I was a high functioning anything at that moment and I spared him a small smile before spinning on my heel and walking off. My phone vibrated in my bag. A text from my friend, and Dena's cousin, Mary Ann. I didn't even bother to read it. I didn't want to deal with her or anyone else right now. I didn't even want to go to the ladies room. I had just wanted a moment to myself to catch my breath. Everything had taken on a hazy quality. The colored lights of the slot machines seemed a little softer and... well, fuzzier. And the laughter of the gamblers, the ringing of the bells... it all took on an almost meditative quality. So much noise and stimulation all designed to keep you from thinking anything through. No wonder I had acted on impulse, recklessly signing a $250 check to a stranger just so he could confirm some bad news. Reckless impulsivity was what Vegas was all about. It all made sense—particularly after you've thrown back five glasses of Evil.

Abruptly I changed course and went to the elevators that would take me up to the sixth floor.

As I rode up, I tried to find some level of clarity despite the intoxication. Would I really hit him? What about her? She hadn't really done anything wrong. It was all him!

And yet it really would be fun to slap her.

I found room 608 easily. *I'll listen first,* I thought. *Find out if they're—in the middle of anything.* The thought made me nauseous, although the vodka was probably partially to blame for that. I leaned forward and pressed my ear against the door...

... and stumbled forward as the door opened with the slight pressure of my body.

45

It had of course been open the whole time. The deadbolt had been pushed out so that the door wouldn't automatically lock. If I had been sober, I probably would have noticed that before pressing my head against it.

Yet I wasn't quite so drunk as to miss the fact that I was the only one in the room. Just me and a bed that clearly hadn't been touched since it had been made up earlier in the day.

But it was Anatoly's room. That was his jacket draped over the chair by the window.

If this was his room and the bed was still made then he hadn't slept with her after all! I half skipped, half stumbled over to that jacket and took it up in my arms. He hadn't even taken her anywhere because if he had, he wouldn't have left his jacket...

Wait a minute.

I sat down on the chair and stared at the door that was still being forced slightly open by that deadbolt. Why had he left the door open when his stuff was here? That didn't make sense. I squeezed the jacket closer to my body. It smelled like him, and it felt—lumpy. Why did it feel lumpy?

I reached into the inside pocket and pulled out his iPhone. He left the room without his iPhone? That wasn't like him. I sat there for a moment staring at the device. This would be a confusing situation even if I weren't drunk. As it was, I was completely stupefied.

"Okay, think about this," I said aloud. "He left the room. He also purposely left the door open, and he left his jacket and iPhone here. Those are the facts."

I was quiet for a moment. Listing off the facts hadn't been as helpful as I had anticipated. Maybe I needed to list even *more* facts. "I'm in Anatoly's room, and there are no bimbos in it, and the bed hasn't been slept or fucked in recently."

These facts weren't any more helpful, but they were much more fun to say. I closed my eyes and enjoyed the mild dizziness. Things didn't always need to make sense. As long as he wasn't letting Mr. Happy go spelunking everything was okay. I opened my eyes and let my gaze lazily move around the room.

And then I saw something on the desk. I stood up and went over to it. Carefully, I touched the cool silver metal of the money clip I had given Anatoly last year, his initials clearly engraved on the front of it. Inside the clip were five twenty-dollar bills and four fifties.

He left three-hundred-dollars in the room. He left the door purposely open. He was nowhere to be found. These were not fun facts.

I was beginning to feel more sober. Now clutching both the money clip and the jacket, I checked the bathroom. No one there. The towels were still perfectly folded which meant the shower hadn't gotten any more use than the bed. There was a travel toothbrush and toothpaste set next to the sink that were still in their original packaging and...a small bottle of Aveeno Positively Radiant Daily Moisturizer cream.

Anatoly didn't use Positively Radiant Daily Moisturizer. Of course he *should* use it. I loved that particular product, and I was of the firm belief that *everyone* should have a strong skincare regiment, regardless of their sex. But Anatoly never listened to me about that kind of stuff, and when you considered why I threw him out, it seemed unlikely that he would try to win me back with newly radiant skin. And yet *someone* had to bring the Aveeno here and that someone obviously wasn't me.

I backed out of the bathroom and then turned to examine the room again. I spotted Anatoly's duffle bag on the floor. Hesitantly I opened it up. On top were a couple of his T-shirts, some jeans, under that a few pairs of boxer briefs and under that...

Under that were two rounds of ammunition. The ammunition Anatoly used for his snub-nose revolver.

With a new sense of urgency, I started rifling through the bag and running my hands along the lining. His gun wasn't in there. It's fairly rare that someone packs ammunition without packing their gun. So he had left his iPhone and three hundred dollars behind but taken his gun? That suggested he wasn't out filling an ice bucket.

Why would he have brought his gun to Vegas anyway? And if he had his gun on him now it was undoubtedly loaded; Anatoly never carried an unloaded weapon. So that was at least three rounds of ammunition. For God's sake, how many things had he planned on shooting?

My heart was beating a little faster now.

Maybe the gun was in the drawer. I opened the top drawer of the dresser. What I saw there did NOT make me happy.

Women's underwear! *Son of a bitch*! He hadn't just picked up some random, drunk, slut. He had actually checked in with her! Less than a week after we broke up! Even Dena would take issue with that! And I knew this chick was a slut because of this stupid skimpy thong... actually, it wasn't that skimpy. I had the exact same one at home.

I also had the same pair of bikini panties that were underneath those and I owned those same bras too. My head was spinning as I opened another drawer.

There was the Michael Stars T-shirt that I had left in my dresser at home along with my BCBG knit top and my scarf that I had bought with Anatoly at the North Beach street fair.

In yet another drawer were two pairs of my jeans.

I looked down at my hands. They were shaking and this time it had nothing to do with the cocktails.

That's when instinct took over. As quickly as possible I took out every item of clothing and stuffed it all in Anatoly's bag. I ran into the bathroom and snatched up the Aveeno and threw that in his bag as well. I didn't know what was going on other than that it looked like someone wanted others to think that this was my room and I had a very strong feeling that if that's what they wanted it was *very* important that no one ever reach that particular faulty conclusion.

I could barely feel the effects of the alcohol anymore. Adrenaline had taken over. I grabbed a washcloth from the bathroom and wiped down everything that I had touched.

"Anatoly, where are you?" I asked the empty room. I desperately wanted to leave but then what if he came back?

I glanced over at the closet. Would more of my clothes be in there? I rushed over to the closet door and threw it open.

There, underneath a few of *my* sundresses that were hanging from the rod, and on top of *my* beat-up overnight bag that I never used anymore, was the blonde bimbo.

She was just lying there—with a bullet hole in her forehead.

"No." I said the word out loud, but this time it didn't feel like I was talking to myself. It was more like a prayer. "No!"

I said again and then pressed my fist against my mouth.

She was dead! Dead and draped over *my* overnight bag! As if I was planning on packing her or something!

And Anatoly was nowhere to be found.

I had to do something right now! But what? I started to reach my hand towards the woman, as if to feel her pulse but quickly withdrew it. People with bullet holes in the middle of their foreheads did not have pluses.

I felt myself gag against my fist. I tore my eyes away from the woman and yanked my dresses out of the closet. I had to get the bag too. I gagged again but forced myself to pull it out from underneath her. She flopped forward, and I nearly screamed before I finally resolved to shove her back in the closet with my foot and then slam the door.

Someone wanted it to look like this was my room and now a woman—a woman who was recently hitting on my boyfriend, a woman who I had paid a stranger to *follow,* was dead in the closet.

Calling the police was simply not an option.

I bit down harder on my fist. What *were* my options?

Leaving. That was the only option. I had to get out, now.

I threw my dresses and Anatoly's jacket in my bag and with effort managed to scrunch his duffle bag in there too. Using my foot, I opened the door then thought better of it and used the washcloth to wipe down the doorknobs and undo the deadbolt so the door would actually lock behind me. Swiftly, and keeping my head down, I walked toward the elevator.

And with each step toward the elevator, the same thought rang through my head.

What happened to Anatoly?

CHAPTER
FIVE

"I'm a very forgiving person… particularly after I've made my enemies pay."
—Death of the Party

Anatoly was still the only thing on my mind as the elevator doors opened to the main lobby. If he could just be down here, waiting for me… even if he was with another woman, I just needed to see him! I stepped out and scanned the room.

"There you are!"

I froze and turned toward my sister's voice. She was no more than fifteen feet away and by her side was my friend, and Dena's cousin, Mary Ann Bettencourt. Mary Ann's chestnut brown curls bounced loosely around her porcelain features complimenting her green hoodie and light grey knit, straight-legged pants. Leah's chemically straightened hair was pinned up, and she was wearing a knee-length charcoal-grey pencil skirt paired with a bell jacket cinched neatly at the waist.

"Oh yay!" Mary Ann squealed. "We didn't know your room number and I was beginning to think we'd have to spend the whole night looking for you! How come you didn't answer my text?"

"My room number?" I asked blankly. I had fallen through the looking glass, no doubt about it. First I had been confronted by a dead body in a closet, and now I was being faced off by Mary Ann and my sister... who was apparently trying to channel a 1980s version of a bitchy Joan Collins. I wanted to throw up. I wanted to run away screaming, I wanted to cry—what I didn't want to do was stand here in this lobby having a conversation.

"I don't know why you're here," I said as calmly as I could manage, "but we've got to leave."

"What do you mean, you don't know why we're here?" Mary Ann asked. "Leah said you guys were turning this trip into my bachelorette party!"

A flash of guilt crossed Leah's face, but when she looked at me, her expression switched to panic. "What's wrong?" she asked. "Oh dear Lord, tell me you're not married!"

"I didn't get married," I said, grabbing her arm and pulling her toward the door. Mary Ann fell into step beside us. "Mary Ann, call Dena and tell her you're here with me and that she and Marcus should meet us back at our room at the Encore right now."

"Encore?" Leah asked, confused. "But isn't this where you're staying?"

"Why would you think that?"

"Because I called and the front desk confirmed that you were a guest here—did you book rooms at two hotels?"

I froze, still twenty feet from the main exit. Pivoting toward her, I met her brown eyes with my own. "There's a room booked under my name here?"

"I called five different hotels asking to leave a message for guest, Sophie Katz. This is the one that had a reservation for you. I figured there'd be a good chance that this is the place you'd pick, seeing that they have a movie theater that shows Hitchcock and all that other stuff you're into—"

"They said they had a room booked under my name," I said again.

"I don't get it," Mary Ann interjected. "You said this was all arranged with them, Leah. Didn't they tell you which hotel they were staying at?"

"She didn't arrange anything with any of us," I snapped as I quickly scanned the lobby. Was the green-eyed man around? Did he have anything to do with this? "You really need to call Dena and tell her to get out of this hotel. It's important."

"Okay," Mary Ann agreed, uncertainly as she reached for her phone

"Come on, we're getting a cab back to the Encore."

"Can't we just walk?" Leah asked.

"Look, you're crashing my party," I hissed as I resumed my march to the door. "You are not in a position to complain to me about my itinerary and right now I'm telling you that the next thing on the itinerary is getting out of here as fast as possible. Do you understand that or not?"

"But you're not married," Leah said, as she followed me out into the cold night air.

"Fucking hell, Leah, *no!*" I stepped close enough to whisper into her ear. "I didn't get married again, but I did find a dead body in a closet."

Leah stared at me as she processed the information. "Why do you keep doing this?"

"What?"

"*What*? It's gotten to the point that when I see the words *body discovered* in a news article, I immediately start scanning for your name, that's what!"

"Keep your voice down," I hissed and started pulling her toward a cab. I could hear Mary Ann talking to Dena on the phone. I could tell from Mary Ann's side of the conversation that Dena was pissed, most likely at me, but I was just going to have to explain later. Right now the most important thing was to get everybody out.

We all piled into the car and I gave the driver our destination. As we pulled onto the strip, Mary Ann hung up and looked over at me and then the overnight bag that was now squeezed between the front seat and my knees. "Something bad happened, didn't it?"

I stared out the window at the overly bright lights of the city. "You have no idea."

"Okay, so help me understand this," Marcus said, slowly. I was standing by the window in his and Dena's room at the Encore, my arms tightly crossed over my chest and the troublesome overnight bag by my side. Mary Ann and Leah were sitting on one of the double beds, and Dena was sitting at the desk refusing to look at anyone but Marcus who was standing in the middle of the room. Marcus turned to the two newest arrivals.

"Why are you here again?" he asked.

"I thought Sophie might do something stupid," Leah

explained, "and I wanted to be here to chaperone. I knew that if I brought Mary Ann with me, Sophie wouldn't be able to just send me home."

"And you thought *Sophie* would do something stupid?" Dena muttered, but Marcus pressed on.

"And Sophie, you went up to Anatoly's room?"

"It wasn't his room," I said, quickly.

"It was the blonde's room?" he asked.

"No, not really… I don't think so."

Dena gave me a withering look. "You barged in there like a first-class stalker and you don't even know whose room it is?"

"Go easy on her," Marcus murmured, "drunken heart-break makes people do crazy things."

Dena didn't look like she wanted to take it easy on me. "So I take it you went up to his room and found him with the blonde and now you—what? You stole his overnight bag to get revenge?"

"This isn't his overnight bag, it's mine." I unzipped it and pulled out the duffle bag. "*This* is his bag. It was in the room, but he wasn't."

"Maybe this isn't a good time to say this," Mary Ann hedged, "But I'm so sorry to hear about you and Anatoly. If it makes you feel better, I really don't think it's a permanent break. True love always finds a way!"

All of us in the room took a second to stare at Mary Ann like she was an alien from outer space—a real possibility—before turning back to the subject at hand.

"So the blonde let you in?" Marcus asked.

"No! No! She didn't let me in! She couldn't let me in because she was in the closet!"

There was a long pause before Mary Ann clapped her hands happily. "This is great news! Anatoly couldn't have been having an affair with a lesbian! He still loves you!"

Leah dropped her head in her hands and sighed.

"You're not understanding me," I said, slowly. "She was literally *in* the closet!"

Dena cocked her head to the side. "Really? That's a new one for me. Usually when people talk about a closet fetish, they don't mean it literally but..."

"Oh dear Lord, Dena, not everything is about sex!" Leah burst out. "What Sophie's trying to tell you is that there's a dead bimbo in Anatoly's hotel room closet!"

"Whoa, whoa, whoa," Dena held up her hands. "Have you gone mental? How the hell did you come up with that?"

"No, she's right," I said, fighting back tears. "I found her in there with a bullet hole in her forehead. And look," I reached into Anatoly's bag and pulled out the ammunition. "Anatoly's got bullets in his duffle bag."

Marcus' coloring went from mocha to milky latte. "Anatoly killed the bimbo?"

"No! He would never do that! But..." I looked down at the bullets, "someone did and Anatoly's nowhere to be found."

"Oh, wow." Mary Ann shook her head. "I was so much happier when I thought he was making friends with lesbians."

Marcus pressed the base of his palms against his forehead. "We have to call the cops."

"There's more," I said quickly. "As I was saying before, it wasn't actually Anatoly's room." I took in a deep, shaky breath. "I think it was mine."

I proceeded to tell them everything. I had to stop once to throw up, but my friends were too shocked to mind much.

"So that's it," I said when I had finally finished.

"This," Marcus said slowly, "is incredibly bad. The police are going to be looking for you."

I shook my head. "I cleared all my stuff out of the room and I wiped off my fingerprints."

"But if it's registered under your name..." Leah's voice trailed off.

"Eventually they'll figure out that I didn't book it! And... and there's nothing to place me there!"

"Except the security cameras in the hallway outside the room," Leah pointed out, "and the stranger who gave you the room number. But aside from that, nothing."

Security cameras! I hadn't thought of that.

"Maybe whoever booked the room did so for a really long time," I suggested. "I don't think hotel maids vacuum closets. And they always keep the air conditioning up so that'll keep her from getting too smelly. It could be more than a week before they find her!"

Dena banged her cane on the floor in frustration. "Could you go throw up again so I can talk to sober-Sophie? It's a cool hotel room, not a fucking meat freezer! And you said you kicked her back into the closet with your shoe! That means she is *on* your shoe right now!"

I screamed and ran into the bathroom to wash off my shoe... and to throw up again.

When I got back, I flopped down on the bed and pressed my face into a pillow. "Why is this my life?" I wailed.

"Yeah," Marcus mused, "why *is* that?"

"And what about Anatoly?" I gasped looking up. "What

if something happened to him? What if he's *hurt?*" I knew that it could be worse than hurt, but I couldn't go there. Couldn't even entertain the possibility.

Mary Ann moved to sit next to me. "He isn't. If he was hurt you'd feel it," She patted her heart. "You'd feel it in here."

"Oh for God's sake," Dena muttered. "No need to make us *all* throw up."

"Yes, and honey," Marcus said gently, "it's possible that Anatoly is a murderer."

"I'm telling you that's not *possible!*" I propped myself up on my elbows. "I should never have kicked him out! I shouldn't even be in Vegas! All he asked for was the chance to explain! Six years we've been together and I didn't even give him that!" I started crying, crying so hard that it even brought out the nurturer in Leah who handed me Kleenex and mumbled a few sympathetic words.

"I want to call him!" I cried.

"Sweetie, you have his phone," Marcus reminded me.

"I don't care! I just have to hear his voice." I snatched up my phone and dialed Anatoly's number. I listened to his phone ring. I had programmed a special ringtone for myself into his phone so he would always know it was me—"Wild Horses" by the Rolling Stones. He had kissed me for my efforts. As it played now the memory of that kiss came hurling at me like a brick. When his voicemail eventually picked up, I put it on speakerphone and clutched my hands in my lap as I listened intently to the sound of his voice.

"I'm unavailable right now. Leave your name and phone number after the beep."

I swallowed my tears as the beep sounded. I leaned over

the silent phone and screamed, "You son of a bitch, where the fuck are you?"

Dena clicked the phone off with a sigh.

"What am I going to do?" I moaned.

"I think there's only one thing we can do," Marcus said. "We wait to see what the morning brings."

Sleep was not a possibility. I lay in bed staring at the ceiling. I had managed to puke out most of the alcohol. That left my head a little clearer than I wanted it to be. Dena and Marcus were sleeping... well, probably sleeping, in the adjoining room. Before arriving in Vegas, Leah had booked a room at Hotel Noir after "confirming" that I was staying there. Now she had canceled that—grumbling the whole time about the hefty last-minute cancellation fee—and Mary Ann had booked a room at the Encore for the two of them, although they hadn't been able to get one on the same floor as us. Of course the fact that there was now a record that my sister had booked a room at Hotel Noir was going to make it even harder for me to convince anyone that the room apparently registered under my name was never registered by me.

At around three a.m. I gave up and pulled myself together enough to go out. I didn't want to wake my friends, but I couldn't bear the idea of sitting alone.

In jeans and a tank top, I went down to the lobby with a book that I knew I wouldn't be able to focus on and sat down on a cushy chair that gave me a full view of everyone coming and going. Even at this hour, the place was bustling.

No one seemed to be paying any attention to me, except one redhead in a little black dress sitting about thirty feet away from me. She seemed to be glancing over in my direction every few minutes before returning her attention to a magazine she was reading. Or maybe she wasn't looking at me. Maybe she was looking behind me toward the casino. Was I being paranoid?

I shifted slightly in my seat and tried not to be too obvious about examining her. Even from across the room I could tell she was pretty with a perfect little figure. The hot pink stilettos suggested that she wasn't a cop or a lesbian, so my suspicions about her checking me out were probably unfounded.

And then she looked up and we locked eyes.

Shit.

I watched, frozen in place, as she closed her magazine, got out of her seat and crossed the room to where I was. "Excuse me," she said as soon as she was only a few feet away. "But are you Sophie Katz?"

Was there any reason to say no? Again, there was no way a cop would wear heels like that. It would be like a lifeguard wearing chainmail. But if she wasn't a cop she might actually be dangerous...

... and she might know where Anatoly is.

"Yes," I said after I had let *way* too much time pass for my response to sound natural. "I'm Sophie."

The redhead smiled and sat down in the seat next to me. "I recognized you from the picture on the back cover of your books. I just finished your last one."

She was a fan? I let out a little-relieved laugh. "If you can recognize me when I'm this much of a mess, I am in serious need of a new publicity shot."

Again, the woman smiled and let my self-deprecating comment pass without correction. That in and of itself was a little odd. "I also just read this really interesting article in USA Today," she said. "It was about how some mystery authors have real life experience with crime. Like, you, Pamela Cope and Amanda Preston."

"Yeah," I said cautiously, "but Cope and I have worked to expose crimes while Preston actually beat a woman to death when she was a teenager. I really feel that's an important distinction."

"I see your point." She crossed her legs and looked up at the ceiling thoughtfully. "But that certainly makes Preston qualified to write about murder, doesn't it? She knows what it *feels* like to take another person's life. Do you think you're as qualified as her?"

The question took me off guard. "No," I said quietly. "I'm not."

"So you've never killed anyone?"

I had. I had shot him at close range. It had been self-defense so technically it wasn't murder—but still, I took a life. I had expected my actions to haunt me. I thought that after the shock had worn away I'd be overcome by remorse or at least some level of guilt.

But I didn't feel any guilt at all. Most of the time I didn't even think about it. And that meant that it was possible that Preston and I had more in common than I cared to contemplate.

And a disturbing little voice in my head told me that if there was someone out there who had harmed my Anatoly I could kill again, with no guilt whatsoever.

And *another* little voice told me this was a very strange question for a reader to be asking. "Are you asking if I'm a murderer?" I asked. "Because obviously, the answer to that would be no."

"Interesting," the woman mused, "and yet you write about it so convincingly. Have you ever interviewed anyone who does have experience with killing? Like, have you interviewed ex-cons, or cops, or military guys?"

"I think the experience of a soldier fighting to defend his country is significantly different from the experiences of someone who kills for personal interest," I glanced toward the entrance. Perhaps when a pink stiletto-wearing stranger tries to start up a conversation about murder, the appropriate response is to just get up and leave.

"True, but I didn't necessarily mean American military," she continued. "You know in some countries there's a lot of crossover between the police, military, and crime families. In Russia for instance—"

I snapped my head back in the woman's direction. "Excuse me?"

"I was just saying that in Russia being part of the military doesn't preclude you from involvement in crime or even in the Russian Mafia—or as they call it the Bratva."

I felt myself go rigid. "Who are you?"

Her smile broadened. Leisurely, she checked her diamond Cartier watch and stood back up. "You should go back to San Francisco and write another one of your wonderful books. Vegas is no place for a novelist. It doesn't provide a conducive ambiance for creativity."

"What are you saying?"

"I'm saying that there's nothing for you here. Go back to

San Francisco. Tomorrow morning if you can."

She started to turn, but I immediately got up and grabbed her arm. "Where's Anatoly?" I hissed.

"I don't know what you're talking about."

"The hell you don't! Who are you?"

"Do I need to call security over?" the woman asked, her voice sweet and sympathetic. "They might even call the police. Would you like to talk to the police tonight?"

I let go of her arm. "Just tell me where he is."

"There you are!" Marcus' voice carried across the lobby tinged with notes of anger and panic. I turned to see him striding toward me. He grabbed me by both my arms and squeezed a little too tightly. "I can't believe you just took off like that! Tonight!"

"She knows where he is! This woman knows everything!"

Marcus gave me a puzzled look and then glanced behind me. "What woman? You mean that redhead you were just talking to?"

I broke free of Marcus and whirled around just in time to see my new acquaintance step out the front doors of the lobby.

"No, no, no, no!" I cried and then took off after her at full speed, Marcus close on my heels.

"Who are we chasing?" he asked as we ran outside.

I came to an abrupt halt and swiveled my head back and forth trying to get a glimpse of red. No one should be able to move that fast in stilettos.

"Do you see her?" I asked urgently.

"No, she must have jumped into one of the cabs or something. Who is she?"

Desperately I stared out at the street that was littered with cabs of various colors. "She's gone," I whispered.

"Who!" Marcus demanded again. "Who's gone?"

"I don't know. But she gave me a warning. She told me to go back to San Francisco first thing tomorrow."

"Or what?"

"Good question. But I guess we'll find out because I'm not going anywhere."

Marcus released a heavy sigh. "Are you really going to stay here and risk our lives to rescue your horny, married, mafia-lovin' boy toy? Because that song's even too pathetic for Nashville."

"Anatoly is *not* a boy toy." I snapped.

Marcus brought his fingers up to the bridge of his nose. "You need sleep, Sophie. You're not going to be able to do anything without that."

I bit down on my lip. I knew he had a point. I could feel the exhaustion tugging at me, and without sleep, I would be left with a debilitating hangover when the sun came up. Perhaps if I had been more rested, I wouldn't have allowed Little Miss Evil to get away so easily. But I knew that if I lay down the images of that woman in the closet would come back to haunt me and yank me out of unconsciousness. I sighed and started walking toward the strip.

"Where are we going now?" Marcus asked as he matched my pace.

"Isn't it obvious?" I asked. "I'm going to see if any of the local drug dealers peddle Ambien."

CHAPTER

SIX

"The vibrator was the fifth domestic appliance ever to be electrified and was introduced more than a decade before the vacuum cleaner. It's comforting to know that every once in a while society gets its priorities straight."
—Death Of The Party

We never did find a dealer who sold Ambien, but we did find a very nice prescription drug addict who allowed me to bum a couple of Valium off her and after twenty minutes more of staring at the ceiling of my hotel room, I was finally able to get to sleep.

I dreamt I had a closet full of monsters and standing between it and me was the redhead in her pink stilettos... and in her hand was Anatoly's gun.

"Who are you?" I asked.

"You know who I am," she replied, coyly. Behind her, the monsters scratched at the closet door.

"Are you guarding me against the monsters?"

"I haven't decided," she whispered. In the real world the whisper would have been too soft to hear, but in my dream, it was as clear as a scream. "The problem is," she went on,

"I'm a monster too."

And that's when I woke up. The room was empty and completely silent. It took me a moment to put together what was a dream and what wasn't. There were no monsters in the closets. Just dead bodies. The mysterious woman wasn't here—but she had to be *somewhere*—and so did Anatoly.

That was unsettling on several different levels. I propped myself up on my elbows. The door adjoining my room to Dena and Marcus' was open but from what I could see both of them were out.

I closed my eyes again and tried to predict what the day would bring. There was a distinct possibility that I was about to be arrested for murder. I glanced at the clock. 9:45 a.m. Would I have time to get a Frappucino before going to prison? I was pretty sure impending incarceration justified splurging on a Venti.

I heard the door to the other room open and close and I immediately tensed. *Oh God, what if I get arrested before I've had my coffee?*

"Sophie?" Leah called out. I exhaled loudly as she appeared in the doorway, a Frappuccino in one hand and a small brown Starbucks bag in the other. "Marcus gave me his key. I thought you might be hungry."

She sat down on the edge of the bed and handed me my breakfast. Gone was the suit from the night before. Now it was twill white pants, a fitted white tank, a cotton/silk blend navy pointelle cardigan and a short strand of pearls that looked fake but I knew were real. She was dressed perfectly, assuming her day's itinerary included jumping on a yacht to win America's Cup.

"Thank you," I breathed, jamming a straw into my drink.

"Are they coming for me?"

"Is who coming for you?"

"I don't know, the police, the mob... anyone really. If anyone is coming for me, I'd like to know about it."

"Are you planning on going on the lam?"

"No, but if I'm going to be arrested, I need to do my makeup. I want a cute mug shot."

"Naturally," Leah said with an understanding nod. She ran her hands over the pristine white trousers. "You think I shouldn't have come."

"I did tell you not to."

"You did, but you need my help."

"I already have Marcus and Dena."

"You need me too," Leah insisted. "When the man you were living in sin with turns out to be married and then murders a bimbo and sticks her in a closet... well, it's times like these that a girl needs her sister."

"Anatoly didn't kill the bim... that woman. He's not capable of that."

"If you say so," Leah said, mildly. "Perhaps he was one of the few pacifists employed by the Russian Mafia."

"Leah—"

"I don't think you're going to be arrested this morning," she said cutting me off. "There's nothing in the news about a murder taking place at the Hotel Noir or anywhere else."

"Maybe the maid hasn't cleaned the room yet."

"Well... it was the sixth floor, right? Those lower floor rooms usually get cleaned pretty early in the morning unless... did you put a Do-Not-Disturb sign on the door?"

I slapped my forehead in frustration. "No! Why didn't I think of that?"

Leah wrinkled her nose in disgust. "Ugh, that means that housekeeping probably has been in the room and they just didn't clean the closet. Do you think housekeeping ever cleans the closets? Maybe they don't! That's it, I'm never going to hang anything in a hotel closet again. Just think of the germs!"

"Yeah," I said, my mouth full of cinnamon sugar coffee cake. "Lots of germs on a dead body."

Leah shuddered at the thought. "Well, hopefully, they at least had the professionalism to do a thorough cleaning of the rest of the room. If so your fingerprints have been wiped away and any strands of hair that you might have inadvertently left behind have been vacuumed up."

"There's still the security cameras."

"True," Leah admitted. "But the longer it takes them to find the body the harder it's going to be for them to pinpoint the time of death. You might be able to argue that when you were in the room, everybody was alive and well... or better yet, that they weren't there at all."

"Listen to you! You sound like an old pro at this."

"Please. You can't be related to Calamity Jane without learning how to clean up a mess."

I smiled. For once, everything my sister was saying was making sense.

"Where's the rest of our little group?"

Leah rolled her eyes. "Mary Ann slept in, but she's getting ready now to join Marcus and Dena at that awful trade show. She's actually excited about going... well, I suppose it's not completely inappropriate since this *is* supposed to be her Bachelorette weekend."

"I can't believe you tricked her into thinking we all came

here for her. And now she's getting the worst Bachelorette weekend ever."

"In my defense, I thought I was crashing a pity party, not a mafia perpetrated homicide."

"Still—"

"Still what?" Leah snapped, cutting me off. "When exactly *were* you going to plan her Bachelorette party? Even before this most recent mess, you were absorbed with the mess of your breakup, and if Dena had planned it, we all would have ended up in some horrible sex dungeon getting ball gags as party favors. This way Mary Ann gets her little celebration and Dena doesn't have the chance to plan a party that would end with the eternal damnation of all our souls."

"We're Jewish," I reminded her. "We don't really have an eternal damnation place."

"Well, being stuck in a sex dungeon for an evening would be a pretty close second." She got up and opened my closet. I bit down on my lower lip. It was going to take some time before I was comfortable with closets again.

"You should get dressed. They're expecting us."

I laughed but then stopped short when I realized she wasn't joking. "Are you kidding? I know you don't want to go and I sorta have other things I have to deal with."

"You're right, I'd rather run a marathon... and you know how I feel about running. But if our story is that you didn't see a dead body last night we can't act like you did. And that means sticking to your precious itinerary." She turned back to the closet. "What is one supposed to wear to a sex toy trade show, anyway?"

I eyed her outfit and smiled. "Probably not Brooks Brother's."

"Don't be ridiculous, Brooks Brothers works for everything." She pulled a pair of wide legged pants out of my closet and a loose, silk, red tank from my dresser and laid it out on the bed next to me. "Get yourself together. I'm going to go see what's taking Mary Ann so long."

I sipped my Frappuccino as she left the room. She had a point. I needed to keep up appearances even though I really, really didn't want to. I got up to take a shower, but the ring of my phone stopped me. My mother's number flashed across the screen.

"Hi, mama. Checking up on me?"

"Mommellah, something terrible has happened!"

My heart dropped as I lowered myself back down on the bed. "Are you okay?"

"Yes, yes, I'm fine."

"Mr. Katz? Is Mr. Katz okay?"

"What is this? You ask after a cat before asking after your own nephew? Not that there's anything wrong with your nephew, or your cat for that matter, but still, what would people think of your priorities? Is this how I raised you?"

Maybe this wasn't the time to tell her that she had apparently raised me to hang out at sex toy trade shows. "So if everybody's okay, what's the problem?"

She hesitated a moment before continuing. "I came to your house to feed the kitty but... oh, mommellah, someone has been here!"

And again, my heart went diving toward my toes. "Someone's been—in my house?"

"And such a mess they left!" my mother went on. "The cushions on the couch are slashed open, the books are on the floor, it's—"

"But Mr. Katz, you're sure he's okay? Is he with you?" my hand clenched the sheets beneath me.

"Your cat's with me. He was hiding behind the curtains."

"Oh, thank God!" I breathed. I bent over holding my stomach with one hand, literally overcome with relief.

"I'm surprised they didn't tear up the curtains too!" Mama went on.

"What's missing? The television? Stereo? Did they take my computer?"

"No, no, not all that. These were strange burglars. They took the computer but as far as I can tell that's all. Who does something like this? I think it's all that MTV the young people are watching these days."

"Mama, the young people who used to watch a lot of MTV are now middle-aged people watching Ellen. All they took is the computer?" I silently thanked the writing gods that I had taken my MacBook with me. I was only three chapters away from completing my next manuscript.

"All your checkbooks are here, your jewelry, the Waterford Leah gave you... they even left that Lennox Kiddush cup! And I paid a pretty penny for that! I tell you, these crooks are meshuggeneh!"

"Yes, that or they were looking for something specific," I muttered. "Mama, the desk my computer was on, is that still there?"

"Yes, it's here."

"And the USB stick that was in the top drawer... is *that* still there?"

"Hold on..."

I bit my lip and waited as she made her way through what I imagined was my trashed living room. The thought of *anyone* violating my home like that made my skin crawl.

"Such a mess! They dumped everything in that drawer onto the floor. Real schmucks these people are!"

"Have the police already been there?"

"Oh, the police, they always make such a mess of things. I called you first."

That was silly. But in this particular case, I was glad she had been imprudent. Eventually the Vegas cops were going to find that body. The last thing I wanted to do was to bring myself to the cops' attention now. Reporting the burglary might also put Anatoly on their radar. Anatoly who was armed, M.I.A., and might easily be considered a murder suspect too.

"Are you sure you kept the USB sticks in that drawer. Those are the little grey sticks, right?"

"Yes, it looks just like the one I gave you to back up your recipes… what about CDs… or any discs at all? Are any of them there?"

"I don't see them. So what was it these people were after? USB sticks? You told me they weren't very expensive!"

"They're not valuable," I said distractedly. But whoever took them clearly thought that what was on them was. Of course the only thing that was really on them were my manuscripts. I had a hard time believing that this whole fiasco stemmed from the Russian Mafia's interest in expanding into plagiarism.

"Listen Mama… I don't think you should call the police. As you said, they usually just make a mess of everything."

"Yes, but on second thought this place is pretty messy already! Listen, I didn't call the police until I was sure the kitty was okay and your jewelry was safe, but when someone breaks into your house and turns it into a pigsty, you call the cops."

"Normally, but they didn't take anything very valuable —"

"They didn't take *everything* very valuable, but the computer is still quite a pricey item! Just because you can afford to replace it doesn't mean you should give it away to hoodlums!"

"Trust me on this. I just need you to hold off on telling anyone anything," I said firmly. "Take Mr. Katz back to your place and don't let Jack torture him."

"What have you gotten yourself into this time?"

"Nothing too bad, I just need a little time to think, okay? Love you!"

I hung up the phone before she could start interrogating me. There was a knock on my door. Leah and Mary Ann stood there looking polished and ready to go.

"I'm so excited about this!" Mary Ann squealed. "It's going to be so interesting! Don't you think it'll be really, really interesting?"

"Someone broke into my house," I said quietly.

They both stood in my doorway with blank looks on their face. Finally, Mary Ann raised her hand as if she was in a classroom.

"Um, didn't we already know that? I mean, that's how they got your clothes and old overnight bag, right?"

So even Mary Ann had thought this through more than I had. Fabulous. Not only was my life in jeopardy, so apparently was my IQ.

"They stole my computer," I added. "And all my storage devices but nothing else of value. My diamond studs, my flat-screen, my state of the art speakers, all still there."

"Maybe they were in a hurry?" Mary Ann suggested.

"They were looking for information," Leah whispered

"I wasn't exactly storing state secrets."

"Was it Mama who called to tell you? Was… was Jack with her when she was at the house?" Leah asked weakly.

"I think so, but mama assured me he's totally fine," I replied, quickly. "There's nothing to worry about there."

Leah swallowed hard. "I hate to think of him running around a messy house."

I searched her expression of some sign of jest. "I'm thinking that's not our biggest problem." I raised my fingers to my temples and tried to massage away the tension. "I don't want the police involved yet… not until I cover my bases."

"Sophie, someone has broken into your house!" Leah exclaimed. "If you wait to report this, how's it going to look?"

"Why do I have to report it?" I retorted. "Do you really think the police are going to get my computer back from the mafia? If they start poking around the chances of them learning about my writing a check to some stranger to get him to follow a…" I lowered my voice, "… a future murder victim… well, that's a little worse than losing a computer!"

For once no one argued with me. We all knew that check could sink me—unless I could get it back. A new plan started to form in my mind. It was vague and very—me.

"I have a migraine," I said, making a point of massaging

my temples again. "I know we're trying to hold up appearances but let's face it, even if nothing went wrong I was going to drink too much on my first night here which means that the normal thing would be for me to arrive at the trade show later in the day. I'll meet you guys there, okay?"

"You really have a migraine?" Leah asked suspiciously.

No. I'm in free fall and I'm about to do something desperate. But I didn't say that. If one thing was clear it was that things were becoming increasingly dangerous... and Dena had a cane because she had been shot not too long ago. I had been there when it happened, and there was no way I was going to be responsible for her or anyone else getting shot again.

"Yes, I just need to lay down for a little bit," I said, keeping my eyes on the floor. "Really, go on ahead. I'll meet up with you in about an hour or so."

"Mary Ann can go. I'll wait here with you," Leah said quickly.

"No," I snapped. "You dragged Mary Ann here, so the least you can do is be her chaperone while she learns about vibrating cock rings. I'm just going to pop a few Advil and take a nap," I went on. "I don't need you here for that."

"And you'll meet us in an hour?" Leah asked.

"Hour and a half tops. Cross my heart, hope to die."

She nodded. "Fine. Just, don't be later than that, OK?"

I returned my eyes to Leah and for the first time noticed the anxiety that was on *her* face. She was scared for me. And as much as I didn't want to admit it, she had reason to be.

Because I was in danger and despite the promise I had just given, I didn't really "hope to die." Not under any circumstances. Hopefully it wouldn't come to that.

CHAPTER
SEVEN

"In Vegas people pay good money to see Masters Of Illusion as if these men are truly special. But really, it's the men who are able to master reality who are the rarity."
—*Death Of The Party*

Hotel Noir looked different during the day. The people milling around the lobby seemed calmer and more ordinary. Miniskirts had been replaced by jeans, Prada loafers with Nikes. It felt like this should be a safe place.

And yet it really, really wasn't.

As I walked up to the front desk, I felt my palms start to sweat. I had to play this perfectly. I had to find Alex Kinsky and get him to give me the check back without letting him know the real reason I wanted it back. That required a certain level of calm and proficiency in lying. I was lacking the former but had an abundance of the latter.

At the front desk a young brunette with heavily mascaraed lashes smiled warmly at me. "Can I help you?"

"Yes," I said, my voice perhaps just a bit too bright. "I'm trying to get in touch with one of your guests, but I think he gave me the wrong room number. I was hoping you might be able to put me through to his voicemail or something?"

The brunette's smile lost a little of its warmth. "We're very protective of our guests' privacy," she explained.

"All I need is to leave a brief message. If I could just reach Alex Kinsky—"

"Oh!" the woman blinked in surprise. "Well, I guess I could page him for you."

That took me off guard. This was not my first trip to Vegas, but I had *never* heard a hotel page a guest over a loudspeaker. "You can do that?"

"Sure. What's your name?"

"Sophie Katz."

"Great, just one moment." She picked up the phone and quickly dialed in a few numbers then, after a pause, a few numbers more. She hung up and smiled at me.

"That… that was a page?" I asked, suddenly feeling panicky. Had she just signaled for security to come and get me or something? Had they been waiting for me to show up so the police could apprehend me? I glanced back at the door. Should I make a run for it?

The phone rang. "Mr. Kinsky?" She asked upon picking up. "There's a guest here who would like to speak with you. A Ms. Sophie Katz?" She paused a moment, clearly listening to the person on the other end of the line. "Great, I'll tell her."

When she hung up, she turned her smile on me again and this time it wasn't just warm. It was the smile you give to someone whom you might have offended *and* who might have the power to seriously mess with your life.

"Mr. Kinsky will be right down."

"He's coming from his room?"

The woman's brow furrowed with confusion. "Um... no. He doesn't live on the premises."

"He doesn't..." my voice trailed off. He worked here! But couldn't he get in *serious* trouble for accepting payment for spying on a guest?

Probably. That's *probably* why he hadn't told me he was an employee. Now I was the one who was smiling. I wondered how much Mr. Kinsky valued his job. Maybe enough to get some security tapes for me?

"Miss Katz, how good to see you again."

My smile widened at the sound of his voice, and I turned expecting to see him in his bellhop uniform or what-have-you.

But he wasn't in uniform. He was wearing a very nice suit. Armani would be a good guess. It was impeccably tailored to flatter his physique. It made him look older than he had looked last night and a lot more intimidating.

My smile faltered. He was management? Why would someone in that position risk his job for a $250 check?

"Why don't we talk in my office," he offered before turning to the brunette. "I'm not sure if you heard, but Tanya Davi handed in her resignation this morning."

"I heard," the woman quickly confirmed. "I can cover tomorrow's shift."

"Thank you, Donna."

He escorted me through the lobby and then through the casino. All the workers acknowledged him. Had they been this deferential last night? But then again I hadn't been given the opportunity to observe that dynamic, and even if I had, I probably wouldn't have noticed. My mind had been on other things.

"What exactly is your position here?" I finally asked as yet another blackjack dealer gave him a courteous nod.

"I'm the GM."

I stopped in my tracks. "Of the *hotel*?"

Alex smiled, and with his hand applied slight pressure to my back, urging me forward. "Did I forget to mention that yesterday?"

"Yeah, I think you did."

"My bad."

We exited the casino, and he took me to a door that led to a very small, private reception area where a woman sat typing on her computer. "Hello Mr. Kinsky," she said quickly.

"Anne," he said, brushing past her and leading me into his office.

I glanced around the room as he closed the door behind us. It was much more opulent than I would have expected. He had a mahogany desk and an abstract painting on the wall from a familiar artist whose work usually sold for several thousands of dollars. A saddle leather, wingback settee was up against the far wall. He gestured for me to take a seat in front of the desk and then walked around to his own, opposite me. "So how are you doing?"

"Not so great," I said carefully. "Someone broke into my house back in San Francisco."

Alex's eyebrows shot up in surprise. "You're kidding! Did they take anything?"

I nodded. "Even with insurance, it's going to cost me a lot to replace my computer. If I had known about this last night, I would have been a little more careful with my money."

Alex looked at me with a blank expression that probably served him well at the poker table.

"For instance," I pressed, "I probably wouldn't have written out any checks."

"I'm sorry to hear about your troubles," Alex said, smoothly. "But it's not all bad, is it? I assume you heard me tell Alison that Tanya Davi is no longer with us?"

"Yeah, I heard," I said warily. "Who's Tanya Davi?"

"She's the woman you saw with your boyfriend last night."

I didn't move. Didn't blink. Didn't breath.

"If you've come to confront her I can assure you that she won't be bothering him again," he continued. "She told me as much when she agreed to hand in her letter of resignation."

"And when exactly did she do that?"

"Very early this morning."

"This morning." I glanced around the room again. In the upper right-hand corner was a tiny little camera. I wasn't sure if its presence made me safer or not. I suspected not.

"Was Tanya checked into room 608 with Anatoly?" I asked quietly.

"608," Alex mused. "That's your room, isn't it, Miss Katz? Or can I call you Sophie?"

My heart was beating so loud now I was sure he would be able to hear it. "I don't have a room here."

"Our records say otherwise. Of course you won't be paying for it. We've comped everything as we do for all our most important VIPs."

"Did you cash my check?"

Alex unlocked the top drawer of his desk and pulled the check out. "I've decided to keep it as a souvenir."

I leaned forward, my eyes on the check. "What happened in room 608?"

He dropped the check back in the drawer and locked it. "It's your room. You tell me."

"Listen asshole, I don't know who you are—"

"But you do know that I'm in charge here and, as far as I'm aware, nothing out of the ordinary happened in your room. Housekeeping has already been up there, and everything is neat and tidy and ready for you. They made the bed, they've given you fresh towels, vacuumed... they even vacuumed the closet."

I opened my mouth but said nothing. I considered running, but at that very moment I couldn't move

"I'm your friend, Sophie. I'm doing you a huge favor."

I held onto the arms of my chair in order to keep myself from shaking.

"What favor is that?"

"I accepted Tanya's resignation despite the staffing difficulties it created. Why?" He took on the tone of exaggerated innocence. "What did you think I meant?"

"Actually," I snapped, my irritation momentarily overwhelming my panic, "I thought you might be on the verge of confessing to murder."

Alex laughed. It wasn't a dark, ominous laugh or even a sarcastic one. Just a genuine chuckle—which, given the accusation, made it all the more chilling. "I'm not exactly an assassin. I'm a GM, and as the GM my only job is to make sure our guests are taken care of and leave here happy." He leaned back in his chair and his voice suddenly became serious, almost tender. "I'm taking care of you now. If you were anxious or worried about—anything, you don't need to be—not anymore."

"Really," I said, flatly.

"You're my guest. It's my job to keep you safe."

I glanced around the room again. Lots of expensive items but not a single personal photo. The only thing the décor gave away was that the occupant of the office was wealthy and had good taste. But I couldn't tell what his hobbies or interests were or if he had a family. He also didn't have any windows.

"I don't need a protector, *Alex.*" I said, spitting out his first name like a curse. "What I need is for someone to answer my questions."

"Which are?"

I shifted away from him and directed my response to the surveillance camera. "Where's Anatoly?"

"Who's Anatoly?" Alex asked.

"You know."

"No, I don't believe I do."

I whirled back on him. "You know he's my boyfriend! The guy you were following last night!"

"Ah," Alex steepled his fingers. "You hadn't given me his name before. So he's still your boyfriend? Even after his recent infidelities?"

"He didn't cheat on me."

"Did he tell you that?"

I smiled, coldly. "That's a very good point. Tell you what, why don't you put me in touch with him and I'll ask him to explain himself. How's that work for you?"

"I don't know where he is," Alex insisted. "All I can tell you is that a cleaner was sent into your room—"

"You mean a housekeeper."

Alex arched an eyebrow. "You say tomato I say... something else. The point is the room was made spotless... for your comfort and Ms. Davi—"

"Is no longer with us. Yeah, I heard you the first time."

"Good, then we're done here." He pulled out a small piece of notepaper and scribbled something down on it. "I hope you enjoy the rest of your stay with us—"

"I'm not staying with you."

He nodded distractedly without looking up from the paper. "Again, our records say otherwise. But regardless, I hope you enjoy the rest of your vacation. Take my card in case you have any follow-up questions—"

"Follow-up questions? But we're not done!"

"I'm afraid I have a meeting to attend. I've also written down the name of one of our guest services representatives. I'll instruct her to get you free tickets to any show you want to see and arrange for you to get complimentary spa services here at the hotel."

"But—" he handed me the notepaper. On it, he had written: *We're being watched. Meet me at this location tonight, and I'll answer the rest of your questions.*

Below that there was an address. I glanced up at him. He was still smiling, but for the first time, I thought I saw a trace of concern behind the cavalier exterior.

"Right," I said uncertainly. "Well, I am in need of some spa services. Do you think they'll be able to fit me in for a facial at seven o'clock tonight?"

"They're open until 11 p.m. and usually they have more

appointments available later in the evening...9ish should work, I think."

"Great… then, um, I'll try to get an appointment around 9ish."

"Sounds good."

I paused for a moment. "I want my check back."

"That's too bad. You gave it to me as payment for a favor, remember?"

"That was a mistake."

"Yeah, but it was *your* mistake, not mine." He cocked his head to the side. "Of course if you think you really are legally entitled to it, we could bring it to the courts. Should we bring it to the attention of a small claims court, Sophie?"

I bit down on my lip.

"I didn't think so. Again, I hope you enjoy your stay." He got up and opened the door for me.

There was really nothing more to say so I walked out, past Anne, who offered me a cursory goodbye, and out into the casino.

I stopped somewhere around the blackjack tables to catch my breath. There was a chance that I had just been talking to a murderer. I found my way to the edge of the casino and called Dena.

"So you're finally awake?" Dena asked upon picking up. But I could hear the accusation in her voice.

"I um, wasn't actually sleeping."

"No shit."

I covered one of my ears to better block out the sounds coming from the slots. "I didn't want to lie, but I had to do this alone," I continued.

"Do *what* alone?"

"I came back to The Hotel Noir." A woman a few feet away lit up a cigarette and the smell of self-destruction overtook me. "I wanted to find the guy I paid the $250 to."

"Please tell me you're kidding."

"I found him," I said quickly.

"Is he a guest at the hotel?"

"Umm… no. He's the GM of the hotel."

Another pause. "The GM," she said flatly.

"Yep."

"Yeah, I'm not a hotelier or anything, but if the GM there is willing to sell out for $250, Hotel Noir might need to put together a more competitive compensation package for its management."

"I don't think he did it for the money. Actually, I can't really figure out why he did it. I asked him…" my voice trailed off as I spotted a woman watching me from halfway across the room. But she wasn't just *a* woman, she was *the* woman. She was standing next to the craps table. This time her dress was purple and black—I recognized it from the Versace ad campaign—and her pink stiletto heels had been replaced by black stiletto boots.

"Dena, I gotta go."

"What do you mean, *you gotta go*? Are you still at Hotel Noir?"

"I'll call you back in a bit," I said. "Promise."

"Sophie!" But I hung up.

The stiletto woman started walking toward me at the same moment I started walking toward her. There was a determination in her step that made everyone around her make way. I had been in a daze last night. I hadn't been able to see through the little sex-kitten act she was putting on, but now that act seemed paper-thin. It couldn't conceal the tough and almost frightening force that lay behind it.

We both stopped when there was no more than three feet between us. At the roulette table next to us, someone shrieked for joy as another groaned.

Simultaneously we asked the same question: "Where is he?"

She hesitated a moment and then glanced around the room nervously. "Let's take a walk," she suggested.

"Why can't we talk here?"

"People might be listening," she explained as she led me toward the exit. "It's not a normal hotel."

"Not normal by Vegas standards?"

"Not normal by *any* standards."

"So what are you saying? It's the Hotel California?"

"Yes," she said dryly. "The Hotel California in Nevada." She pushed open the glass doors leading to the strip. "But the big difference is that *you* can get out."

I followed her into the sunshine and dug into my bag for some sunglasses. "Well we're both outside, so I guess that means you can get out too."

"No, not really," she said, quietly. "Not in any way that matters."

I didn't understand what that meant, so I let it pass for the moment. I watched her open up her handbag, but instead of taking out sunglasses she took out a package of cigarettes. "Want one?"

"I don't smoke. I'm not a big fan of secondhand smoke either."

"Oh?" She asked, blithely lighting up a cigarette. "So you decided to ignore my advice? You're not leaving

Vegas?"

"It sounded more like a warning than advice, but yes, I'm ignoring it."

Stiletto lady shrugged. I was having a hard time keeping up with her without getting winded which was humbling since I wasn't wearing killer heels or sucking in carcinogens.

"Warning you to get out of Vegas was supposed to be my good deed of the week but you've completely messed that up." She took another long drag from her cigarette. "You're probably going to ignore this advice too, but if you *are* going to stay in Vegas, you should at least stay away from Hotel Noir."

"Oh for God's sake, if there's something you want to tell me about the hotel then tell me! I don't have time to decipher codes."

She blew out a long stream of smoke as a family of four hurried past us on the sidewalk. "It's owned by a very powerful family."

The alarm bells that went off in my head were so loud it was surprising other people couldn't hear them. "Are we talking about the Russian Mafia?"

Ms. Stiletto smiled "I don't really believe in labels."

"Riiight, well I guess a turd by any other name smells just as shitty." I tried to take a deep breath, but that ended with a cough. "The woman who was with Anatoly last night —"

"Tanya Davi," she supplied, "my cousin."

I was overtaken by an unwelcome wave of sympathy. "I'm sorry."

"Me too. No one should have to put up with a family member like Tanya. She's awful."

"You're... you're using the present tense."

"Why wouldn't I?" She glanced back toward the direction of the hotel and then grabbed my arm and abruptly pulled me onto a side street. The pedestrian traffic immediately became more manageable. A pudgy middle-aged man at a bus stop flashed us a crooked toothed grin as we passed.

"What happened to Tanya?" I asked carefully.

"She handed in her resignation this morning and now she's gone. But to be fair, she's been dead to me for quite some time now."

I gave her a sideways glance, but she kept her focus straight ahead.

"That's not what happened," I said, firmly.

She shrugged. "Winners write the history books." She shot me a quick, meaningful look. "Tanya isn't the winner here. There is no other story to be told."

I came to an abrupt stop. Stiletto lady followed my example and pivoted to face me.

"Who the hell are you and why can't you talk like a normal human being? Not everything needs to be a fucking riddle, metaphor, or analogy! What. Is. *Wrong with you*?"

She glanced around the area as if there might be spies around every corner. "Who am I," she mused. "At the moment I'm Anatoly's only hope." She then brought her eyes to me. I recognized her expression; after all, I'd seen it in the mirror enough times. It was determination mingled with a healthy dose of fear. "I can help him. I saved his life last night—"

"Wait, *you* saved his life? What the hell happened?"

"—and if you know where he is you've got to tell me because I swear I can save him again. I might be the only one who can."

"You won't even give me your name! Why should I trust you enough to tell you anything?"

"I guess I'm just hoping you have good instincts about people," she said with a sad smile. "I'm not asking you to just give me his location, not if you're not comfortable with that. You can take me there and be there right by my side. If Anatoly thinks I'm some kind of threat to him he can shoot me on the spot—but he's not going to think that."

"Because you saved his life yesterday."

"Exactly." The wind picked up her red hair and it flew almost gracefully behind her shoulders, like a Chinese flag without the yellow stars. I didn't trust this woman, and I didn't like her—but none of that really mattered because I didn't have any information to give her even if I wanted to.

"I don't know where he is."

She studied me for a moment and then took a very long drag off her cigarette. "Well shit," she whispered. "Where the hell could he be?"

"When did you last see him?" I asked, trying unsuccessfully to keep the rising panic out of my voice. "What happened last night?"

She was quiet for a moment as she stared at the cigarette between her fingers. "Are you the reason Anatoly quit smoking?"

I hesitated. I hadn't known that Anatoly had ever smoked. I let my eyes wander to the cars lined up impatiently at the red light. "He… he quit before we met," I hedged.

"Ah." Did she sound relieved? "Well he never smoked much to begin with," she went on. "Just while enjoying a good cognac or after sex."

My head snapped back in her direction. She raised her eyebrows mockingly as she sucked leisurely on her cigarette.

"Natasha?" I asked.

"Ah, you know my name." She craned her neck upward before blowing out a long steady stream of smoke.

"If you see him tell him I can still help him," she said and then added with a sly smile. "Tell him I'll bend over backward for him—just like old times."

I stood there frozen as she turned on her impossibly skinny high heels and walked away.

CHAPTER EIGHT

"They say a good man is worth fighting for. But a man who's good for YOU shouldn't make you fight just for the right to be in his life."
—*Death of The Party*

I called Dena and told her I couldn't stomach going to the trade show today. I couldn't really stomach anything other than going back into my room and hiding under the covers. So I suppose I shouldn't have been surprised when I came back to the hotel and found her and Mary Ann sitting on my bed.

Mary Ann got up and pulled me into a hug. "You're having a hard time, huh?"

I sighed and dropped down into one of the chairs. "My life sucks."

"I've been thinking," Mary Ann said, as she sat back down next to Dena, "maybe things aren't as bad as they seem."

"How is that even possible?" I laughed.

"Well, we know someone broke into your house and brought your stuff to that hotel room, but maybe there wasn't an actual murder. Maybe, just maybe this woman committed suicide!"

Dena shifted her position to look at Mary Ann. "The woman was found stuffed in a closet with a bullet hole in her head, in a room that wasn't hers, and without a gun in her hand. What about that sounds like a suicide?"

"Well, I was thinking," Mary Ann said again, "what if she didn't want her blood and… you know, her… her brains splattering all over the place. So she decided to, like, contain it to the closet? She was just being considerate!"

"And the fact that she didn't have a gun?" Dena asked, dryly.

"Are we sure she didn't have a gun?" Mary Ann pressed. "Maybe she was sitting on it."

"Uh-huh." Dena looked like she was working extra hard not to hit her cousin over the head with the jaguar handle of her cane. "How did she manage to sit on her gun *after* she had just used it to shoot herself in the head?"

"Oh, oh, I've thought about that! I have it all figured out," Mary Ann was bouncing up and down on the bed, pleased that she had managed to anticipate this line of questioning. "I was reading this article in Yahoo News and it said that sometimes bodies have these, like, reflexive reactions right after they die. Like sometimes someone will blink and move their mouth after being decapitated or, um, sometimes their arms jerk around—"

"Those are convulsions!" Dena snapped. "Bodies convulse after the brain has stopped working properly, but they don't stick handguns under their ass! You need to reread that article!"

"I met Anatoly's wife," I interjected. *The woman he was*

claiming to marry for citizenship. Dena and Mary Ann fell quiet, their eyes widened with surprise and curiosity.

"What's she like?" Mary Ann whispered.

"She's a Bond Girl. A bad one. Anatoly married Pussy Galore."

Mary Ann cocked her head to the side, making her curls cascade over her right shoulder. "I thought Pussy Galore was one of the good Bond girls."

"Good or bad," Dena said, "nobody *marries* Pussy Galore. It would be like marrying your battery operated Octopus."

"Yeah? Well, it doesn't matter. She may have married him, but she's not keeping him." My volume was rising, but I couldn't seem to bring it back down. "I will NOT lose everything! I'm the one who's going to save Anatoly from Dr. Evil or whatever. This stiletto wearing, carcinogen inhaling, pussy-galore *bitch* is just going to have to play Russian roulette with somebody else!"

My friends didn't respond right away. I knew I was on the verge of losing it. On the other hand, dealing with any of this while sane might not even be possible. The time had come to embrace the crazy.

"So," Dena said in a voice that was straining for calm, "I guess this means you're not ready to kick Anatoly to the curb after all."

I blinked in surprise. Oddly enough I hadn't really thought about that. I had been so caught up in just making sure he was alive I hadn't worked out what I would do with him if he was.

"I'm not sure," I admitted. "This is putting a lot of strain on our relationship."

"He's hardly been the pinnacle of loyalty," Dena said.

"Maybe not," I agreed, "but… but he's still *mine,* and if anyone's going to kill him, it should be me. Not the extended family of some mafia slut!"

Mary Ann twisted one of her curls around her finger. "In a weird way, that's kinda romantic." Dena shot her a disgusted look, but Mary Ann persisted. "She has to do this. She loves him and… when it's true love you have to do what you can to protect that, right? It's in every good Disney movie."

Dena put her hand over her chest. "Oh my God, what has Monty done to you?"

"And you know what else?" Mary Ann continued, unfazed, "In all the *really* good Disney fairy tales, the princess rescues the prince before he has a chance to rescue her! Monty says that's how Disney honors feminism. The princess gets to rescue the prince before he takes her in his arms, marries her, showers her with luxury, and takes care of her for the rest of her life! It's, like, a Gloria Steinem thing."

I blinked. "Not… quite."

Dena got up and took my hand. "I know you don't want to hear this, but there's a chance that you might not be able to take down the Russian Mafia. Can you at least consider that possibility?"

"But… what if I have to in order to get him back?" My eyes filled with tears. Dena briskly pulled a tissue from the Kleenex box on the desk and handed it over.

"Sophie, what about the GM you gave the check to? What's going on with that?"

I gave Mary Ann and Dena the full rundown of the morning's events. "If he's telling the truth," Dena said once I was finished, "you're out of the woods."

"That's a big if and it doesn't sound like Anatoly's out of the woods at all."

Dena sighed. "Look, come back to the trade show with us. We can talk about all of this while sampling flavored exotic oils."

"I can't. Really, I'm so, so tired."

Dena gave me a severe look. "You used that line earlier this morning, remember?"

"I'm serious this time. Call the room in a half hour and see if I'm here if you like but oh my God, I can *not* go to that trade show right now. Before it was funny but now... if I even look at those toys, it will feel like they're all there to remind me that I no longer have Anatoly here to hold me or... or touch me. People are supposed to see those devices as ways to spice up their sex lives. But for me, they're just grotesque substitutes for what I used to have—to what I really *want*. And Dena, I'm *so* tired. I just can't go."

Dena studied my dark circles and bloodshot eyes. "You better not be bullshitting me, Sophie."

"You're one of the very few people in this world I've never lied to. You know that."

Dena nodded and gestured for Mary Ann to get up. "I'll be calling the room later, just to be sure." Mary Ann gave me one more hug. As Dena opened the door for her, she gave me a sympathetic smile. "Just do me a favor and think about this. Anatoly's married to someone else. He doesn't have to be your problem anymore—unless you need him to be."

I didn't say anything as the door closed behind them. Part of me wanted to shout after her that I didn't need anyone to be my problem. But I couldn't force out the lie. To say you didn't need problems was to say you didn't need love.

I lay down and attempted to sleep, but my thoughts kept waking me up and when I did sleep, my dreams were replaced with memories.

I remembered the day Anatoly had made whipped cream from scratch. I had teased him for not taking the Cool Whip route, and he had responded by picking up the bowl of his homemade concoction and leading me up the stairs to our bedroom. He sat me down on the bed and explained that homemade whipped cream was richer than anything you could buy in a store. He then slid a cream coated finger into my mouth. Next, he pulled my shirt over my head and removed my bra before instructing me on where to place the cream. He watched as I did so as he continued to talk, his voice deep, his pace slow. He told me that, unlike the store bought brands, homemade whipped cream was rich but not too sweet. As I lifted my finger for another taste, he lowered his mouth to my breast. A trail of cream was painted on my stomach as he described the texture of a good whipped cream. It had been hard to listen at that point because his hand had already slipped inside my jeans. As I felt his fingers enter me I...

... woke up. A memory, not really a dream.

I sighed and swung my legs over the side of the bed. Six years. Six years of going in circles with this guy. Our first date had ended with an argument. I had stormed off and less than ten minutes later he was saving my life. That's how it always was with him. Either he was saving my life or driving me insane. It seemed like there should be a middle ground. One that didn't involve fatalities or mental illness.

Dena never yelled at her lovers the way I yelled at Anatoly, not even Jason whom she loved and had sustained a committed but open relationship with for a few years now. While in the bedroom she would occasionally whip him, sometimes tie him up... throw in a ball gag and a blindfold, and it was easy to see how she was able to channel her aggressions into a mutually agreed upon activity. But if she became angry at Jason's behavior outside the bedroom she'd just tell him straight up what her beef was and then she'd walk away until he decided to come around. "Men are not worth frown lines." That was her motto. Her cousin Mary Ann had a whole different approach to love. Love turned her into a doe-eyed fairy princess. She had even wanted to get married in front of Sleeping Beauty's Castle at Disneyland until my sister mercifully talked her out of it.

But for me it was different. I couldn't deal with love in the pragmatic manner that Dena did, and I wasn't enough of a romantic to harbor any Cinderella fantasies. Love, for reasons I could *not* explain, turned me into a fighter. It was like love was the arena, and I was the Matador choosing to wave a red flag in front of a bull. It was a brutal, beautiful, compelling, and totally addictive sport.

And in *my* version of the game, no animals were ever harmed. The only thing that ever got trampled on were hearts —usually mine. The bull almost always got away leaving me with nothing more than a pile of his BS.

I surveyed the room. I could pack up and be out of here by the end of the day. Maybe that's what I should do. Maybe Anatoly wasn't even in Vegas anymore. Wasn't it at least possible that he had gone back to San Francisco? Did he even know I was here?

I opened the drawer of the nightstand and pulled out Anatoly's iPhone. What kind of moron runs out of a room without his phone? No matter what the emergency you *always* grab you phone!

I glared at the screen. "Stupido," I said in what I imagined was a fairly good Spanish accent. I liked the feel of the word. "Stupido," I said again, and this time I reached my arm back and hurled the phone at the door—

—and it was caught—by Anatoly.

CHAPTER
NINE

"My husband and I have a deal. The day he's able to make me a multi-orgasmic woman is the day I stop dragging him to romantic comedies."
—Death Of The Party

He stood in the doorway, with that totally infuriating and totally sexy half smile on his face. He held up the phone I had just inadvertently hurled at him. "Just like old times."

He let the door close behind him.

For a full minute, the room was completely silent.

And then he took one step forward.

"I thought I'd stop by and say hello," he said, his voice shaking ever so slightly.

And that was enough for me. I burst into tears and threw myself at him. He caught me in his arms and kissed my cheeks, my hair, my eyelids, and finally my mouth. I held onto him so tightly he would have had to struggle to get away.

But he didn't try.

His hands moved up my back and then down to my hips and then all the way back up to my hair. "I'm sorry," he whispered.

"Shut up." I pushed myself away from him and put my hands on my hips. "The Russians are out to get you, and there's literally a skeleton in your closet!"

"Tanya," he said the name slowly, his face completely unreadable.

I stood a little straighter and tried to access the courage that was hiding somewhere underneath all my fear. "I need to know something...actually, two things."

He nodded, but his jaw seemed to tighten.

"One, did you sleep with her and two, did you kill her?"

He took a deep breath, but he didn't avoid my gaze. "Which one is the worse offense?"

"Just... answer the questions."

"I didn't even consider sleeping with her. I didn't kill her either, but I wasn't all that upset to see her die."

"Wow." I sat down on the bed and stared at the floor. Was that the answer I wanted? "I have another question."

He sat down next to me. "Go ahead."

"Do I know who you are?" The question came out as little more than a whisper.

He grasped my chin and guided my face in his direction. In a voice that was rich with both pain and warmth, he said, "Yes."

With his free hand he pushed my hair from my face, and for the first time, I realized that he was fighting back tears. "I thought they had you," he whispered. "When Tanya led me to that room, and you weren't there—just a man with a gun —I thought I was too late."

"It wasn't my room! I... wait, there was a man with a gun?"

"He showed up a few minutes after I got there—by then Tanya already had me at gunpoint."

"She…" my voice faded off as I tried to make sense of what he was telling me. "The guy with the gun," I said, slowly, "is he the one who shot Tanya?"

"No, Natasha did that."

"Your wife shot Tanya?"

Anatoly nodded. "She saved my life."

And just like that, he had killed the mood. Again I pulled away and stood up. "I have spent the last eighteen hours *freaking out*!" I snapped. "First I see you with some play-mate from hell then I go up to what I think is your room and find her dead in a closet filled with *my* stuff! Then I'm ha-rassed by your wife and the GM of that stupid hotel—"

"Wait," Anatoly reached out and grabbed my arm. "What GM?"

"That can *not* be the thing you're focusing on!" I yanked my arm away. "Your wife shot your bimbo in the head in a room that was registered under your girlfriend's name! Do you have any idea how fucked up that is? I mean even a US Congressman couldn't come up with something this de-ranged! Do you get that? I mean for God's sake, Anatoly, the only reason I came to this stupid city was to buy a vibrator!"

Anatoly cocked his head to the side. "Are you talking about that trade show? The minute we hit a bump in our relationship you go shopping for sex toys?"

"We didn't hit a bump. I kicked you out of my life!"

"I was worried that you might find some guy to have rebound sex with. But instead, you went shopping for a vibrator. That's…" he paused as he searched for the appro-priate word, "sweet."

"Getting it on with a vibrator is sweet?"

"It means you're still thinking of me and that another man can't replace me."

"What the fuck are you talking about? It means you can be replaced with a dildo."

"No woman uses a vibrator without conjuring up an accompanying fantasy." He stood up and brushed my cheek with the back of his hand. "What's your fantasy?"

"It doesn't involve you, that's for sure. If anything it involves Ryan Gosling and an octopus-shaped bath toy with eight functioning tentacles."

Anatoly laughed, and I was immediately reminded of how much I loved that sound.

"I missed you," he said quietly. "I really—I really thought I had lost you."

I pressed my lips together as the tears broke free again. I wanted to kill him... but... but I was so incredibly relieved that no one *else* had. I reached out and pressed my palm against his chest. "*This* is real." I looked up into his eyes, and I could see that he was losing his battle against tears too. "I take it back," I said, desperately trying to keep my voice even. "I don't want Ryan Gosling, or the dildo or even the octopus. I just want you."

He pulled me to him and his mouth crushed against mine. I felt his arms surround me and there was no space between us anymore. Every part of me was responding to him, and I could feel his desire literally growing and pressing up against me. I felt a surge of power. He wanted me. He had risked his very life to be here with me. "Are we in danger?" I gasped.

"I'll protect you." His voice was slightly muffled by the

shirt I was pulling off him. God, his abs were as perfectly sculpted as ever. Before I met Anatoly, I hadn't even known there were straight men who *had* abs like his!

"But aren't you in danger too?" I breathed as his lips moved down my neck.

He pulled away slightly, pulled my shirt over my head and took my face in his hands. "You're worth the risk."

It was a stupid risk to take. We were waving a red flag in front of a bull; risking our very lives.

And I loved every second of it.

I sucked in a sharp breath as his fingers unclasped my bra.

He pulled the bra from me and gently ran his thumbs over my nipples. "I was so worried I would never feel you again," he murmured. Without a word, I slipped my hand down to the front of his pants.

My fingers fumbled with the button of his jeans and I felt him, hard and perfect, no batteries needed.

I let my fingers trace his ridge and tip and felt him harden more still. "I want to feel you too… inside me, Anatoly. Right now."

And just like that, we were on the bed again. I could barely feel the sheets beneath me. All I could feel was him. He pulled my jeans off and my panties went off with them. I moaned as he touched me. His fingers toyed with me until I could barely contain myself.

"More," I breathed. "I need all of you."

He removed his hand, and I gasped again as I felt his weight on top of me…

… and when he entered me my world exploded.

I dug my fingernails into his back. I didn't care if Anatoly had a harem! I was never letting him go again!

"I love you."

He breathed those words into my ear, and I tried to respond in kind, but I couldn't speak. All I could do was be here feeling this. I wrapped my legs around him as he moved over me and raised my hips to meet him. I scratched up his back as he sped up his rhythm. No one would be able to look at him shirtless without knowing he was mine. He continued to run his hands over my face, my breasts, the curve of my waist. He bit down gently on my lower lip all the while pushing further and further inside of me with increasing force until he finally pushed the words up through my throat and I was able to say, "I love you too."

And that's when I felt him come inside me, my body immediately reacting with an orgasm all its own.

We lay there, breathless and sweaty, too tired to move.

It was perfect.

CHAPTER TEN

"I promised myself I wouldn't sleep with more than ten people in my lifetime. It works for me because I keep going back and sleeping with my ex-boyfriends."
—Death Of The Party

I stared at the ceiling trying so hard to focus on nothing but the feeling of the man next to me. But reality was sneaking back into the room, tapping me on the shoulder, forcing itself into my consciousness.

"They're watching me." I said quietly. "Natasha's tracked me down twice, and there are others... I don't know who they are, but I can sense them."

"You don't have to worry about Natasha, and those others don't know I'm here," he said. He turned on his side and stared down at me. "But you're right, they have been watching you. That's why you have to go back to San Francisco."

"They won't watch me in San Francisco?" I asked incredulously. "You know, they were in my house. They took my computer... with my *manuscript* on it, Anatoly. I don't know if I can really hide from these guys."

Anatoly swore under his breath. "I was in your place several hours before I got on the plane to get here. They must have come in right after I left."

I paused for a second. "You realize that you're confessing to breaking into my house, right?"

"For over a year it's been my home too," he countered and then after a moment added, "You had already boxed up a bunch of my stuff. Clothes, books..."

"I did."

"There were some books I couldn't find. Like my books on soccer—"

"That's because I donated a lot of your books to the library the day after you left."

Anatoly squeezed his eyes closed. "Did you? That's great. What library?"

"The one by the Civic Center."

I smiled to myself as he cursed in Russian. I hadn't actually donated them although I had thought about it. I had even put them in a box marked, "library" and stored them in the garage. I knew how much Anatoly loved his books and I had wanted to hurt him... more to the point, I had wanted to get all the things that helped define him out of my sight. He had hurt me.

And now I had opened my arms to him again and made myself vulnerable despite the hell he had put me through.

The least I could do was let him stress about his books for a day or two.

"What else did they take?" He asked.

"Just my storage discs."

"What about your MacBook?"

"I have it with me."

"OK, you can leave it here for them to take. Then everything will be good."

"*Good?* Then I won't have any copies of my work! I'm two-thirds through the book! That's 280 pages of *bad* Anatoly!"

"Save it in Dropbox. If they know they have everything that you can store an electronic file on, they probably won't be back to your home."

"What are they looking for?"

"Evidence," he said with a sigh. He sat up and rested his back against the wooden headboard. "Working for the mafia… it's not the kind of job you can just walk away from. I had to prove my loyalty and that I could keep my mouth shut."

"And they weren't convinced of that?"

"They *were* convinced. But for some reason, they've changed their minds. All these years I've been silent. I have information that could be catastrophic for them if I shared it with the wrong people."

"So why do they think you're going to start talking after all these years?"

"It might not be them—not entirely."

"We're dealing with the mafia and… and then some? Who else?"

Anatoly tightened his arm around me. "It doesn't really matter. What matters is that there are people who know I have damning information. They know there's a chance I've stored it in some kind of written or electronic medium. Once they have that, all they have to do to suppress the information is kill me."

I sat up next to him. His eyes wandered down to my bare

breasts, and I snatched up the sheet to cover myself. "Stay focused! If these guys can assure themselves that you don't have any files on them, they can kill you... and you want me to leave them my MacBook? Are you suffering from a head injury? Let them think there's a file!"

"If they think there's a file they will either come after you because they'll suspect you can lead them to it, or they'll come after you to make me tell them where it is."

"Anatoly—"

"I'll do what I can to get your stuff back, but Sophie you have to go back to San Francisco. They have to think we're completely through with one another. Otherwise, they'll use you to get to me."

I shook my head, refusing to accept that. "What was the deal with Tanya?"

Anatoly sighed and rested his hand on my thigh. Although the sheet kept our skin from actually touching I could still feel the warmth of his palm. Again I shook my head. I would stay focused even if it took every last bit of willpower I possessed.

"Tanya had a crush on me while I was with Natasha," Anatoly explained. "I thought I could get her to help me and lead me to you. But apparently she was still bitter that I rejected her back in the day."

"So she tried to kill you."

"She has a tendency to overreact."

I glanced at the open door that connected my room to Dena and Marcus'. Either of them could walk in at any minute. "But was this all her plan?" I asked rushing my words together. "Is she the one who made the mob lose faith in you?"

"No, she just agreed to lead me into a trap. She was never a big planner."

"Anatoly, we may not have much time," I said. "Tell me now what the evidence is that they're looking for."

Anatoly hesitated. "I don't want to lie to you anymore."

I smiled wryly. "It's nice to know we can still agree on something."

He nodded and pulled me back toward him so that my head was resting on his shoulder. I waited for him to say more. He didn't.

"Wait a minute," I said slowly, "you don't want to lie to me so as an alternative you're just going to stop talking?"

"If I tell you more it'll put you in danger. Like I said, they know what they're looking for isn't in your house, so if they think I'm out of your life, they'll leave you alone."

"Yeah but the problem is, you're not out of my life. You're not even out of my bed."

Anatoly was quiet for a moment. He shifted his body toward mine and let his fingers run over my now tangled hair. "You're beautiful."

I liked that. It was so much better than, *you look beautiful*. No, with Anatoly my beauty was a state of being that couldn't be disturbed by bloodshot eyes or a tangled nest of hair. I tilted my head toward him and smiled up into his eyes. "Tell me what you're going to do. I promise not to get mad."

He kissed me gently. "I'm going to have to be with Natasha for a while."

I slapped him across his stupid face.

He rubbed his cheek, which was now bright red. "I thought you weren't going to get mad."

"Well gee, I guess you're not the only person who can break a promise! You can NOT go back to Natasha!"

"Sophie, if the mob thinks that torturing someone I love will get them what they want that's what they'll do."

"Sooo....you're going back to Natasha so they'll torture *her*?" Suddenly his plan sounded a lot more appealing. I mean I didn't want them pulling her fingernails out or anything but a little Chinese water torture never killed anyone.

"They won't torture Natasha because of who she's related to. But she might be able to help me convince some key players that I'm not as dangerous as they think I am. And if she can't, she might at least be able to help me kill the individuals leading the crusade against me."

"You're planning on a murder?"

"It'll be self-defense."

"And Tanya? Did Natasha kill her in self-defense too?"

"Tanya had a gun so yes, you could make a case for it."

"*You could make a case for it*? The woman was stuffed in a closet with a bullet in her head! I'm not sure this is one of those times when we should be coloring things in shades of grey!"

"I don't think Natasha needed to kill her." Each of Anatoly's words were carefully measured. "She could have shot her in the leg or the shoulder and Natasha's a good enough marksman to have done that. But still, she saw the gun in Tanya's hand and she had to make a snap decision. If she hadn't shot Tanya, I might not have been able to get away."

I hesitated a moment as I turned this over in my mind. The last thing I wanted was to be indebted to Natasha. "What happened after you left the hotel room?"

"The less you know the better."

"Perfect," I said flatly. "So you're leaving?"

"For a while, yes."

"And you want me to go back to San Francisco."

"On the next plane."

"And if I do you'll be able to defeat the Russian Mafia."

He hesitated at that. "I might be able to get out of this without anyone important getting hurt."

"And who are these important people? You're an important person, right?"

"Sophie—"

"And what are you going to do with Natasha while you're *with* her?"

Again, Anatoly hesitated. "I'll do what I need to do to keep her on my side. No more, no less."

"Oh fuck that." I jumped out of bed, completely naked and started the search for the clothes I had been so anxious to get out of just a short time ago. "I'm not leaving Vegas. I'm not going to sit around twiddling my thumbs while you play Bonnie and Clyde with a Russian psychopath."

Anatoly sat up and pulled on his boxer briefs and jeans. "Sophie, we don't have a lot of options here."

"I thought you said there was no *we*!" I snapped as I yanked on my own pants.

Leisurely he walked over to the minibar and pulled out a small bottle of vodka and a cranberry juice which he poured into a glass. "You're being unreasonable."

"I'm being unreasonable?" I pulled on my shirt then pounded my fist against the wall three times before facing him again. "You just told me you're going to take one for the team with Natasha! Tell me, how many orgasms are you going to have to give this woman to make it worth it for her to double cross the mafia? *That's* unreasonable! Paying $30 for a minibar cocktail is unreasonable. What *I'm* being is hysterical!"

Anatoly handed me the $30 cocktail, and I downed it in three consecutive gulps.

"You're putting words in my mouth," he said. "I didn't say I was going to be sleeping with her."

"You didn't say you weren't either! What you *did* say is that you were going to take off with another woman!"

"If I thought there was another way to do this there'd be something to talk about." He said, taking a seat on the bed.

I took a deep and very shaky breath. He wasn't hearing me. I had to find a different tone... and maybe a different volume.

Slowly, I sat down beside him and clasped my hands together in my lap to better keep them from whacking him upside the head. "I understand that you're trying to protect me but what I don't think *you* understand is that there is no way in hell that I'm going to let you out of my sight until we resolve this. If you even think of trying to leave here without me, I'll barricade the door. I'll scream so loud every mafia thug in the country will hear me. I'll—"

"I got it," Anatoly said resignedly, "and I knew you'd say that."

"Right well... I'm... I..." Something was wrong. My thoughts were becoming jumbled. "I'm dizzy," I murmured

"You just had a glass of vodka."

"No, no, not vodka dizzy," I clarified. The room wasn't just spinning it was spinning at an odd angle... and everything was getting fuzzier. "This... Anatoly this is different."

I was having a hard time making eye contact... it was

almost like there was two of him. But in his four eyes, I thought I saw a trace of sympathy. "I think what you're reacting to is what I put *in* your vodka—other than the cranberry juice."

"You... you drugged me?" I slurred.

"You're just going to fall asleep for a little while. I can't have you following me."

"Wha..." I could barely think. There was something I should do now... something... I needed to... do something very, very bad to Anatoly.

"Go back to San Francisco," I could hear him say as he eased me back on the bed. "I'll call you when things are taken care of. It may take awhile, but I *will* fix this."

"Anatoly," I whispered as my eyes fluttered close, "when I wake up..."

"Yes," I heard his voice through the haze, tender... even loving.

"I am going to kick your ass."

And then the haze overtook me.

CHAPTER
ELEVEN

If you're going to medicate people for being obsessive, you're going to have to drug every person who has the misfortune of falling in love.
—Death Of The Party

When I woke up, Dena was sitting by my side shaking me, and Leah was leaning over me flicking water into my face. Behind her, I could see the slightly fuzzy figure of Marcus and... someone else... probably Mary Ann, a little further behind him.

"Look, look! She's waking up!" Leah said, flicking so much water in my face I had to turn away to avoid drowning. "She's not in a coma!"

"What... where..." I blinked several times until the room came back into focus. "Is he here?" I asked groggily.

Marcus shot Dena a worrying glance. "Sweetie, are you okay?" he asked. "We were just about to call 911. We've been trying to wake you for several minutes now."

"He drugged me," I mumbled.

"Wait," Dena sat up a little straighter. "Someone was here, and they drugged you?"

"You mean like, with a roofie?" Marcus gasped.

"Oh my gosh, I know what a roofie is!" *Yes, that was definitely Mary Ann in the background.* "There was this Lifetime movie and this woman was given a roofie and… oh, Sophie! What did they do to you?"

"I don't' know if it was a roofie," I muttered. "Maybe."

"Oh dear God," Leah whispered.

Marcus kneeled down by the bed. "Sweetie, who did this and… do you know if they… did anything—"

"It was Anatoly… he… he was here, and we had sex."

"What!" Dena was on her feet now. When she stood without her cane she always seemed slightly off kilter, her weight never exactly distributed evenly. But at that moment I could see that if Anatoly had been on the other side of the room, she would have had the wherewithal to slam his head into the window.

"No, no," I corrected quickly, alertness beginning to come back to me. "I mean we *did* have sex, but he didn't have to drug me for that. He drugged me because I wasn't going to let him leave."

Marcus paused for a second and then let his head fall into his hands. "You tried to kidnap him?" he groaned. "And he had to drug you to escape. Sweetie, I've seen this story-line play out on General Hospital."

"Don't be melodramatic." I rubbed my eyes. The haze hadn't fully cleared yet. "I didn't kidnap him. He came to me! I just tried to hold him hostage."

Dena stared at me for what might have been a full minute before she exploded. "*Have you lost your mother-fucking mind*?"

Leah was clearly on Dena's side because she stopped

flicking me with water and just dumped the full content of the glass on my head. As I sat up sputtering she paced the room. "You could already be a suspect in a murder investigation, Sophie!" she snapped. "Isn't that enough!"

"He made love to me and then he told me he was going back to his wife! I had to do it!"

"No, you *really* didn't." Leah countered. "You know I came here to make sure you didn't marry some random idiot, but getting yourself shot might actually be worse!"

"*Might* be worse?" I asked. I raised my fingers to my temples. My head was killing me.

Marcus sighed. "I think it depends on the idiot in question."

Dena was tapping her cane on the ground... actually, it was a little more than a tap... if the people in the room below us were in, they were bound to register a complaint shortly. "You should be trying to get away from Anatoly," she said. "Far away. No man is worth all this. Let's buy you some adult bath toys and get the hell out of Vegas."

"It's worth considering," Marcus agreed.

"Excuse me, guys?" Mary Ann stepped forward, almost timidly. "Sophie seems to have a pretty big headache. Why don't you leave me with her and you can go out while she recovers."

"I can't leave her alone again!" Leah spat. "Every time I do she does something insane!"

"Um, Leah?" Mary Ann said, softly, "you told me we were coming here for my bachelorette party, but there was never a party planned. Even if everything had gone the way you wanted it to, you still would have been lying to me. You sort of owe me?" She phrased it as a question although there really was no question about it. Leah looked appropriately chastened.

"And," Mary Ann continued, "the rest of you sort of owe me for not wanting to include me in the weekend to begin with. I mean, a sex toy trade show in Vegas?" She shrugged. "Leah's right. This really should have been my bachelorette weekend."

Dena stopped banging her cane. "Mary Ann I—"

"No, no, it's okay," she said, holding up her hands to stop Dena's impending apology. "You can all make it up to me by giving me some alone time with Sophie. Would that be okay?"

There were a series of shrugs and muttered apologies.

"You could go get dinner or something?" Mary Ann suggested.

"Dinner?" I asked. "Shouldn't you guys be having lunch?"

Dena gave me a sideways glance. "We did, four hours ago."

"What!" I twisted toward the bedside clock. Sure enough, it was after six.

"We came in here to check on you a few times," Marcus confessed sheepishly. "But you seemed to be sleeping so peacefully we didn't try to disturb you. But when we came back this last time and you were still zonked out we knew something was wrong."

"So you'll give us some time?" Mary Ann pressed.

"*Puppetry of the Penis* starts in two and a half hours," Dena pointed out.

"*Puppetry of…*" Leah's voice faltered.

"It's a show where men turn their penises into puppets,"

Marcus explained. "But we only have three tickets."

"I'm really not up for it tonight," I said. There was only one dick I wanted to look at, and he had just gone back to his wife.

Leah sucked in a deep breath. "If you and Mary Ann really want some time together maybe… maybe I should go to the show in your place."

"You?" Dena took a step back and gave Leah a quick once over. "Have you been possessed by some demon who actually likes having fun?"

"I just don't think we should waste the ticket," Leah said defensively. "And we… we have to keep up appearances."

"By going to a penis show," Dena said flatly.

"Of course I have no interest in seeing men wave their… their peckers around but—"

"Excuse me," Dena interrupted, "but we're not talking about some kind of wood-drumming bird here. They're cocks. It's a cock show."

"Whatever!" Leah snapped. "If we don't use the tickets we already bought it will look suspicious!"

"Leah's right," Mary Ann said. "Have fun at the pecker show."

Dena looked like she wanted to protest but apparently she couldn't think of anything to say, so with a heavy sigh, she led the way out. "I can't believe I'm going to see *Puppetry of the Penis* with The Church Lady."

"Yes, that's right, Dena, I'm the Jewish Church lady," Leah hissed as she walked out behind her.

Marcus flashed us an apologetic smile. "Call when you want to join the party," he said and closed the door behind him.

Mary Ann sighed and went over to the mini bar. "There's a bottle of Advil here... did you leave these out?"

I shook my head.

"Anatoly must have done that for you. That was nice of him." She opened the bottle and took out two pills for me. "He left out some pretzels too."

"Minibar pretzels?" I asked.

"I don't think so—oh and I think he left a note!" She unfolded a piece of paper by the Advil, took a second to read it and then dumped a third Advil into her hand before handing them to me along with the pretzels and a bottle of water.

"What does the note say?" I asked as I downed my three pills.

"It's a boarding pass," she said as she took a seat by my side. "You have a seat on Southwest's 10:00 p.m. flight to Oakland... and he left a little note on the bottom saying he charged it to your Capital One Visa."

"Son of a bitch," I grumbled as I started snacking.

"He's just trying to protect you," Mary Ann assured me. "Dena, Marcus, and Leah... they don't understand."

"Understand what?"

"What it's like to be madly in love."

I thought about that for a second, nodded my agreement and handed Mary Ann a pretzel as a reward for her astute observation.

"Dena thinks it's silly that I'm so excited about my wedding but what she doesn't get is, well—Monty, he's like —like my *everything*. He's my world!"

I smiled and offered her another pretzel. Anatoly wasn't my world. But he was a large percentage of my everything, so I understood her point.

"If I thought someone was going to take my world away from me," Mary Ann continued, "I'd do anything—I'd risk my *life* to get it back. That's what you do for true love."

"Sooo," I said after washing down the pretzels with a little water, "are you saying I shouldn't leave Vegas?"

"You *can't* leave Vegas. You have to stay here and rescue your Prince. That's what you do when you have fairy-tale-worthy love."

I squeezed her hand. "This fairy tale may be more Brothers Grimm than Disney."

"Oh," she wrinkled her brow, "are they the head of Dreamworks or something?"

"No, I..." but then waved my hand in the air as if to dismiss the point. "Look, I want to tell you a little about a man I met today. A man named Alex." I proceeded to give her a very broad description of my interaction with Alex at the hotel, stopping several times for more gulps of water. Whatever Anatoly had given me was wearing off quickly, if you could count four and a half hours as quick. When I got to the part about how Alex gave me an address I got to my feet. "I don't want to wait until nine o'clock to go there," I said. "I want to take this guy off guard. In fact, if I can get to this address before Kinsky leaves work I might be able to do some reconnaissance."

"I want to go with you," Mary Ann pleaded.

"You can't. I need you at the Hotel Noir." I did a quick image search for *Alex Kinsky, Hotel Noir GM* on my Android and showed her a photograph of Alex. "That's what he looks like. You remember where I told you his office is?"

Mary Ann nodded.

"Okay, but he might not be in his office. He might be

just walking the casino or something. Go to the front desk first and ask for an application for employment. Ask a few casual questions about the hotel, ask about the GM, and ask if he's still there. Again, make it casual. You're just trying to get a sense of the place. If they say he's left, text me. If they say he's there, find him, spy on him, and text me. And then, when he *does* leave the hotel, text me, wait a half hour, and then go to the address in a town car. Park… maybe a block away or so. Wait there for no more than an hour and a half. If I don't come out to you by then call and if I don't pick up… call the cops. Oh, and we should have a code word in case I pick up but still need help… like I'll say *see you later gator.* If I say that call the cops."

"But you never say that."

"That's the point. If those words come out of my mouth, I'm in serious distress."

"Wait… didn't you say you needed to keep the cops out of this?"

"I do. But if I can't get out of there by then I'm in the kind of trouble that the police can't make much worse."

"I don't know about this…" Mary Ann hedged as she studied Alex's picture. "You don't know what this address he gave you is…"

"That's why I'm going early, to find all that out before anyone's prepared for me. And yes, it's a little risky, but I'm going to great lengths for the man I love. You approve of this kind of stuff, remember?"

Mary Ann nodded. It was obvious she was having second thoughts but not enough to get in my way. She looked at the picture on my Android again. "Okay, I'll look for him… you'll be careful?"

"Totally," I said. Of course careful meant different things to different people.

And as if to prove it, I *carefully* put my MacBook in its carrying case and draped it over my shoulder. This was coming with me.

CHAPTER
TWELVE

"New studies suggest that, contrary to popular wisdom, IQ scores can change over the course of one's lifetime. I'm pretty sure mine drops twenty points every time I fall in love."
—Death Of The Party

My Jamaican cab driver was all smiles and chatter as he drove me away from the strip and toward Alex's home. I liked the sound of his accent. At that moment any accent that wasn't Russian was comforting.

The address took us outside the main part of town. Way out of it. We passed rows of houses, half of them in foreclosure. God, I missed San Francisco. I missed the smell of the sea air, the tightly packed houses... hell at this point I even missed the nudists and the traffic-blocking protesters. Anything familiar would have been comforting. But this was a suburban desert inside a city. I didn't know anything about this.

I got a text from Mary Ann:

He's here. He seems to be having a meeting with

someone at the café.

I texted her back a *thank you* and stared out the window. As we continued our journey, the houses got nicer. The foreclosure signs were replaced by For Sale signs and soon even those became less prevalent. With each block, the homes got bigger. There wasn't enough land for places like these in San Francisco. But here? It was as if they had so much land they felt the need to fill up as much of it as possible. So they just kept adding pools and guesthouses. One house even had a tennis court. The home we pulled up in front of was modest by comparison but would still shame most houses in Pacific Heights. It also had a security gate.

Was this Alex Kinsky's home? My $250 wouldn't even pay for his monthly air conditioning.

"Do you want me to drop you off here or should I give a name," the driver asked waving at the little box where we were supposed to announce ourselves.

"Drop me off here," I said. I reached into my bag and took out the fare plus $50. "I don't think anyone will ask if you saw me but if they do…"

"I didn't," the driver said with a wide smile as he took the money. "Always happy to help a sister out."

I smiled nervously. It was tricky this instinctive commonality between people of the same minority group. Sometimes it held up. Other times it encouraged a level of trust that hadn't been earned or deserved. Just ask the Jews who invested with Bernie Madoff.

I stood on the side of the road as the car drove off and then carefully walked up to the gate. Could I climb it? It seemed unlikely. Still, I was anxious to peek inside the windows before Alex arrived. He said there were things he could tell me, but at the moment I was more interested in what he *wouldn't* tell me. I walked along the sidewalk as if going for a stroll. No one in the front yard that I could see. It was a little hard to tell because it was dark, the only illumination coming from the streetlights and a porch light. Plus the yard was... well, *huge.* Neatly trimmed trees shaded benches nestled between rose bushes. It was right out of a Jane Austin novel.

I turned and started to walk along the side of the house. My cell phone beeped. It was Mary Ann again.

> *He's done with his meeting. I think he's going back to his office. I'll tell you if he takes off.*

Again I thanked her and continued my exploration of the perimeter. Everything was enclosed within a tall iron fence but against the fence at one spot was a bench and on my side of the fence, there was a large rock. I could climb up on the rock pull myself over the top, and then, if I was really careful, I could drop right down on the bench so it wouldn't be such a big fall.

I hesitated a moment. The consequences of breaking into the home of a possible gangster were pretty big, and I didn't even know what I was looking for. But it seemed that no matter what I did, my life was in danger. One look inside the windows might give me a sense of who I was dealing with and if there was anyone else living there—or if an ambush was being set up. These were good things to know before walking into a private meeting.

I leaned my MacBook against the iron bars. If I got over, I could easily pull it through. Then I took my shoes off and slipped the straps over my wrists. I climbed up on the rock, which didn't quite give me as much leverage as I had hoped. The rock's ridges pressed into my feet, not enough to cut them but certainly enough to cause considerable discomfort. I stretched my arms over my head and grabbed the iron bars. They were slick. But if I could just somehow pull myself to the top...

I crouched slightly and then leaped up, grabbing the bars with both hands, my whole body banging against the gate.

I missed grasping the top of the gate by about a foot. I tried to move my hands up the bars. My hands did move, as did the rest of me. I was sliding slowly down, back to the rock.

So that didn't work.

But giving up just wasn't an option. I leaped again, grabbing onto the bars.

And I slipped again.

This went on for about five minutes. I was so bruised up you would have thought I was a battered wife. My phone rang in my handbag and in utter frustration I sat down on the rock and answered it despite the unknown number.

"What?" I snapped.

"Why don't you just announce yourself at the front gate?" Alex asked.

I fell silent.

Seriously?

"Where are you?" I asked.

"I'm at work, but I have a security feed. I also have a panicked housekeeper who is damn near ready to call the cops. She's waiting for you at the front gate. Go there, tell her you're not a murderer, and she'll let you in and make you a cup of tea. I'll be there in about an hour."

"Is this a trick?"

"Look, if you'd rather throw yourself against the fence for the next hour be my guest. All I'm suggesting is that there are easier ways to do this."

"Just so you know, I have mace," I lied.

"Don't mace the housekeeper. Other than that, mi casa su casa. See you in a bit."

Reluctantly I got off of the stupid rock and went to the front gate where a very irritated and *very* beautiful woman was waiting for me.

"Mr. Kinsky says I should let you in," she said. Her Mexican accent was subtle but recognizable.

Mr. Kinsky can shove it, I thought, but out loud I said. "That would be great, thanks."

Hesitantly she pressed the button that operated the automatic gate. "You want something warm to drink? Mr. Kinsky has very good hot chocolate."

"That would be great, thanks."

She nodded and led me to the front door. She reached into her oversized pocket and handed me a small ice pack. Embarrassed I took the pack and held it to my right elbow.

"I'll draw up an Epsom Salt bath."

"That's really not necessary—"

"Mr. Kinsky insisted." She shot me a withering look as she opened the front door. "He's very kind to his guests. Even one's who try to break in."

"I wasn't trying to—" but one more glare told me that there would be no convincing her of my innocence. Chastened and in not a small amount of pain, I followed her into a foyer that was every bit as opulent as the lobby of my five-star hotel.

"Don't touch anything."

I nodded as she disappeared through a door. She was speaking in what sounded like stilted English, but she pronounced each word perfectly. It was almost as if she was playing a part that she hadn't quite perfected.

Maybe she was.

She was only gone long enough for me to glance around the room and take in the original artwork and dark hardwood floor... the kind of floor that would gleam if it had been properly cleaned and cared for which it clearly hadn't... which once again made me wonder about this housekeeper.

She returned with a steaming cup of hot chocolate. It smelled heavenly, and if I hadn't been worried about being drugged again, I would have downed half of it instantly. As it was, I just used it to warm my hands as she led me up a curving staircase then through the master bedroom and finally to a bathroom that was slightly larger than my hotel suite.

I stood awkwardly in the corner as the woman drew up the Jacuzzi bath, pouring a huge amount of Epsom Salts into the stream. I desperately wanted to go back and take another peek at the bedroom that we had so quickly strode through.

"You don't like hot chocolate?" the woman asked.

"I was going to drink it in the bath," I explained.

She crossed over to me. "Mr. Kinsky said that if you didn't drink the hot chocolate, I should do this." She took the cup from my hand and took a long sip, smiled and handed it back.

Okay, that was unexpected. "You're proving to me it's not poisoned?" I asked.

She shrugged. "Mr. Kinsky just told me to do that." She returned to the bath and turned off the water.

Tentatively, I took a sip of the chocolate and almost choked. "Rum?" I squawked when I was able to speak again.

"He said you would need a drink."

I nodded and glanced past her to the tub. "Look, I really don't need a bath... I'm sorry, I didn't get your name."

"I see you banging against the gate!" she snapped ignoring my question. "Over and over again. You need Epsom salts."

There it was again, the stilted English with polished pronunciation. Weird.

"When will Mr. Kinsky be home?"

The housekeeper looked up at the wall clock. "In a little over an hour, I think. You have time for your drink and bath. There's a robe behind the door," she said, gesturing to a pink terrycloth robe as she walked out. I stood there for a moment, unsure of what to do. I really was a mess. My clothes were dirty, and there was a new hole in my pant leg. My cell beeped, and I read the text from Mary Ann telling me Alex Kinsky had just left the hotel. No surprise there but I texted back another *thanks*.

I placed my MacBook carefully on the floor, far away from the bath, and took some time to explore. On the counter were an electric razor, cologne and a single Sonicare toothbrush. I opened the top drawer next to the sink gingerly. Shaving cream, men's antiperspirant, a nail clipper but no nail polish or any other evidence of a woman living here. More drawers revealed mouthwash, aspirin, a comb and some hair gel, nothing all that interesting. Not even a bottle of prescription medication.

Which made the robe the housekeeper lent me a bit more interesting. If it belonged to a wife or live-in girlfriend, she certainly wasn't using this bathroom, which implied she wasn't using the room attached to it either.

I took another sip of my drink, savoring the warm and pleasing effects of the rum and chocolate. It was expected that I would immediately get in the bath. That wasn't going to happen, at least not yet. For one thing, I wanted to make sure there wasn't a security camera in here. I couldn't see one, but that didn't mean much. It seemed to me the best way of ensuring that I was unwatched was to do things I wasn't supposed to do and then wait and see if this broom-wielding-super-model came back in to stop me.

With that in mind, I went into the bedroom. It was well appointed and very masculine with its dark, earthy color tone and mahogany furniture. On his nightstand was a copy of Simon Singh's latest book about the universe and on his desk, a half finished New York Times crossword puzzle. Mounted on the wall was a shotgun. I didn't know much about guns, but this one looked old... from an entirely different era. I stepped up to it and let my fingers touch the steel of the trigger. It was a collector's item... but people who collected old guns usually had new guns too. I went over to the nightstand and there it was, a small handgun. I picked it up. A quick check confirmed it was loaded. If there were a security camera, this would be the time someone should be coming up to deal with me. But no one did.

Holding the gun in my hand, I went back to the bathroom. I placed the weapon and my drink by the side of the tub and, gingerly, took off my clothes. With each piece I removed, I found a new bruise or tender spot. I sank into the heavenly bath and closed my eyes.

But I kept my fingers on the handle of the gun—just in case.

CHAPTER
THIRTEEN

"I don't date men for their money or the gifts they may give me. But if a guy has the skills to fix my computer he might be marriage material."
—Death Of the Party

I only stayed in the bath for ten minutes. As good as it felt I hadn't come here for a spa day. I put my bra and panties back on but hesitated before putting on my clothes. They were such an unholy mess. I glanced at the robe and then, with only a moment of hesitation, slipped it on. It was plush, warm and perfect… and it had pockets big enough to hide the handgun in. I went back into the bedroom and was considering looking through a few more drawers when the housekeeper walked in. "You finished the bath?" she asked sounding slightly surprised.

"I'm not really a bath person," I lied. I looked down at a Marc Jacobs shopping bag in her hand. "What's that?"

"Mr. Kinsky's home. He's waiting for you in the study, but he got this for you." She held the bag out for me, but I took a step back.

"He's buying me gifts?" I asked suspiciously. "Why?"

"Your clothes are all torn up."

"So he bought me Marc Jacobs?"

"He bought you Marc by Marc Jacobs."

See, right there, what kind of housekeeper puts emphasis on that kind of distinction? Who was this woman?

I took the bag from her and tried to force my lips into a smile. "Thanks for lending me your robe," I said as casually as possible.

She broke out laughing. "It is not mine. Mr. Kinsky likes to have a spare robe around just in case."

"Just in case?" I repeated. "Wait… are you telling me he keeps a woman's robe on hand just in case he happens to get lucky?"

"Each girl gets to keep her robe, he always gets a new one."

"A new robe or a new girl?" I asked, dryly.

"Both. I'll wait in here while you change in the bath-room."

"You don't need to wait for me while I change."

The housekeeper simply stood there. It looked like I wasn't going to have the chance to do any more snooping. With a sigh, I went back in the bathroom.

I put on the clothes Alex had selected for me. I really hated to admit this, but they were cute. The tank was made from an incredibly soft cotton and it had four little buttons at the neckline that I made sure were buttoned right up to the top. The shorts were elegant, and the silk felt luxurious against my skin. He had even bought me a skinny leather belt to go with them. The only problem was that he hadn't gotten me a bra, and the black lace number I was wearing did show through, but not by much. He might not notice. Of course there was no way I could carry a gun in the pocket of these shorts without it being noticed, so I put it in the shopping bag and my ripped clothes on top of that. Then, after slipping the strap for my MacBook case over my shoulder, I stepped back out, and the housekeeper nodded her approval. She adjusted the collar of her shirt, and for the first time, I noticed the pendant around her neck. It was made up of very clear diamonds arranged to form three linked circles. It was an impressive piece—particularly since it was hanging from the neck of a woman who supposedly cleaned toilets for a living.

"I like your necklace."

She fingered it gently. "It's very special to me. Three circles of six diamonds."

Three circles of six... so 666? How very Dante-esque.

"Mr. Kinsky is waiting."

We found him in a room that could have been ripped from the pages of Architectural Digest; dark brown leather furniture and an expensive oriental rug over a Brazilian cherry hardwood floor. In one corner was a piano and in the other a bar. Quick inspection revealed it was fully loaded with expensive bourbon, scotch, gin, cognac, and a mini fridge. Alex was sitting in a leather armchair, one ankle slung over his knee.

When our eyes met his lips curled into a bemused smile. "So did you enjoy going through my stuff in the bathroom and bedroom?"

My breath caught in my throat. Had there been a security camera after all? If so the gun was going to come in handy. I would definitely have to kill him. "What makes you think I was snooping?" I asked, carefully.

"I'm pretty sure it's what anyone with an ounce of curiosity would have done." He shifted his eyes to the housekeeper who nodded curtly at her employer before turning around and leaving the room, closing the door behind her. "Besides, the way you tried to get in," Alex continued once we were alone, "it doesn't imply that you have a lot of respect for my privacy."

I felt my shoulders relax. He had a point.

"Margarita tells me you took an Epsom Salt bath?"

"Her name is Margarita?"

"She didn't tell you? She probably kept it to herself because she knew you would make fun of it."

"I wouldn't have done that." I snapped.

"I see," Alex said sagely. "So breaking into my home, that's okay, but making fun of someone's name is beneath you."

"I wasn't breaking into your home! I was just going to sneak into your backyard and peek in your windows."

Alex's smile broadened, and he got up and walked over to the fireplace. The flames behind him gave him a devilish aura. "Why did you want to peek in my windows?"

"I wanted to see if anyone else lived here."

"They don't."

"Well that's not exactly true, is it? Margarita lives here."

"No, she just works here. She'll be going home soon."

I hesitated for a moment as that sank in. "We're going to be alone in the house?"

"Does that frighten you?"

"No," I lied. "If you're the GM of Hotel Noir why did you agree to follow Anatoly up to his room?"

"You gave me a check."

"It doesn't look like you need the money."

"Ah, but I didn't want your money, I wanted your check."

I crossed my arms over my chest. "Should I be worried about that? Is there some kind of identity theft scheme going on?"

"No. You know you have a nasty bruise on your forearm. Would you like another ice pack for that?"

"Oddly enough, this bruise isn't ranking all that high on my list of worries. Someone broke into my house, *went through my underwear drawer*, stole all my computer equipment, brought a bunch of my stuff to some hotel room in Vegas that was registered *under my name* and then killed someone in there… with my underwear in the dresser."

"You seem particularly concerned about your underwear."

"No one goes through my underwear drawer, not even my boyfriend."

"Would that be the boyfriend who cheated on you?"

"Why was the room registered under my name?"

Alex held my gaze for a moment and then took several steps toward me. As he got closer, I had to fight the urge to take several steps back, but I was determined not to allow him to intimidate me. When there was less than a foot between us I had to crane my neck up to meet his eyes. He was studying me. Examining my expression, my features, my hair… what exactly was he up to?

That question was answered a second later when he unexpectedly grabbed the Marc Jacobs bag from my hand. I tried to take it back, but he immediately moved away from me, while reaching his hand inside the shopping bag. I stood there panicked as he pulled out his gun.

"Listen—"

Alex put up his hand to stop me. "I would have been surprised if you hadn't taken it," he said. "You don't have a lot of reasons to trust me, and you're in my house, in an unfamiliar city, and we're alone." He held up the gun with the barrel pointing toward the ceiling. "You wanted to protect yourself. The good news is that I didn't ask you here to harm you." He unloaded the gun and put it on his desk, tossing the bullets in a drawer. "Do you know why I told Margarita to draw you a bath?"

I shook my head although I barely heard the question. He had unloaded the bullets to calm my fears but what if he had another gun on him?

"I asked her to pour you a bath because you can't *take* a bath if you're wearing a wire. I picked out those shorts because you can't hide a wire under silk without it bunching and I chose that tank because you can't hide *anything* under it... not even a black lace bra."

I was actually too surprised to be offended. "You thought I was going to come here wearing a wire?"

"And you thought I was planning on hurting you. You tried to protect yourself by taking my gun, and I protected myself by buying you new clothes. My way is nicer."

I glanced down at my outfit. "How did you know my size?"

"I saw the clothes that were brought to the Hotel Noir. You're a size four. And before you ask, I didn't look through your underwear." He smiled mischievously.

There was a knock at the door, and Margarita entered

without waiting to be asked in. I glance at Alex to see if that irritated him, but it didn't seem to.

"I'll be leaving now," she announced.

"All right, before you go could you please take Miss Katz' handbag, shopping bag, and computer and put them away in the coat closet off the foyer?"

"Wait a minute, what? She can't take my things!"

"They could be bugged too," Alex explained.

"Um, I'm not going to just leave my things lying around your house where I can't keep an eye on them. What if you're the one lying to *me* and there *is* someone else in this house."

"Fine, keep the purse on you, but you'll have to let me search it."

I weighed my options for a moment before thrusting the purse into his hands. "The most dangerous thing I have in there is a Tweezerman."

I watched as he looked through my things, my lipstick, tampax and all the rest of it. It really wasn't any more of an invasion of privacy than what you would expect at any airport security station but still, having *him* do this made me uncomfortable. Margarita continued to stand in the doorway, looking bored.

Alex pulled out my cell phone and then Anatoly's. "Two phones?"

"One of them isn't mine."

"They're both going to have to wait in another room."

"Why don't you want me to have a phone?" I asked nervously.

"Because they can be easily used as recording devices. So your choice, you can give the phones and that laptop to

Margarita for her to store in the other room and I'll tell you what I know, or you can take your new outfit and leave. Seems to me you win either way, but you may not see it that way."

I hesitated, my hand gripping the strap of my MacBook case. "Yes to the phones, but I want to keep the MacBook with me."

"Very well. It was nice of you to stop by, Sophie. Hope you enjoy the rest of your stay in Vegas."

I exhaled loudly. "You really have information that will help me?"

He shrugged. "I have information that you want. Whether it's helpful or not depends on what you choose to do with it."

I thought about it for a moment and then carefully took the MacBook out of its carrying case. I put it on a side table near the chair Alex had been sitting in and opened it. "Examine it if you like. Assure yourself that it isn't on while we talk. It can be by your side for as long as I'm here. But I just had my home computer stolen along with all the storage devices that I had my latest manuscript on. I'm not letting this thing out of my sight now. You and I know I can't make a MacBook into a recording device if it isn't on."

Alex hesitated, clearly not pleased with the compromise. I stepped forward and took my phones from him and placed them firmly in Margarita's hands and then handed her my bag of clothes. "Go ahead and put those in the foyer." I turned to face Alex. "See? We're both making compromises here."

It was a compromise I wouldn't have made if I hadn't already noted where the landline phone was in the room.

Besides, Mary Ann knew that if I didn't answer my phone she should call the cops, so if Alex's plan was to keep me from calling for help, he was in for a surprise.

Reluctantly, Alex nodded at Margarita.

"I will put the phones on the table in the foyer," she said woodenly. "Goodnight Mr. Kinsky."

She left the room without bothering to say goodnight to me.

Alex examined my MacBook and then moved it over to a spot on the floor near a speaker and then turned on the stereo. Then slightly eerie, intriguing and intense music filled the room.

"Zola Jesus," Alex said. "A Russian, American singer. She's known for combining goth, industrial, classical, electronic, and experimental rock influences."

"That's a lot of influences."

"It is. She'll also add a layer of protection in case you *are* trying to record this." Alex smiled wryly. "Seems like we both could use a drink, yes?"

I struggled with myself for a second too long before answering, "No."

"Are you always this bad of a liar?"

I couldn't help but smile at that. "Do you have vodka?"

He opened up the mini fridge and pulled out what looked like a large bottle of cologne. It was beautiful. Clear with perfectly elegant curves and a sparkling silver lid that came to a graceful point.

"That's vodka?" I asked. "It looks like art."

"It's Kauffman Luxury Vintage Vodka," he said, holding the bottle out for my viewing pleasure.

I sucked in a sharp breath. I had heard of Kauffman but

had never actually seen it. It was almost impossible to get in the States. It also cost $250 per liter. "Is it as good as they say?"

"There's only one way to find out." He served me a glass, neat. "Vodka this smooth shouldn't be mixed with anything. It's a sipping vodka."

I had never heard of "sipping vodka" before. I had been raised with the belief that vodka was for drinking—relatively quickly—or consuming in shot form. I watched as Alex poured himself a glass, which he then raised for a toast. "To new friendships."

I rejected that with a shake of my head. "To answers."

His eyes darted over to the piano, and for a split second, he looked somber. "To answers."

I brought my glass to my lips; I had *never* tasted vodka like this before. It was perfection, and it made me trust him a little more. I had a bad habit of trusting people who had good taste in liquor. "So can we talk now? Have I appeased your paranoia?"

"I don't see it as paranoia. I see it as being cautious." He sat down on an oversized leather armchair. "I think Anatoly and I have that in common," he mused. "We're both very cautious men."

I laughed until I realized he was serious. "He rides a motorcycle, married into the mob and then ditched his gun-wielding wife for a life with me—and I'm not exactly known for my ability to stay out of trouble. So in what dictionary does that fit the definition of cautious?"

"He takes risks," Alex conceded, "but only after he's weighed the odds and all that. Because of that, he was a huge asset to the family."

"What family?"

"The Russian Mafia… at least for this syndicate." He waved this revelation away as if it had no bearing on my predicament. "The only way to make a cautious man careless is to play on his emotions. Last week, when they found out that you had broken up with him—"

"Okay, stop right there." I scooted to the front of the couch. "How did you know I had broken up with him before I came to Vegas?"

Alex ran his finger along the rim of his glass. "You got a lot of calls from Anatoly in the days leading up to your Vegas trip but—have you gotten any voicemails? I'm guessing no."

"You're beginning to creep me out, Alex."

"They tapped your phone, and they've been erasing his voicemails after they listened to them."

It took me almost a full minute before I found my voice. "So when you said my phones *might* be recording devices you meant they *are* recording devices."

"No, they tapped the line, they didn't bug the phone and to be honest they're not even listening into the calls anymore. Anatoly knows better than to call you now so there's no reason to monitor your phone conversations. But not too long ago, there was."

"Wow, that is just so pragmatic of you."

"Not me," Alex said quickly. "I had nothing to do with it. All I do is run the hotel. I deal with the legal side of the mafia's investments."

"The legal side," I repeated. "Does that include covering up murders that take place in your hotel—legally?"

"I like to call that crisis management. That's why I wanted your check. If... *they* weren't able to clean up their mess as quickly or discreetly as they hoped I could have used your check to prove that you had the victim followed and then there would have been a quick arrest and little damage to the hotel's reputation."

I gripped my glass with both hands. "What are you saying?"

"If plan A didn't pan out, which it did, I was going to set you up for murder."

CHAPTER
FOURTEEN

"Being with a man who is protective and caring is kind of like owning a gun. It gives you a sense of security... right up until it's unexpectedly used against you and shoots a hole through your heart."
—Death Of The Party

"YOU WERE GOING TO SET ME UP FOR MURDER!" Outside the wind blew hard enough to sway the small trees that were planted along the exterior of the house. I could hear their branches thumping against the walls, as if testing their strength.

"I didn't know you then," Alex calmly replied.

"Oh, and you know me now?"

He put his glass down carefully on a coaster. Dubious tales about pink robes aside, I wondered if he was gay. He *had* to be, right? Otherwise, there would be a line of women waiting for their turn with the I-use-a-coaster guy who shopped at Marc Jacobs and stocked up on the good vodka.

"I know that you're impulsive," he said slowly. "I know that you're passionate about the people you care about and protective of them even when they don't seem to deserve it. I know that you're brave to the point of being foolish. I know that you're scared but are very good at hiding it. And you don't seem to ever let fear get in your way. I know that despite your impulsivity you don't panic in a crisis. I know that there's enough money in your bank account that you can write a $250 check without thinking about it. I know that you're a size four, shop at Victoria Secret, and are wearing a black lacy bra. So yes, I'd say that I know you."

"So you did look through my underwear drawer."

Alex looked surprised and then laughed long and hard. "I also know that it's hard to get anything by you. You remember what's been said and are always looking for contradictions."

"Uh-huh. Stop looking at my bra."

"I'll make an effort."

Okay, so maybe he wasn't gay. "You said the mob was playing on Anatoly's emotions?"

Alex nodded and sipped his drink. "They made him believe you were here... well, you *were* here so that made it an easy sell. Luckily for the mob, you registered at Encore under your friend Dena's name. When Anatoly checked to find out which hotel you were staying at the only one that had your name on file was mine. He came here to rescue you —and then was distracted by a blonde."

"That blonde told him she could take him to my room."

"He could have found it without her."

I set my mouth in a thin line. I sensed that Alex might be trying to turn me against Anatoly. Considering what had happened earlier today that shouldn't have been a tough task, but knowing that someone else wanted me to turn on him made me hate Anatoly less not more.

"Why is the mob after him?"

"When Anatoly came to the States it was with the understanding that he would only be doing a few jobs for the
mafia. But certain people in power liked him—Natasha liked
him *a lot*."

"Is she a person of power?" I asked, rejecting the bait.

"Her father, Vadim Ignatov, is and that matters in this
world. So they kept trying to pull him in further and further.
Anatoly wasn't very resistant at first, but eventually I guess
it got to be too much for him."

"How could anyone turn down the opportunity to sell
heroine to school children and murder people for money?" I
asked.

Alex tensed. For the first time that night it seemed I had
hit a nerve. "Everyone *should* walk away from that. Eventually, if I can, I'll walk away from this God damned hotel.
But the money and power the mafia can offer…" Alex shook
his head, "it's hard for some people to resist. They just can't
see past it, even when their lives are at stake."

"Was Anatoly's life at stake?"

"No," he said after a long pause. "But he knew he wanted out. It was assumed that was why he got on so well with
the new guy."

"What new guy?"

"Daniil," Alex answered, his voice growing colder.
"There's some disagreement as to who originally introduced
Daniil to the Ignatovs, it was either Anatoly or Kenya—"

"Kenya?" I was going to have a hard time remembering
all these names.

"Like the country. It's not an uncommon Russian name.
It means, innocent." Again, Alex fell silent as his expression

became distant.

"Sooo, Kenya-like-the-country," I pressed, "he liked Daniil too?"

"Yes, Daniil was capable, eager and seemed to be ready and willing to take Anatoly's place in the organization. Again, Anatoly had already gotten a promise from Vadim that he would be allowed to walk away. Daniil just made it a little easier for Vadim to keep that promise."

"The promise of freedom," I said, for clarification.

"Yes," Alex's mouth curved into a smile that could almost be construed as sarcastic. His fingers drummed against the deep brown leather of the armrest.

"So Anatoly found himself a replacement, what's the big deal?"

"Oh, it wouldn't have been a big deal at all—if his replacement hadn't been an undercover FBI agent."

"Oh... Shit."

"Yep, you pretty much summed the situation up right there. Oh shit."

"But Anatoly didn't know!" I stammered. "He couldn't have!" *And why couldn't he have?* A little voice in my head asked. Anatoly didn't have the same visceral reaction that I had to the police, which was odd because of the two of us he was the only one with a hardcore criminal past. Why would someone who used to work for the Russian Mafia feel comfortable talking to the cops unless he already knew that he had some kind of pass—the kind of pass you might get in exchange for helping the FBI get information?

"There are a lot of people in the...organization, who don't think he *did* know. It's a matter for debate."

"What about Kenya? You said he might have been the

one to introduce Daniil to the mafia. What does he have to say about all this?"

Alex shifted his weight so that he was looking into the fire. "Kenya's dead."

"Oh." I swallowed hard, "because of the FBI agent?"

"In a way, yes. Daniil went to Kenya's house. There was a gas leak that *coincidentally* led to an explosion at that very moment. It looked better for the mafia to lose one of their own at the same time the agent lost his life. Not that it fooled anyone but they weren't able to make an arrest and there's been no admission of guilt, not even to the rest of us affiliated with the organization. It was just... one of those things."

For a few minutes we sat in silence, listening to the wind's fruitless attempts to push itself inside and the fire crackle and flicker as it struggled to stay alive. I still had a lot of questions but the enormity of what I had just been told... well, it was going to take me a bit to wrap my arms around it. And there was still a lot about this that didn't fit.

"Why are they being so... so James-Bond-Super-Villain about this?"

Alex raised his eyebrows, clearly confused by the question.

"If they want Anatoly dead why haven't they just shot him? Why the elaborate ruse to get him to the hotel? Why not just keep it simple instead of staging this... this almost comically elaborate trap?"

"Well, for one thing, killing Anatoly in the hotel *would* have been simple. The hotel is tightly controlled by people they can trust—"

"You."

"And a few others," Alex conceded. "That makes getting

rid of the body and altering security tape footage exceptionally easy. A drive-by shooting in San Francisco would have been messy. Messy crimes usually end with someone doing jail time."

"How about a gas leak?"

Alex smiled humorlessly. "We can't have too many of those, can we? It might make the *just-an-accident* argument go from unbelievable to prosecutable."

"So that's the only reason?"

"No." Alex put his glass down and leaned forward. "Anatoly is a cautious man."

"You said that."

"Cautious men take out insurance policies."

The evidence Anatoly was talking about. The reason they had taken my computer. I knew, in the most general sense, what Alex was talking about but letting on that I knew would mean admitting to seeing Anatoly. So instead I threw my arms up in feigned frustration. "You know I'm not wearing a wire so if we could just leave the metaphors at the door that would be great."

"He made copies of certain records," Alex explained. "Transactions of the Ignatov family."

"Records that they don't want the Feds to see."

"It would be catastrophic for a lot of very powerful people." He took a sip of his drink again, and if I didn't know better, I'd say he was hiding a smile. "It would be worse," he continued, "if certain... business partners saw them. That's the problem with criminal organizations. You have to do business with other criminal organizations. And if you're dishonest in your business dealings, as criminals so frequently are, you can get yourself in a lot of trouble."

Now I really was confused. What organization on earth could intimidate the Russian Mafia? Maybe another Russian Mafia group? After all, there had to be lots of Russian Mafia crime families, right? It wasn't a chain like The Gap where there were lots of little stores but only one corporate head-quarters that called all the shots. It had to be more like a franchise… a really dangerous messed up franchise.

"How do we know that Anatoly still has any records? Even if he had them once he could have destroyed them years ago."

"He wouldn't do that because—"

"Because he's a cautious man," I finished for him.

Alex smiled and tapped the side of his nose with his index finger. "When he realized he might be in trouble he let it be known that he *does* have those records and that he's willing to use them."

"He could be bluffing. This is Vegas, after all."

"You think?" Alex asked, with what appeared to be legitimate curiosity. "In that case, if the Ignatovs just kills him—"

"Or maybe he's holding a full flush," I added quickly. "Hard to tell."

"It always is with a good poker player. If he does have the evidence then the question is where's it stashed?"

"Beats me."

Alex studied me. "When I met you last night it was clear that you still cared about this guy. If you know where this information is you should get it because in the not too distant future you may need to trade it for his life."

The mafia would do a trade? That didn't sound likely. I glanced up at the clock. I had been here for too long. In a moment Mary Ann would call, and when I didn't answer, she'd call the police.

"I gotta go." I got to my feet and put the MacBook back in its case.

"Look, things are sketchy right now. You're welcome to stay here."

I laughed as I slung the carrying case over my shoulder. "Yeah, um, I'm gonna pass. But really, thanks for the offer." I picked up my purse and walked out into the foyer where I immediately spotted the bag with my clothes and my phones on the key table.

"You'll be safe here."

"Bye-bye Alex." I collected the rest of my things and walked briskly toward the door, my heels clicking against the hardwood floor.

"Sophie, wait.

I turned. "What?"

"If I'm wrong about your wanting to reconcile with Anatoly and you're looking for someone to... distract you —"

"Fuck you."

Alex smiled. "I was rather hoping you would after I bought you Marc Jacobs."

I held out the strap of my tank top for his examination. "It's *Marc* by Marc Jacobs. No one gets fucked for bridge-wear!" I whirled around, but as I opened the door, he reached over and closed it again. Keeping my eyes glued to the door, I growled, "I swear to God if you try to lock me in here—"

"Take my jacket."

I turned slightly to see that he had taken off his blazer

and was offering it to me.

"Why would I want to do that?"

"Because otherwise you can see your bra through your shirt."

I thought about that for a moment and then pulled out my dirty messed up red tank from the shopping bag and put it over the tank I was already wearing. "There, problem solved. Keep the jacket."

"I'll call you a cab to take you back to the hotel." He said as I started to open the door again.

"I got it, thanks."

"One more thing?"

"Alex, I really have to go!"

He held up a hand, requesting one last moment. I watched impatiently as he went across the room and un-locked the drawer of a console by the stairs.

As he pulled a gun out, I found myself really wishing I hadn't waited.

"Listen," I whispered, trying desperately to think of a way out of this.

Alex simply put his fingers to his lips. He moved across the room. I hadn't noticed how graceful he was before. He should have been a dancer not a killer. It was probably a little late to suggest a career change, though.

He took my hand so that my palm was facing up. I held my breath not sure what his next move was going to be. Slowly, carefully, he put the gun in my hand.

"This one's a little smaller than the one you tried to steal, but it should be enough to keep the bad guys at bay. Protect yourself." I stared down at the gun and watched as my fingers instinctively closed around the handle.

"Put it in your purse," he instructed. "Concealed weapons are legal in Vegas, and if you have it in your hand, there's a good chance the cab won't stop."

I smiled slightly at that and did as he suggested. "Thank you... but I won't be back."

"I don't believe that for a second."

I didn't know how to respond so I simply turned and walked out.

The front gate opened for me automatically, and I spotted a town car parked at the end of the block. Mary Ann got out of the back and waved me over.

"I was just about to call the police," she admitted once I got within hearing range.

"I'm glad you didn't." I climbed into the backseat to find that Marcus was there too. "I thought you were at *Puppetry of the Penis* with Leah and Dena," I said, turning to him as Mary Ann got in beside me and asked the driver to take us to the Encore.

"I was, but I left after five minutes... and those five minutes will give me five years of nightmares. Your sister seemed to be enjoying it."

"You're joking, right?"

"Oh, you think that's odd? Because I think it's odd that you would go to the private residence of a possible murderer."

"But I always go to the homes of possible murderers," I pointed out. "It's kinda my thing."

"Marcus tracked me down at the Hotel Noir," Mary Ann explained.

Marcus held up Dena's iPad. "I borrowed this, and I've been using it to do some research on your new friend," he said. "Do you have any idea who you were just talking to?"

"Of course I know. I was talking to Alex Kinsky."

"Yes, Alex Kinsky… general manager of Hotel Noir, well-known philanthropist and half-brother to a woman who legally changed her name from Fedora to *Fawn.*"

I froze in my seat and Mary Ann grabbed my arm, squeezing it so hard I actually winced.

"Ewwy Fawn?" Mary Ann asked.

"The Fawn who called me collect from prison to tell me that Anatoly was married? *That* Fawn?" I added before Mary Ann chimed in again.

"The Fawn who slept with my ex-boyfriend… back when he was still my boyfriend, before he got all creepy?"

Marcus nodded. "That's the one… but honey," he locked eyes with Mary Ann, "that boy was *always* a creepy mess."

"Are you sure it's the same person?" My voice was shaking now.

"Sweetie, how many convicted felons do you know named Fawn?"

"But what does it mean?" I whispered.

"It means he's fucking with you." His eyes dropped to my outfit. "Wait a minute, two mismatched tanks… what did those drugs do to your brain? You've forgotten how to layer!"

"I know how to layer," I snapped. I pulled up one of the tanks to show him how the other was too sheer for my bra. "*This* is why I'm wearing two mismatched tanks!"

"Right," Marcus said slowly. "Obviously you couldn't wear a shirt that showed the outline of your bra because nobody dresses promiscuously in Vegas."

"This isn't that kind of vacation," I retorted.

"No, this is a working vacation. Spend an afternoon or two at a sex toy trade show and then put in a few hours toward defeating the mafia. Why didn't you match your tank to your bra if it was a problem for you... wait, are those new shorts too?"

"Alex bought them for me."

"They're lovely," Mary Ann said distractedly. Her mind was clearly still on Fawn.

"It's Marc by Marc Jacobs."

Marcus looked at me blankly. "Sophie, this isn't the red carpet. I didn't ask you *who* you were wearing. I just want to know why you're wearing it."

"Well, um..." I ran my hands over the tan silk of the shorts "I actually tore my clothes while trying to break into Alex's backyard."

Marcus's mouth dropped open.

"But it's okay, he didn't mind!"

"He didn't mind your trying to break in," he repeated, flatly.

"Not so much. He bought me this outfit to replace my clothes... although he then insinuated that I should repay him with sexual favors."

Marcus balked. "For bridge-wear?"

"I know!" I threw my hands up in disgust.

"Did you at least learn anything useful?"

"As a matter of fact, I did. Alex tells me that the Russian Mafia thinks Anatoly helped an FBI agent infiltrate their operations."

Marcus took a while to digest this. "Was this recent? Because he hasn't exactly been acting like a man in Witness Protection."

"It was a while ago," I explained. "Alex also knows that Anatoly has some incriminating evidence that could get the top people in this particular mob family into a lot of trouble."

"So does that mean he *will* have to go into Witness Protection?" Mary Ann asked. "Will he have to change his name? I love the name Anatoly."

"It won't come to that. Alex says Anatoly has proof of some of the mob's illegal activity. That evidence *is* Anatoly's protection—assuming Alex is telling me the truth."

"Which is doubtful considering his family's track record," Marcus reminded me.

"Yeah," I admitted, softly. I shifted my position so that I could look out the window at the starless sky. If Alex was on the up and up why hadn't he mentioned Fawn?

But then again, *I* hadn't mentioned Fawn either. I had barely given her a second thought since she called to tell me Anatoly was married. Was she even relevant at this point in the game?

"He gave me more than information and a new outfit," I whispered.

"What else did he give you?" Marcus asked. "A migraine?"

I glanced up at the driver. He seemed to be completely uninterested in us as he tapped his fingers in time to the Top 40 tune playing on the radio. I took a deep breath and opened my bag so my friends could see the gun. They gasped simultaneously, and I snapped my purse shut.

No one said anything for the rest of the ride to Encore. When we arrived, I paid the driver—picking up the tab was the least I could do—and we all piled out of the car. Marcus dragged me to the fountain with Mary Ann close on our heels. I noticed that his jaw was set and his shoulders were tense. For a full minute, we all just stood there, Mary Ann and I looking at Marcus expectantly. But he just stared silently at the fountain as it shot up toward the night sky like an aquatic version of the northern lights.

"Why do you think he gave you that, Sophie?" he finally asked, his voice icy and controlled.

"Because he wants me to be able to protect myself," I said. "What other reason could there be?"

"Do you know if that gun has been recently used?" he asked. "Like maybe on someone named Tanya? Do you think that maybe the reason Alex booked a room under your name and gave you that gun is because he's helping his sister get revenge?"

The question froze me in place. I tried to come up with a reason his theory was ridiculous. I couldn't.

Now I was the one staring at the fountain. It really did remind me of a smaller version of the northern lights, and the building behind it looked like it was made of solid gold. *But it wasn't.* It was an illusion. Nothing in this town was what it seemed to be. It was designed to entrance. Its goal was to make you throw caution to the wind. It *wanted* you to lose track of your own common sense.

"I'll get rid of the gun," I whispered.

"Where?" Marcus snapped. "You can't just throw it in a trash can."

"She could bury it in the desert?" Mary Ann suggested. "In those mobster movies, they're always burying things in the Vegas desert."

"There you go then," I said hopefully. "I'll... I'll bury it in the desert first thing tomorrow."

"Tomorrow might be too late," Marcus pointed out. "As far as you know the police might be coming for you right now."

With effort, I swallowed down my rising panic. "I don't think Alex wants to draw the police's attention to this whole thing any more than I do. If he's setting me up, he's setting me up so that he can point the finger at me if and when things go sour, and we have no reason to believe that's going to happen tonight. Tomorrow we'll figure out what to do with the gun. One step at a time."

Marcus tapped the tip of his shoe against the pavement. "Anatoly... your hot little Russkie? He drugged you."

"Yes, he did."

I could see little stray drops of water from the fountain settle onto Marcus' hair. "He lied to you too, Sophie."

"I know," I said softly.

"You're risking your neck for an asshole."

"I am," I admitted. The fountain was now a blur as the wind played with the carefully structured pattern of the water. "But here's the thing... he's *my* asshole."

"Is this about ownership?" Marcus asked incredulously, "Or is it about love?"

"It's about love," I whispered. "Marcus I... I love my asshole, okay? I love him so much."

"That's almost as romantic as it is disturbing," Marcus sighed. "So I guess we'll just focus on the basics. Try to find Anatoly, try not to get implicated in any crime, and try not to die."

I bit my lower lip. One of those things should have sounded easy.

CHAPTER
FIFTEEN

"I rarely play by the rules. Unfortunately the rules I break most frequently are the ones I set up for myself."
—Death Of The Party

We got back to the hotel room right around the same time Dena and Leah were returning from *Puppetry of the Penis*. Leah had apparently been traumatized and had gone directly to her room. The rest of us were in Dena and Marcus' room. Dena had bags full of goodies from the trade show and she and I were sorting through them while Marcus continued to Google information on Dena's iPad. I hadn't owned up to going to Alex's house, but we did tell her about what Marcus had found out. Once Marcus got to the part about Alex being Fawn's brother, Dena got up and left the rest of the sorting to me.

"Okay," Marcus said, a vodka tonic in one hand and the iPad in another, "here's the results of the forty dollar background check. Fawny-Dearest changed her name four years ago and she has one half-brother, Alexander Kinsky. Then there's a list of a whole bunch of people she may or may not have a connection to... people with crazy names like

Inno...Innokenty? Whatever, that part's not all that reliable, but she's *definitely* Alex's sister."

"Maybe she's estranged from him?" I offered. "Maybe that's why he never showed up at her trial."

"I think it's possible," Mary Ann agreed.

"If I had a sister like Fawn I wouldn't want anything to do with her," Dena whispered. She was leaning her weight against the desk and staring out at a night that had been made grey by the neon lights of the strip.

Marcus turned to me. "Do you really think it's a coincidence that you met Alex a week after his sister called to tell you about Anatoly? Seriously?"

"Maybe Fawn wanted out of the mafia world, and she cut off contact with Alex because he wouldn't get out too," I offered. I examined a package of dog-bone shaped paperclips that Dena had in one of her bags. "I don't get it. What's dirty about these?"

Dena walked back over to me and put one of the paperclips on the strap of my MacBook carrying case. When in use the "bone" looked a hell of a lot like an erect penis with two balls. Dena shrugged unenthusiastically and went back to the window. "What part of the mafia do you think Fawn objected to?" she asked. "She's in jail for attempted murder so obviously it wasn't the violence."

"Maybe she didn't like working with other people?" Mary Ann offered. "She does seem to have some social issues."

"Yeah," Dena replied, "maybe she just didn't like the corporate culture. She's an individualist. Like Ayn Rand with a Quentin Tarantino edge."

"Oh come on, guys," I said with a sigh. "So they share a

parent, that doesn't automatically make them co-conspirators."

Marcus was studying me intently, but I couldn't figure out what he was thinking so I plowed ahead.

"He wasn't at the trial. When she was arrested, no one posted her bail. She had to go with a public defender because she couldn't afford a lawyer. Does that sound like a woman who has a close relationship with her wealthy brother?"

Marcus was still staring at me. "You like him."

The comment was just shocking enough to shut me up. Both Dena and Mary Ann froze in place.

"I what?"

"You like him. You don't want him to be in league with Fawn…"

"Of course I don't want him to be in league with Fawn! He's offering to help me—"

"Yeah, but you're pissed at Anatoly. And what better way to get back at him then—"

"There is no way Sophie would ever even think of touching Fawn's brother," Dena said, her voice as cold as ice.

"Of course not!" Mary Ann crossed her arms over her chest. "Sophie is madly in love with Anatoly!"

"All right," Marcus said, holding up his hands in a request for calm. "I'm not implying that you're going to sleep with him, but you're not looking at this objectively—"

"I'm *looking* at the evidence!" I yelled. I threw Dena's jar of nipple warming cream at the wall. "Your problem is that you have trust issues."

"I agree!" Mary Ann said. "Alex is the only one who has given Sophie any information at all. You think that just because someone works with the mafia, they're a criminal!"

Marcus stayed mute and let the awkward moment do his talking for him.

I leaned my head back against the wall. "I'm angry with Anatoly. I have the right to be. And I know Alex is totally ruthless, and I would be stupid to trust him but..."

"But?"

I walked over to Marcus and sat down next to him. "I don't think he's petty. Evil? Maybe. But not petty. And what you're suggesting... that he would set up an elaborate plot just to give his sister an eye for an eye... I know that's beneath him."

Dena raised her thick Sicilian eyebrows. "You got all that from your one meeting with him at his office?"

"Um... I might have been in contact with him tonight too."

"You might have?"

"You know," I said, crossing back to her bag of goodies and holding up some of the lingerie, "this leather bra and panties set is actually kinda cute."

"What's going on, Sophie?"

"Nothing! It's been a while since we've heard from Leah. I think I'll go check on her."

Mary Ann silently handed me the room key, and I hurried out before Dena could ask any more questions although undoubtedly Mary Ann and Marcus would break under her interrogation.

When I got up to Leah's room, I knocked but there was no answer so I let myself in.

"Leah?" I called out as I stepped inside. All the lights were on but Leah didn't seem to be there.

Leah always turned the lights off before going out. Always. "Leah?" I said again. I looked over to the bathroom. The door was closed but if she was in there she would have heard me come in, right? And I didn't hear the shower.

"Leah?" I called out again, this time louder. Again, nothing.

And then I saw Leah's purse sitting on the desk. Just sitting there unattended. Kinda like how Anatoly's money clip had just been sitting there right before I discovered a dead body in a closet.

A wave of nausea washed over me. I reached into my handbag and pulled out the gun. I put my hand on the closet door and said a quick and fierce prayer before throwing it open.

Nothing in there but clothes.

I exhaled… but still…

Terrified I let my eyes slide back to the closed bathroom door. I called out her name and again got nothing for my efforts. I slowly approached the bathroom, gun raised.

She has to be okay, she has to be okay, she has to be okay.

And then I heard a thump of something falling to the ground and my sister cried, "Oh dear Lord!"

I cocked the gun, threw open the door and jumped inside ready to shoot.

Leah let out a bloodcurdling scream… from the bathtub. The bottle of conditioner she had apparently knocked over rolled on the floor and her earbuds were firmly in place and attached to her iPod. As she quickly grabbed for a towel, I noticed that there was a battery-operated octopus in her hand.

"Sorry!" I squealed and rushed back into the bedroom, slamming the door behind me.

Two minutes later Leah stormed out, wrapped in the white hotel robe. "What the hell were you doing?!"

"I'm so, so sorry." I was sitting on her bed with my head buried in my hands. "I just heard you and... well, I've never heard anyone say Oh dear Lord while having an orgasm before and—"

"Sophie!"

"I'm sorry! I mean, I've heard *oh my God* and—"

"I get it!" she snapped. "Are you really critiquing how I —"

"No, no! In fact, I think the best thing is for us to both pretend I didn't see or hear anything."

"I don't even like sex toys!" She pushed a wet strand of hair away from her face. "But... but..."

"But each tentacle has a different function," I finished for her. "I was rather impressed by that too."

Leah's skin was a little darker than mine, but I could still see that she was blushing. "Look," I said, trying very hard to be the mature one, "this is not a big deal. Every woman has at least one sex toy."

"I don't. Or I didn't until today. I've never even owned a vibrator."

"Really?" I asked, honestly shocked. "Well in that case, Congratulations! You finally have what you need to... um... unwind."

"It's disgusting."

"Please Leah, in the beginning of the twentieth century they were selling vibrators in the Sears Roebuck catalog. It's normal."

"It's not a *me* thing to do," she insisted. "It's a you thing to do. You're the one who faces down dangerous criminals, who goes to Vegas on a moment's notice, who marries someone you've been dating for a month. You're the one who gets it on with octopuses and rabbit vibrators!"

"Oh come on! I don't even own a battery operated octopus or a… well, I don't own an octopus!"

"When I lost my husband… when he died less than a day after I discovered he was cheating on me… well, I went a little crazy."

The ninety-degree change of direction knocked me off balance, but I managed a sympathetic nod. "I remember."

"I… I got a belly button piercing, I got burgundy highlights in my hair, I slept with a man I barely knew… a man who was practically a member of the Black Panthers!"

"Um, no, just because someone occasionally makes a fist and doesn't wear Ralph Lauren Polo… that doesn't actually make him a Black Panther."

"Well, all right, I'll give you that… but still… I barely knew him."

"I remember," I said, again.

"I was out of control."

"A little bit."

"It was fun."

I didn't answer that time. I sort of thought Leah had already had and discarded this particular epiphany.

"I knew you weren't going to marry a stranger… no matter how drunk you got."

I shifted my position and sat cross-legged on the bed. "Then could you tell me why you're here?"

"Because I wanted to come to Vegas!" she burst out.

"Why were you so adamant that I stay home? Why didn't you want to include me?"

I blinked in surprise. I hadn't even considered that possibility—then again, I had been distracted.

"I want to have fun too, you know! I've never been to a sex toy trade show! Didn't it ever occur to you that was something I might want to do before I died?"

"A sex toy trade show," I repeated slowly, "that was on your bucket list?"

"It wasn't on yours?"

I stared at her, too baffled to come up with an answer.

"And then that show…"

"*Puppetry of the Penis?*"

"I haven't seen anything like that in years."

I laughed. "Leah, I've *never* seen anything like that. Not many have."

"I mean a man's penis."

"Oh."

"I have a horrible life!" She cried.

I shook my head quickly to clear it of the confusion that was gathering there. "Leah, you realize that I'm in the middle of a life or death situation here, right? The Russian Mafia might be after me."

"Oh, there you go again, making everything about you," Leah snapped, then hearing herself, she blushed a little harder. "I know you have a lot on your plate, but when you told me not to come to Vegas, all you were dealing with was a breakup."

"You told me you wanted to come just so you could chaperone me!"

"You're saying that if I had phrased it differently, you

would have wanted me to come?"

"Look, our friends are downstairs—"

"*Your* friends," Leah corrected. "That's how they would define themselves."

She was right. Marcus, Dena, Mary Ann... they would all say that Leah was their friend's sister. It was also true that Leah was always considered an attachment to somebody or something. She was Jack's mother, Bob's widow, that crazy woman's daughter—although, to be fair, we were both stuck with that one. God knows she sat on enough boards, promoting the opera, the symphony, the cultural WASPification of San Francisco—which was quite a feat for a black, Jewish woman—but her social connections never seemed to extend past the planning meetings. Leah had come here because she had wanted to be part of my Vegas getaway and when she had arrived and realized that things had taken a dark turn she could have left. But she had stuck by me. Leah often drove me nuts but she loved me, and she was loyal...

... and I wasn't always nice to her.

"I'm glad you got the octopus," I said, sincerely. "And I'm glad you got to see men play with their dicks. You deserve it."

Leah giggled. "You think?"

"I'm certain." I ran my fingers back and forth over the duvet. "Look, I don't really know what I'm doing right now. I don't even know what I *should* be doing, but while I figure that out, you should try to... to fully experience Vegas."

Leah eyed me warily. "What do you mean, fully experience Vegas?"

"Tomorrow morning I'm going to come up here at... let's say, 9 a.m., and we're all going to order a room service breakfast with Bloody Marys."

"I can't drink at 9 a.m.! I have to maintain *some* sense of propriety!"

"Propriety? Five minutes ago you were sitting in the bathtub with an oversexed octopus! This is Vegas. Fuck propriety."

"But—"

I held up my hand to stop her. "Once you're a little liquored up you should take Mary Ann down to the casino. Shoot a couple of games of craps or something. Then go to the last day of the sex toy trade show before hitting the clubs...preferably clubs that feature men in various stages of undress as entertainment. Live a little."

"And if you need help?"

"I promise to ask for it as long as you promise to have fun until I do." I glanced at her robe and dripping hair. "I'll go and let you put yourself back together... or whatever."

As I got up and walked to the door, Leah called out to me. "Sophie?"

"Yeah?"

"If you tell anyone about the octopus you won't have to worry about the mafia. I'll shoot you myself."

I smiled. Of all the threats I had been dealing with that was the only one that seemed justified.

CHAPTER
SIXTEEN

*The best revenge you can reap on the "other woman" is
to let her have him.*
—Death Of The party

The next morning Dena, Mary Ann and I had a Bloody Mary
breakfast up in Leah and Mary Ann's room. Marcus chose to
sleep in. Dena also agreed to accompany both Mary Ann and
Leah down to the casino for a bit of gambling before escort-
ing them back to the trade show. She was clearly irked with
me for going to see Alex without telling her—Mary Ann and
Marcus had ratted me out—but she didn't make a big thing
out of it. I figured she had basically given up on the idea of
talking sense into me… or maybe she was just trying to be
nice because it was clear I was in a bit of a funk. Anatoly
was in danger and I had no idea what my next move should
be… worse yet, he was probably with his wife.

So while my friends went to the casino I stayed behind,
picking at my breakfast in Mary Ann and Leah's room and
tried my damnedest to come up with a plan. The best way to
find Anatoly was to find Natasha. Would she be at Hotel
Noir again? What about this information everyone seemed to

think Anatoly had on a storage disk somewhere? Did it exist and if so where *would* he hide it?

There was a knock on the door. I smiled as I stood up. Marcus no doubt… unless…

My heart caught in my throat. Anatoly? Had he come back?

I practically flung myself at the door but then stopped right before opening it… what if it wasn't Anatoly or Marcus. What if it was someone… bad.

"Hello?" *Please, please, please let it be Anatoly.* I leaned my ear against the door and waited for a response.

"Hello to you too. Do you still have my gun?"

Alex. I took a step back. Should I be afraid? How did he know about this room? I went back to my purse and pulled the gun out. I took a steadying breath and opened the door. "Yep," I said, pointing the gun at his chest. "Got it right here."

Alex smiled. "Can I come in? Feel free to continue to hold me at gunpoint if it makes you more comfortable."

I waved him in, keeping the gun trained. He smiled and closed the door behind him before taking a seat in a chair by the window. "I thought I'd make it simple for you," he explained. "If you shoot me it'll be easy to clean my brains off the glass."

"Funny," I sat down on the bed and gave him a blatantly fake smile. "So, how's Fawn?"

"Ah, you know." Alex sighed and shook his head. "I should have told you she was my sister. I know you two have a troubled history—"

"You mean the history in which she tried to kill me? That history?"

"Fawn tries to kill everyone," he said offhandedly, "you shouldn't take it personally."

"Believe it or not I didn't… until she called from prison to tell me about Anatoly."

"Yeah, I heard about that too."

The light from the window was reflecting off his hair giving him an almost angelic quality… of course they say Lucifer was once an angel too. "You heard about it?" I asked, "or you were behind it?"

Alex only hesitated a moment before answering. "Both."

"Oh my God, you're in league with Fawn!" I stood up and held the gun with both hands. "I should shoot you right now!"

"No," he said without the slightest note of fear or anger.

"No? No what?"

"No, I'm not in league with Fawn and no, you're not going to shoot me. I put Fawn up to that call because the Ignatovs instructed me to do so. They've been bugging your house, you know."

"What? You mean in addition to tapping into my phone?"

"No point in doing a half-assed surveillance job," he pointed out. "Usually the mafia doesn't have a hard time making people talk. But Anatoly is different. They thought if you confronted him he might tell you things that he wouldn't tell them even under threat of torture. Especially if he thought he was at risk of losing you."

"Wait, you're saying that the goal was to piss me off so that I would confront Anatoly and he would… what? Confess to helping the FBI infiltrate the mafia? Why would he confess to something like that when all I was questioning him about was his relationship to Natasha?"

"To be honest, I'm surprised he didn't," he said, his brow wrinkling with confusion. "Don't you think you would have been more inclined to forgive him if he had told you that he was helping the FBI take down the mob? Instead, he told you... what was it? Ah, yes, I understand he told you that he had worked for the mafia because he wanted American citizenship and the chance to sleep with Natasha. And he was surprised that didn't go over well?"

He had a point. I took a second to really *look* at Alex. He was completely relaxed. I might as well have been pointing a banana at him. "I don't trust you," I said simply. "You say you're a legitimate businessman, but you cover up murders for the mob..."

"I told you, I don't see it that way," he interrupted. "I look out for the interests of my guests and my hotel. What do you think happens when people commit suicide in a Vegas hotel after losing all their money? The mob comes in at the hotel's request and relocates the body off premises and they make sure that when it's eventually found, it looks like a murder. That way no one can blame the hotel or its casino. And the mob doesn't just do that for Hotel Noir, they do it for every establishment in Vegas. Dead bodies are bad for business and I'm a very good businessman. No one will ever find a dead body on a property I manage regardless of how the dying happened. That body *will* disappear, for the sake of commerce."

"Wow," I breathed, truly impressed. "You're a master! You're, like, the David Copperfield of bullshit!"

Alex rubbed his chin thoughtfully. "I think I'm going to take that as a poorly phrased compliment."

"It was a compliment… of sorts, and I phrased it perfectly. You seem to have convinced yourself that you're a law-abiding citizen. You treat covering up a murder like it's jaywalking or letting the registration slip on your car."

"I've never let the registration slip on my car."

"You're not a law-abiding citizen. You're dangerous."

"To some, perhaps. But not to you."

"Well no, not as long as I'm the one holding the gun."

Alex laughed. The guy actually laughed in the face of death. "You're really considering shooting me with my own gun?"

"Happens all the time. It's one of the main arguments used by gun control advocates."

There was a definite twinkle in his green eyes. "You don't want to shoot me."

"What I *want* are answers and since I have the gun what I want counts for something. *That's* the argument used by *pro*-gun advocates and at the moment I find it so appealing I'm seriously considering donating to the NRA."

"It's a good feeling, isn't it?"

"What?"

"Power." He stood up, his eyes still trained on mine. "Danger." He took another step forward

"Don't move," I whispered.

He took yet another step and then another. Gently he put his index finger against the barrel of the gun. "I like danger too." His voice was softer now, seductive and absolutely terrifying. He let his finger slide along the barrel, then the handle and then to my shaking hand. "You are definitely a force to be reckoned with."

I jerked away and glared into his smiling eyes.

From his jacket pocket I heard a phone ring. He pulled it out without bothering to ask if that was all right. "This will be quick," he promised as he glanced at the screen.

I walked away from him and leaned against the dresser. The gun *really* wasn't having the effect I had hoped for.

Alex answered with the standard "hello," but what came next was a string of rapid Spanish. Not Russian, Spanish… which reminded me of Anatoly.

I had only discovered a few months ago that he also spoke Spanish. It had been a disturbing revelation and not because I had anything against his being fluent in three languages. That was sexy as hell.

Oddly enough the problem was that it *was* sexy as hell. When a guy speaks three languages he usually lets you know by the third date. It made no sense that he would hide something like that from me.

And yet he had, only inadvertently letting it slip after we had been living together for over a year. Why had he done that?

Alex got off the phone and stuck it back in his pocket. "Someone from my staff," he explained. "Vegas is an international city, helps to be multilingual."

I didn't answer. Obviously it was useful for a hotel's GM to be fluent in as many languages as possible. But there was something more than that going on here.

Alex flashed me another grin. "Now, I believe you said you had some questions for me?"

"Yeah, why didn't Anatoly want me to know he spoke Spanish?"

What happened to Alex's face then was—interesting. I had expected him to burst out laughing or just look at me like I was crazy. He did both of those things but there was a split second before that—the moment when his face registered the question and at *that* moment he looked—cornered.

"Oh my God, you actually know the answer."

"How could anyone know the answer to that?" He peeled off his jacket and carefully draped it over the chair by the window. "I like these chairs but I wonder if they'll seem a little dated in a few years."

"Alex, why didn't Anatoly want me to know he spoke Spanish?"

Alex continued to study the chair as if it was the most fascinating thing in the room. "It's possible," he said eventually, "that he used some of that Spanish while working for the family."

"Why would Anatoly need to know Spanish to work for the Russian Mafia?"

"Because some of the people in the old neighborhood, people who worked with the Ignatovs, weren't Russian. Most were but... the Ignatovs wanted to expand the drug business into the Spanish-speaking immigrant communities."

I felt my heart drop down into my stomach. "Anatoly helped bring drugs into low income, immigrant areas?"

"I didn't say the neighborhoods were low income," Alex said as he finally turned his attention away from the furniture.

"Oh, I'm sorry," I snapped. "Was Anatoly bringing the drugs into high income, immigrant areas? That would give him a pretty small market, wouldn't it?"

Alex chuckled and sat down in the attractive, but-soon-to-be-dated, chair.

"For a guy who just deals with the legal end of things,

you sure do know a lot about the illegal stuff," I noted.

"You can't do business with the Ignatovs without knowing what's up."

"Really?" I asked. "See, if I were running a mafia family, I'd keep everything on a need to know basis. This company-wide memo business seems counterintuitive."

Alex smiled. "I have friends who trust me enough to share certain things."

"They trust you and yet here you are spilling the beans."

"Do you want me to keep secrets from you?"

"No, I'm I just trying to figure you out."

Alex nodded and glanced down at my hand. "Forgive me for harping on this, but how long *do* you plan on holding the gun?"

"It gives me a sense of security, gun rights advocate argument number two."

Alex shifted the chair and stared out the window. "You know, I used to have a brother."

"Used to?"

Alex nodded. "I don't have a brother anymore. Just my sister, Fawn."

"Oh." I drew up a mental picture of Fawn. "Sex change?"

"Um… no. My brother's dead."

"Oh… sorry. How?"

"The Ignatovs needed to make a point." Outside the world was still bright and cheery. The perfect contrast to Alex's sudden change of mood.

"A point… to you?"

"No, I had nothing to do with that particular conflict."

"How can you still work for them after they killed your

brother?"

"I don't have a choice. If they're not convinced that I'm more loyal to them than my own flesh and blood, I'll be a marked man."

"Your brother... did he die quickly?"

"I don't know."

"Oh."

Alex got up, crossed the room and leaned on the dresser next to me. "I want to help you... and Anatoly. Not because I'm nice but because I'm angry."

"Angry with the mob..." I said for clarification.

He nodded. "I shouldn't be forced to prove my loyalty every fucking day by kowtowing to my brother's murderers." He stared at the carpet and I noticed that his hand was now in the form of a fist. "They've been nursing a viper in Rome's bosom," he muttered.

"Yeah, okay, you gotta go now."

"What?" Alex blinked himself back to the here and now. "I was just telling you why I want to help you and Anatoly defeat the mob. I'm on your side."

"You're also crazy," I noted.

"I'm your only chance. If the Ignatov family finds Anatoly before we do they'll kill him."

That doesn't make sense! A little voice in my head screamed. I *knew* I was smart but I was having a hard time following this whole thing. I tried to put everything in order in my head. Fawn had been told to give me enough information to get me to confront Anatoly about his mob days. That argument was recorded. Then, when I announced I was going to Vegas, they set a trap for Anatoly. But Natasha, the mafia princess, saved him—bitch. And now everyone was trying to get their hands on some information Anatoly had on the mob.

And supposedly this all started because of an FBI agent who Anatoly may or may not have helped infiltrate the mob...

It didn't come together the way it was supposed to. It was messy. "Einstein taught that the most accurate equations are usually the simplest ones," I muttered.

"He didn't call them simple," Alex corrected. "He called them beautiful."

"Yeah, well this equation is a big ugly mess. Too many people have tinkered with it and now I just can't trust it at all."

"I'm not sure I'm following you."

There was a knock at the door. "Sophie, are you in there? I forgot to ask for Mary Ann's key card."

Dena was back. I glanced up at Alex. "You really need to go now."

Alex shrugged. "You know where to find me if you need me... *when* you need me."

He pushed himself away from the dresser and got the door. "Careful," he said as he ushered in my surprised friend, "she's packing heat." Alex turned back and winked at me before leaving. Dena turned to me and then lowered her eyes to the gun, which I quickly put away in the top dresser drawer. "So, Leah and Mary Ann are down at the casino?"

"I left them at a blackjack table... who the hell was that?"

"The viper being nursed in Rome's bosom."

Dena gave me a look. "Caligula?" she asked flatly.

"That is who that quote references. Anyway, he's the

one who equated himself to Caligula, I'm just taking him at his word."

Dena put a little more weight on her cane. "Caligula was psychotic."

"Yes, but he built some very useful aqueducts."

"Well, I guess that makes up for throwing all those innocent people to the lions... you know, I think I've seen him before."

"My Caligula? Where? At Hotel Noir?"

"No, I think I saw him in the lobby just a little while ago, when we were going down to the casino. He was talking to this really gorgeous Latina woman and this other guy. Normally I wouldn't have noticed them but again, this woman was a showstopper."

"Really," I drummed my fingers against the dresser. "I wonder if that was his housekeeper."

Dena laughed. "Trust me, she's not anyone's housekeeper. She's still downstairs. I saw her on the way up."

"Wait, what?"

"She's..."

But I didn't wait for her to finish the sentence. I grabbed my purse and was immediately out the door and rushing toward the elevator.

"Sophie! Where are you going?" Dena called after me.

"No time to explain, I'll be back later!" I called back. It was questionable whether or not she heard me but I couldn't worry about that. I jumped on the down elevator. I had to see if it was Margarita... and if so, was she the woman Alex was speaking to on the phone? What was the significance of that? Why would he bring her here?

When the elevator got to the ground floor, I rushed out

and practically ran to the lobby. Once I got there, I swiveled my head this way and that trying to spot Margarita... but I didn't see her. I didn't even see a single Latina woman who Dena would have considered a showstopper. "Fuck," I muttered. I turned around ready to walk back to the elevators and smashed right into Marcus.

"Caught you," he said. "Dena just called me. She said you took off like a bat out of hell to find a Latin love thang."

"She's not here," I said, disappointedly.

"She? Are we playing on a coed team these days?"

"Come on Marcus, that's not what's going on here, and you know it."

Marcus shook his head and pulled on one of his locks. "All I know is that you can't just run off on Dena like that. She can't keep up with you anymore."

"I didn't want her to keep up," I said irritably. "I wanted... Marcus!" I grabbed his arm and pulled him into the arbor trees the hotel had placed along the outskirts of the room.

"What are you—"

"Shh!" I tried to hide behind a five-inch-wide trunk. Keeping my head low, I gestured toward a woman dressed in what looked like a very expensive outfit walking past us with a man who had an arm full of tattoos. The woman was Margarita.

"Who's that?" Marcus asked.

"Margarita, she's a housekeeper."

"Yeah right. Seriously, who is she?"

"I told you, she's... oh just come on!" I grabbed his hand and walked him through the trees until we were forced to be in the open again. By then Margarita and her friend were walking out of the hotel.

"We can't let them get away!" I cried, still yanking Marcus along.

"Could they be dangerous?"

"Maybe, but so am I! I have a gun… oh, wait I forgot to bring it."

I wasn't looking at Marcus but I could actually feel him rolling his eyes. I threw the doors open as we walked outside. I didn't see them.

"They probably got in a cab," Marcus said, but just then I spotted them walking and turning toward the strip.

"Perfect! Let's go!"

"What's perfect about this?" Marcus asked. "If I'm understanding correctly, we're following potentially dangerous criminals and we're unarmed."

"Yeah, but they're on foot and it's not like they're going to shoot us in the middle of the Vegas strip."

"Really? Tell that to Tupac."

"Shh!" I said, more out of frustration than necessity. "I don't see them, do you?"

We had just turned onto the strip. There were people everywhere but I couldn't spot Margarita or the tattooed man to save my life.

"Maybe they finally got in a car," Marcus suggested again.

"Or maybe they turned down a side street." I pointed to the nearest one and gestured for Marcus to follow me. There were still people on the street when we got off the strip but their numbers dropped off dramatically.

I didn't see them.

"This is not happening," I moaned.

"Good," Marcus said with relief. "Besides, I thought we were fighting the Russians. When did we switch nationalities?"

"Well, maybe not everyone who works for the Russian Mafia is Russian."

"Really? From what I've heard, the Italian mob is only open to Italians. I know the Chinese gangs are only open to the Chinese. But you're telling me that the Russian Mafia is an equal opportunity employer?"

"Maybe?" I said, doubtfully. I kept walking, not because I expected to spot them now, but because walking helped me think. There was something very familiar about that tattooed guy... had I seen him at Hotel Noir? But so much of that night was a blur. I just couldn't be sure.

"I'm texting Dena and telling her we're all right," Marcus said as he pulled out his phone while keeping pace with me. "But I do have another question."

"Shoot."

"Why is the mafia so intent on hunting Anatoly down?"

"I told you, the FBI agent—"

"Yes, yes," he said, stepping over a discarded plastic bag on the sidewalk. The pedestrian traffic was getting lighter and lighter. "But it's not like he could introduce *another* FBI agent to them now and he hasn't been involved in the crime family for a while so he has no new information to pass on to the Feds. Why are they so intent on coming after him *now*?"

I hadn't thought of it in those terms. "A show of strength? A warning to others who might try the same thing?"

"Maybe," Marcus conceded. "Or maybe someone's just fucking with us."

For a brief moment, I felt giddy. It's not that what Marcus was saying hadn't occurred to me but having it come from his mouth gave it validity. It was possible that we were dealing with individuals rather than an entire crime organization. Individuals I could deal with.

I was on the verge of doing a little happy dance when a limo pulled up beside us and a door opened. Natasha stepped out, a tight smile on her face. "Just the people I was looking for."

Marcus and I exchanged looks. I wasn't ready to give up my newfound hopefulness quite yet, but Natasha showing up out of the blue probably wasn't a good sign. "Is Anatoly with you?" I asked.

"No. But come take a ride with me anyway."

In fact it was a very bad sign. "I have a gun, you know."

"Really?" Natasha asked, as if somehow charmed by this. "Can I see it?"

"Well, I don't actually have it *with* me but if you give me a second I'd be happy to run back to my hotel room and —"

"Not necessary." She knocked on the roof of the limo. From the passenger side of both the front and back seat two very large men stepped out and stared down at Marcus and me.

"They have guns *on* them," Natasha explained. "So we won't be needing yours."

And now my giddiness was completely and absolutely squelched. I threw a questioning glance at Marcus who looked absolutely terrified. "You can't kidnap us right here in the open!" I said hopefully. "Someone will see."

We all looked around. The only one anywhere near us

was a homeless guy who seemed very intent on not noticing anything.

"We're gonna risk it," Natasha said, sweetly. "Get in the car, please."

I swallowed hard and allowed Natasha to usher us into her limo.

CHAPTER
SEVENTEEN

"I don't mind that my husband still enjoys bumper cars.
I just wish he would refrain from the sport while on the
freeway."
—Death of The Party

Marcus and I sat stiffly against the leather cushions as Natasha and one of her gun-toting bodyguards got in after us. At Natasha's instruction, he searched my purse and kept it by his side. Then she rapped her knuckles against the patrician and within seconds we were moving down the street.

For the first few minutes of the drive, Natasha just stared at me. I met her gaze without flinching. My life expectancy might not be very good at the moment, but I sure as hell wasn't going to go out sniveling.

Finally she graced me with a smile. "Anatoly thinks you're a victim in all this, maybe even a pawn."

I studied her expression carefully. "You don't agree."

"I don't. I think you're a manipulative whore who has been sleeping with my husband." She leaned forward. "I think that maybe you know a lot more than you're letting on.

I *think* that you might very well have booked that room at Hotel Noir after all."

"And why would I do that?"

Natasha shrugged. "I don't know... revenge maybe? I know a little about that." She pulled a switchblade out of her purse.

"Oh dear, God," Marcus gasped, "she's about to go all West Side Story on us."

"A couple of weeks ago a man was killed," Natasha said. "I saw them hold him down. I watched as he begged before my friend pushed a gun into his mouth and blew his head off." She paused for a moment. "I know what you're thinking."

"Really?" Marcus asked, weakly. "Then you know you're going to have to pass me a barf bag in about five seconds."

"You're thinking that the scene I just described is brutal," she continued, completely ignoring Marcus' warning. "But brutality has its place. Sometimes you have to send a message. The guy Igor killed was stealing from the family and he had to pay for that. He had to pay in a way that let everybody else know that his mistake should never be repeated."

Marcus pressed his lips together, probably battling his urge to vomit.

"Did you order the hit?" I was surprised at how steady my voice sounded, particularly since what I really wanted to do was jump out of this moving vehicle, drop, roll, and run for my life... it always worked in the Mission Impossible movies.

"That's dad's job, not mine... sometimes my uncle gets

to make the call." She shifted her body and stared out the tinted windows. "I considered running off with Anatoly and rejecting the violence altogether, but it turns out rejecting violence isn't like dieting. You can't just cut down on it. It's more like giving up smoking. You can pretend that you're not really a smoker because you only have a cigarette or two while you're drinking but it's obvious to everyone else that the only way you can be a nonsmoker is if you stop smoking entirely. No cigarettes, no cigars, and definitely no chewing tobacco."

She seemed to expect me to comment on that but I couldn't think of a single thing to say.

"When it comes to violence," she continued, "Anatoly is a smoker, just like me. The only difference between the two of us is that I *own* it. I was raised in it, I was nurtured by it, and I embraced it. I know who I am and what I'm capable of. Anatoly's life with you is nothing but a facade to help him hide the truth about his nature from everyone—including himself. But when offered a stick of violence he will *always* inhale."

Marcus was now looking more than a little green. I clasped my hands in my lap and sighed loudly. "I'm sorry, am I here for a satellite course in criminal psychology, or do you actually have something important to say?"

Watching the anger distort Natasha's features was fun... probably dangerous, but definitely fun.

But Natasha pulled herself back from the brink quickly. The bodyguard next to her was looking at Marcus with what appeared to be concern. "Are you okay?" he asked him, which was enough to make all of us do a double take.

"Bo, he's fine," Natasha snapped before Marcus could

answer. She turned to me with a glare. "It was Innokenty who brought in the FBI agent who went by the name of Daniil... you've heard about this?" she asked.

Innokenty? I thought Alex had told me that someone named Kenya had brought the FBI guy into the fold.

"That name sounds familiar," Marcus said quietly.

Again Natasha ignored him. "Anatoly was as clueless as the rest of us. He never wanted to hurt my family. Not even for a second."

"Okay," I tried to keep a poker face but my mind was spinning. Why would Alex lie about the name... or was Natasha lying now?

"But Alex didn't think so. I believe you've met Alex, the GM at Hotel Noir?"

I didn't even begin to know what to do with that. Who was telling the truth? Natasha had obvious reasons to mess with me... but if Alex was Fawn's brother then maybe he did too...

Natasha noted my confusion and smiled. "Innokenty was Alex's brother."

I wished I had a mirror so I could check on my poker face because inside I was freaking out.

"Of course no one called him Innokenty," Natasha went on. "We called him by his nickname."

"Which was?"

"Kenya."

Oh shit. "The two names don't sound even remotely alike," I whispered.

"And Dick sounds like Richard?" Natasha countered.

Marcus, still green, leaned his head against the window. "I prefer dick," he said to no one in particular. The bodyguard giggled.

He giggled. Bodyguards aren't supposed to giggle. Natasha shot him a death glare and even Marcus gave him a funny look... a funny, appraising look.

I was about to be killed by my boyfriend's violence-loving wife and Marcus was about to out a hot hired gun. This was so fucking typical.

Natasha inhaled deeply as she tried to take back control of the limo's dynamics. "Let's not pretend that I'm telling you anything new. You already know about Alex and his brother, don't you? You're working with Alex to get revenge. You want revenge on Anatoly because you found out about me and you knew that in the end, he would come back to me. And Alex wants revenge too—but I think his target is a little bigger than my husband."

I had to hand it to her; Natasha had thrown out so much bait it was hard to figure out what to nibble on first. My instinct was to start by telling her that Anatoly had matured in the years since he'd left her and was no longer sexually attracted to mob affiliated psychopaths. But that probably wasn't the best tack to take.

"Who would Alex want revenge on?" I asked carefully. "And he hasn't done anything vengeful, has he?" *You killed his brother,* I thought to myself, *did you really think he was going to just sit on his hands and interview a few more Food & Beverage managers?*

"Not yet. My family provides him with his livelihood so he'd be smart to keep his loyalty with them rather than with his poor, dead little brother. My family thinks Alex is smart," Natasha explained.

"What do you think?"

"I think he's intelligent, in a bookish kind of way... but I don't think he's ever been very *smart*."

I shook my head, trying to clear out all the unnecessary information so I could get to the heart of what was being said. "What do you think is going on here, Natasha?"

"The issue of the FBI agent was settled some time ago. The only person who thought Anatoly knew something was Alex and his brother. But now Anatoly has come to Vegas. He's killed someone who works for the family. He says it's because he threatened his life. I can vouch for that, but even if that's true, why was Anatoly's life being threatened to begin with? There was no hit ordered on him. And now Anatoly is defending himself against charges that no one has made. It's kind of like a criminal who insists that they weren't at the scene of the crime before you tell them there was a scene to be at. It makes him look guilty. Now the family is beginning to wonder if Alex and Innokenty were telling the truth."

"But what good would any of this do Alex?" I asked.

"Well, if Alex really thinks Kenya took the blame for Anatoly that would be enough to make Alex want to hurt him. But the beauty of what's happening now is that if Anatoly thinks the mob is after him, *he* might launch a preemptive strike. If Anatoly hurts my family, Alex gets his revenge on them. If my family kills Anatoly in retaliation, Alex gets his revenge on Anatoly. So Alex gets everything he wants while the rest of us have to deal with a war."

"There's a simple answer to this," I said.

"Really," Natasha said, dryly.

"Yeah, *kill Alex*! You said you have guns, use them! It's not like you don't know where to find him!"

"Eventually," Natasha said. "But the problem is that my family doesn't like my theories right now. Until they do, I can't touch Alex. But I can touch those who he's enlisted to work with him, like you. No one will care what I do to you."

"You're going to kill me?"

"I'm going to take you to a lovely little hideaway. It's secure and very private so there'll be no risk of interruptions. You're going to tell me what I need to know about Alex's plan."

"I don't know anything about Alex's plan."

"That's too bad because if you don't tell me what I want to know, I *will* kill you and your carsick friend. And it won't be a painless death."

The thug threw Marcus a sympathetic look. So he wasn't going to stop his employer from torturing us to death but at least he felt bad about it.

"I really think I'm going to be sick," Marcus said again.

I reached for his hand but just as I did the limo was slammed from the side and we swerved off the road. Natasha and I were thrown to the floor and Marcus ended up in the thug's lap… not that the thug seemed to mind. In fact, and I *saw* this, the thug grabbed Marcus' hand while Natasha was struggling to right herself and placed it on the door handle. Marcus didn't have to ask what to do. He jerked open the door and grabbed me. My purse had fallen right in front of me (or had Bo thrown it there?) so I grabbed it too. The limo was already starting again but had virtually no speed. Marcus and I leaped out of the vehicle before Natasha could do anything about it. The thug might have been able to do something about it, but he was moving rather slowly.

I had been so focused on Natasha I hadn't even noticed

that we had driven out into the middle of nowhere… there was nothing to be seen but desert… and the tinted glass Hummer that had sideswiped us. We started running. The limo backed up as if it meant to run us over, but the Hummer backed up too and sideswiped the limo again.

I could hear Natasha screaming, but whether it was in anger or pain, I didn't know. I couldn't take the time to figure things like that out. Right now Marcus and I just needed to run.

I heard another vehicle coming for us. I risked a glance behind me and saw the Hummer once again.

"Oh God," Marcus muttered, but the Hummer passed us and then swerved and screeched to a stop directly in our path. The glass was so dark I couldn't see who was driving. And then the driver's side window was cracked open. "Get in," a voice instructed.

Anatoly's voice.

Without a second thought, I dived into the back seat and Marcus got in right after me. From there it took some maneuvering for me to climb into the front seat next to Anatoly, particularly since he was already back on the road, going at a breakneck speed. But I needed to be next to him. Hearing his voice hadn't been enough. Seeing the back of his head certainly wasn't enough.

"Get your seatbelt on," Anatoly said in lieu of hello.

"Oh, so now you're worried about my safety? Were you thinking about that when you drugged me?"

"Did you think about the danger you were putting us both in when you refused to leave Vegas?"

I shot him a glare before glancing in the side mirror. "Why aren't they following us?"

"I think that last hit disabled the vehicle."

"You realize," Marcus said, as he struggled to catch his breath, "that we wouldn't have been able to get away if it wasn't for Bo-Bo the gay mafia thug, right? You did see that?"

"Bo-Bo? You mean Bo? He was in there?" Anatoly asked, concerned. "Did you notice if he was hurt in the crash?"

"You know him?" I asked and then shook my head in disgust. "Of course you do. You're all hooked up in the mafia world, aren't you?"

"I used to be a part of that world, Sophie. I was honest with you about that."

"Oh right, you were very honest after you were caught lying. Your friend Bo-Bo is fine!"

"Yes," Marcus muttered, "he is that."

I glared out the tinted window. "I wonder if Natasha has any injuries."

"If we're lucky," Anatoly said quietly.

I gave him a sideways glance. The corner of his mouth was twitching. I broke out into a full smile and grabbed his hand. "I love you, Anatoly."

"I love you too, Sophie."

Marcus groaned. "I swear you two make Catherine and Heathcliff look like a well-adjusted couple."

I sighed and turned back to the window. The desert was beautiful but it frightened me. It had to be every bit as foreboding as an English moor. "I've memorized whole passages from Wuthering Heights," I admitted aloud.

"Have you?" Anatoly asked, his eyes still firmly on the road.

In an affected voice, I took on the personage of Catherine. "Nelly, I am Heathcliff! He's always, always in my mind: not as a pleasure, any more than I am always a pleasure to myself, but as my own being."

My Heathcliff smiled and squeezed my hand as he drove us into the depths of the desert.

CHAPTER
SEVENTEEN

"I learned how to fight but no one ever taught me how to walk away."
—Death Of The Party

It took me a few minutes before I was truly thinking clearly again. My first worry was for my sister and friends but Anatoly assured me they were safe. Natasha had no interest in messing with any of them, and she probably would have preferred not to bother with Marcus but since he was there when she nabbed me she had to take him along. Still, Marcus called Dena and suggested that she, Leah and Mary Ann stay in public spaces and be on the alert. He also told Dena she might want to keep one of her whips and a pair of her fur-lined handcuffs handy just in case.

"Where are we going?" I asked as we drove further and further away from the Vegas I knew.

"Somewhere we can talk."

I accepted that for no other reason than that I didn't have the energy to interrogate him. Apparently Marcus was exhausted too because he remained silent in the backseat.

"I called the Civic Center library," Anatoly said, casually.

I laughed. "Oh yeah? What did they tell you?"

"That I would have to wait until Tuesday to get my books. That's when the person who deals with donations will be back at work."

"Well then, I guess you'll have to get all this wrapped up by Tuesday, huh?"

He smiled wistfully. "If only."

We were approaching mountains now but they weren't the green mountains I knew from Northern California. These were bare and jagged. As we drew nearer I could see the red soil and rock that covered the peaks and ridges of the land ahead of me. It was as if the very earth was angry.

I didn't know how to survive out here. I didn't know the rules.

Eventually we came to a giant rock on the side of the road. On it were the words "Red Rock Canyon National Conservation Center" painted in bold, black letters and a little after that we reached a parking lot outside a closed visitor center. There were a few cars in the parking lot but no people to be seen.

Anatoly turned back to Marcus. "I need some time to talk to Sophie alone. Do you mind if we take off for ten minutes or so?"

"I'll stay here," Marcus said, with relief. "Not moving sounds very, very good."

Anatoly nodded and got out of the car. He was actually gentlemanly enough to come around to my side and open my door for me.

Without protest I let him lead me toward the hiking trails.

For a few minutes we didn't say anything. We knew that as soon as the words came so would the accusations. So we kept our mouths shut and just walked, red dust rising up with each step and settling on our shoes. We were just... feeling each other's presence. How many times had we walked like this and not even thought about it? Sure we argued, occasionally we even broke up but when it came time to walk down one of life's dusty little paths we always found a way to do it together. It was just natural.

But now for the first time I was acutely aware that my hold on Anatoly was tenuous. Not because he didn't love me, but because the forces that were keeping us apart were just *so big*!

A lizard darted out from under a rock, took one look at us and darted back under again.

Anatoly sighed. He was going to break the silence. "So now do you see why I need you to leave Vegas?"

"Do you see why I can't?"

The sun was getting a little lower in the sky, making the rusty red surroundings look almost luminous.

Anatoly stopped and took my hands in his. God, I loved his hands and I couldn't help softening a little as he caressed my skin with the subtle back and forth movement of his thumb. "I was married before and I lied to you about it."

Oddly enough, it didn't feel wrong for him to use this moment to state the obvious. It was the confession that I needed. Simple, straightforward—even the pain the words caused felt—right.

"I was married before," he said again. "But I've never been in love before. Sophie—you have to leave Vegas. For me."

"You are so selfish," I whispered.

He furrowed his brow. "I'm sorry?"

"You act like your feelings are the only ones that matter here. You want me to leave Vegas because you don't like thinking about me being in danger. Well, have you ever considered that I don't like the danger *you're* in?"

"Sophie—"

"Forget it," I said, cutting him off before he could even start his rebuttal. "I can't leave Vegas until I know you're safe. That stresses you out? Tough. Pop a Valium and learn to deal."

Anatoly's mouth was twitching again. He was really trying to scowl at me but it just wasn't working for him.

"Do you think Kenya's brother is behind all this?" I asked.

"You know about Kenya." By the tone of his voice, I could tell he didn't want me to know about him. Clearly he didn't want to answer the question either.

His eyes moved to the horizon. "I've heard Natasha's theory, but Alexander Kinsky's motives seem weak to me."

"Weak? They killed his brother! If someone killed Leah, I'd go vigilante too!"

"So he gets revenge, but if the theory's right, the revenge he's after will probably end up getting him killed along with everyone else."

"So you *don't* think he's involved."

"Until I can figure out why he would be, I can't point any fingers," he said. His jaw tightens a bit before he added, "Natasha tells me that you and Alexander Kinsky have become close."

"Not that close," I said harshly, "it's not like he's my

husband or anything."

I knew that was a cruel twist of the knife but for him to listen to *Natasha* about what other men I was or wasn't getting close to… it just made me want to scream.

"I can't accuse him of much at this point, but he's not a good guy. Look at who his employer is."

"Yeah, he works for your old boss. How about you can just call him Kettle and I'll call you Pot. How 'bout that?"

Anatoly's jaw was so tight at this point I was a little worried that it might lock in place. But after a deep breath, he managed to relax it enough to talk. "Even if this guy isn't the cause of all this, he's still involved and now I am too. That's why you need to get on a plane and as far away from both of us as possible—until I say it's safe."

"And that will be when? After you've taken down the entire Russian Mafia?"

"Natasha doesn't think the mob set up that trap at Hotel Noir. Which means Tanya was either working on her own or she was working for someone else and *that's* weird. If you work for a crime family it's really not a good idea to free-lance, and to what end? It's got to be about more than re-venge."

"Oh, wait! I just thought of another possibility!"

The sun was in my eyes and I had to squint to look up into Anatoly's face. "What's that?" he asked.

"Maybe Natasha's full of shit!"

Anatoly chuckled. "Let's keep walking."

"I'm not kidding!" I insisted as we continued down the path. "Maybe Natasha is behind all of this! She could have lured you out here and set up a situation that made her look like your savior."

"She has no motive."

"She has a huge motive! She wants you back!"

"You think she set up a situation that ensured the death of two people just so she could play the hero?"

"Oh, I'm sorry, would that be beneath the mafia princess' code of ethics?"

"One of those people was her cousin, Sophie."

"Please, did you ever watch *The Sopranos*? Cousins kill each other."

"Natasha isn't behind this."

I looked around at the landscape and studied the large boulders that decorated it. Each one was way too big for me to throw at Anatoly's head. "You're defending her."

"No, I'm..." his voice trailed off as he tried to find an alternative explanation. Unfortunately there wasn't one. "I don't think she's behind this, that's all."

"She was going to kill me, Anatoly."

"It wouldn't have gone that far."

"You *are* defending her!"

"As moronic as this sounds, she believes you're working with Alexander to get me killed."

"You still care about her!"

"I risked her safety in order to get you away from her. If she has whiplash, it's because she deserves it. And if she had actually hurt you? I would have killed her."

Immediately I felt better about things. "Thank you."

"But she wouldn't have."

And then I felt worse about things. "Oh, what-the-hell-ever. Just tell me what information you have on the mafia."

"Some corners were cut and if the wrong people find out, it will be a big problem for the mafia."

Could the man *be* more vague? "A life or death kind of problem?"

"No, just death," Anatoly said, his voice becoming so quiet I had to strain to hear him. "Kidnapping, torture, decapitation... even the family members, the kids, and the wives... everyone will be in danger."

"Oh."

"That's why it doesn't make sense that Alexander would be behind this. Why would he want to risk getting caught up in that? But you should still stay the hell away from him," he quickly added. The sun was even lower now. I had never seen the sunset over the desert and I wondered if it would be as red as the dirt we were standing on.

"I have to go," he said.

"No. You're not leaving me again."

"Natasha didn't have her family's permission to do what she did today. I can use that to make sure she doesn't come near you again. If you go back to San Francisco, it'll look like the break-up is permanent. You'll be safe."

"Anatoly—"

"I have to figure this out. Natasha can help me but she won't if you're by my side." He ran his hands over my hair. "You can't tell anyone you saw me."

"Obviously."

"Please leave Vegas, Sophie."

"No."

Again he sighed but this time he pulled me to him, kissing my lips so gently that at first it felt like the tickle of a feather. But then it became deeper, more passionate... I felt myself melting against him and automatically my hands went up into his hair as I tried to pull him even closer, to make my Heathcliff part of "my own being."

But of course there was no way of doing that... not in a physical way, and as his hands moved up and down my back I felt him gently pull away.

"Have you forgiven me?" he asked.

"I don't know."

He traced my jaw line with his finger and then lifted my chin so I was looking up into his brown eyes again. "You don't have to," he said hoarsely. "But I want to fix this."

I could hear the concern in his voice and I wanted to tell him it was all going to be okay but that would be like one agnostic trying to convince another that there really was a heaven. I *wanted* to believe in our future—more than anything. But I wasn't sure anymore. Our lives were in danger and he was about to walk away from me and into the waiting arms of his ex-wife who had just tried to kill me... no, that wasn't right. She wasn't his ex anything. And if all that wasn't enough to drive a wedge between us, he was also keeping secrets from me.

"Anatoly, what's the real reason you learned to speak Spanish?"

He hesitated, but only briefly. "I'm good with languages. When I got to this country, I could see that Spanish would be useful."

"That's all?" I didn't even try to disguise the severe skepticism in my voice.

He smiled, almost apologetically. If there was more to it, he wasn't going to tell me. "I'm going to have Marcus call a car to come pick you up. I'll stay until it arrives. Believe it or not, we're only about thirty minutes away from the center of the city."

"And then you're leaving again."

"I have to, Sophie."

"In that case have Marcus text me when the car arrives. I'm going to sit here by myself for a while."

"Sophie you shouldn't—"

"Either stay with me or stop telling me what I should and shouldn't do."

He winced "At least you're traveling light."

I didn't know what that meant, and as he stepped away from me, I wasn't sure I cared. What mattered was that he was leaving again.

"If you really want to help me, you'll get out of Vegas so I know you're safe."

I stood stalk still as he turned around and walked away. In a whisper too soft for him to hear I said, "The only way you can know that is if you stay by my side."

Within minutes he was out of sight.

CHAPTER
NINETEEN

"Hell has no fury like a writer whose hard drive has crashed."
—Death Of The Party

True to my word, I didn't immediately go back to the parking lot. Instead, I found a rock to sit on and watched the clouds move across the sky.

I tried not to think about the personal aspects of things. I tried not to think about how it had felt to kiss him or how betrayed I felt now. I had to separate myself from all that and focus on the bigger picture.

The information Anatoly was holding onto sounded nuclear. That was good and bad. On the one hand, sane people didn't mess with individuals who had their finger on the button. So the best-case scenario was that this could turn into a cold war. The mafia could destroy Anatoly and Anatoly could destroy them. We could have a lifelong stalemate. It was a stressful way to live but it was doable.

But if the mob wasn't what the international community would call a "reasonable player," it could decide to push the red button regardless of the consequences. It only took one crazy fanatic and really, was it so unlikely that the leader of a crime family might be a little crazy?

Eventually Marcus called to tell me the car had arrived. When I got back to the parking lot, Anatoly was gone.

"He could have at least driven us back to the strip," I grumbled as Marcus held open the door for me.

"He said he would have but it was a bit risky since the Hummer was stolen."

"You're kidding."

"I know, he took us for a ride with his hot Hummer. How can you not love that?"

I wasn't sure I loved that. I would have thought it was too conspicuous a vehicle to sneak away with but if anyone was capable of carrying off the feat it was Anatoly. As I sat down in the backseat, I decided to keep that last thought to myself. I didn't feel like giving Anatoly accolades, even if they were in regards to his ability to act like an accomplished criminal, particularly since he *was* an accomplished criminal.

As the car pulled onto the street, Marcus leaned his head back against the seat. "Anatoly assures me he can keep Natasha from coming after us again."

"I wouldn't count on that," I replied.

Marcus was quiet for a moment before adding, "If he really is going to keep Natasha from killing us, he's probably right about needing to be apart from you for a while."

"You know what?" I asked, my volume rising. "I don't care what stupid excuses he gave you. We're supposed to be a couple. We're supposed to see things through together. No matter what."

"Maybe we should leave Ve—"

"No!"

Marcus raised his eyebrows but didn't say anything more. After we had been on the road for about ten minutes, he called Dena to make sure everyone was okay and to tell her we were heading back to the hotel. He was wise enough not to try to engage me in conversation once he hung up so the only sound in the town car was the instrumental jazz the driver had playing on the radio.

I hated instrumental jazz. I hated everything about this trip. This was not the Vegas from the brochures. We were weekending in a war zone.

When Marcus and I finally got back to Encore, we decided to go up to Leah's room first. I had the key but I still made a point of pounding on the door before using it.

"Are you knocking or trying to knock it down?" Marcus asked.

"I just want to make sure she can hear me in case... in case she's listening to her iPod."

"Okaay," Marcus said, giving me a confused look.

"Yeah, um, you know what? Let me go in first." I let myself in and held out a hand indicating that Marcus should stay back. But the lights were out and the bathroom door open so after releasing the breath I had been holding, I ushered him in.

"What's up with the extreme caution?" Marcus asked.

"I don't know what you're talking about. This is always how I enter hotel rooms." I opened the top dresser drawer. The gun was still there. It had been so unforgivably careless of me to leave it here. I should have buried it at Red Rock.

"Let's go back to my room," I suggested. Little memories kept creeping into the forefront of my consciousness: the first time he kissed me up by Coit Tower; holding his hand the first time we went to see a movie together… Hitchcock. He loved Hitchcock just as much as I did.

I hated that it was the fond memories that were breaking through the wall I was trying to put up in my mind. Why couldn't I hate him? *Really* hate him? What was wrong with me?

We walked down the hall and waited for the elevator. I was remembering the first time I rode on the back of his Harley. By the time we were stepping onto the elevator, I was reliving the first time he saved my life, the first time he held me while I cried.

Let him go, Sophie. Just let him go!

But when the elevator doors finally opened I was already lost in the memory of the first time he told me he loved me.

I was barely even aware of Marcus as I slid my key card into the door. The last time he said he loved me had been less than an hour ago. But that couldn't be the last-*last* time! There had to be—

My brain froze in mid-thought as the here and now came crashing down around me. Marcus gasped.

The room was trashed. The blankets pulled off the bed, the drawers were all open, and my clothes were scattered on the floor. I stood perfectly still and listened for the sound of an intruder. He would know I was here so he'd be trying to stay quiet too. Still, all I needed was one small tell, a jagged breath, the sound of something rustling, a creak coming from the bathroom, behind the curtain, anywhere that should be silent.

"I don't hear anything," Marcus breathed as if reading my mind. He insisted on walking ahead of me so I clung to the back of his shirt as we moved forward.

I spotted two suitcases on the floor, the one I had brought and the one they had brought to fool Anatoly. Marcus knelt down by the former... the lining had been ripped open. They probably would have slashed open the lining in both bags if the latter hadn't already been torn.

My knees buckled underneath me and I dropped down onto the stripped bed.

Marcus checked inside the bathroom "Uh-uh, no!" he cried.

I was immediately on my feet again. The bathroom was a mess. They had dumped my leave-in conditioner into the sink. "That's just fucked up!" Marcus snapped

I spun around and went back into my room, trampling my own clothes as I went to the closed door that adjoined mine with Marcus and Dena's. Marcus wasn't far behind, muttering—more to himself than to me, "They better not have gone through *my* stuff because if they lay a hand on my Bumble & Bumble *no one* will be safe."

I put my hand on the doorknob...

... and heard the jagged breath.

Right behind the door in the next room. It hadn't been loud but I had *heard* it. A quick glance at Marcus' face told me he had heard it too.

My heart, which had been breaking all the speed limits, came to an emergency stop.

I instinctively reached inside my purse. I felt the cool steel against my fingers.

As I pulled out the gun my hand was shaking so badly you would have thought I was going through a heroin withdrawal.

I heard the door on the other side of mine creak. Was he

closing it or was he going to come into this room? I glanced down at my shaking gun and then at Marcus. I mouthed the word, "*run.*"

"You run," he whispered as he gently took the gun out of my hand. "I'm going to get my Bumble & Bumble."

"Wait!" I hissed as he cocked the gun, threw open the door and leaped into the room, his arms straight in front of him pivoting this way and that in the way we had all seen people do in every action movie ever made. Clothes were strewn all over the floor but the room was empty.

I turned toward the door leading to the hall. It was slowly closing the way weighted doors in hotels do when you let them close behind you on their own. The intruder had already left. I rushed to the door and Marcus rushed to the bathroom, gun outstretched. "Clear!" he shouted. But I wasn't paying attention. I pulled open the door and jumped into the hall. No one to my right. I heard the sound of an elevator ding at the far end of the hall to my left. I turned just as the doors opened. A dark haired man with his back to me, wearing a long-sleeved black T-shirt, stepped onto the elevator. He was carrying the case to my MacBook.

At least you're traveling light.

That's what he had meant! I had left the MacBook in my room!

"Son of a bitch!" I screamed.

But, the elevator closed before I could even get close.

Marcus came up beside me, the gun now lowered at his side.

"I thought losing Anatoly was the worst thing that could happen to me," I said.

Marcus put his arm around my shoulders. "It's going to

be okay. They didn't mess with my products so we can share tomorrow."

"I'm not worried about my hair, Marcus! They took my MacBook which means they now have every electronic copy of my unfinished manuscript and I don't *have* a hardcopy!"

"Oh... you don't use Dropbox?"

"Fuck these assholes!" I turned to Marcus and he literally stepped back from the force of my anger. "They want to go nuclear?" I asked. "Fine, I'm ready to blow this shit up, Right. Now."

CHAPTER
TWENTY

"I hate it when my loved ones give me a hard time about my reckless behavior. So now I pick up all my dates outside of Al-Anon meetings. The trick is to get 'em before they walk in the door."
—Death Of The Party

Marcus called Dena and caught her up. She was hightailing it back to the hotel from the trade show while we went down to the casino to look for the rest of our party. We spotted Leah and Mary Ann at the craps table and Leah was jumping up and down like a little girl who had just been told she was going to get an unlimited, lifetime supply of ice cream. I found myself hanging back. After all, Leah's room was still intact. The intruder got what he wanted from me so it was best not to interrupt my sister's rare moment of giddiness. Marcus and I found a spot against the wall and ordered drinks from a passing cocktail waitress.

"I have to go back to Alex's," I said as I watched Leah take the dice again.

"Why?" Marcus asked. He was leaning against the wall as if it was the only thing holding him up. In his hand was a plastic bag filled with his hair products. He had decided they wouldn't leave his sight for the rest of the trip.

"If Natasha's right and he's behind this then I have to get close enough to prove it. If she's wrong, then he's the only one who has offered to help me. And I have to find out where in the hell Anatoly stored that information."

"Well, they've stolen both your computers and your storage devices and undoubtedly they've stolen his laptop too so…"

"So Anatoly's not stupid! These people have totally underestimated him! If he was going to store top secret information, he wouldn't put it on his girlfriend's computer and he wouldn't store it with all our other USB sticks."

The waitress arrived with our two cosmopolitans and we clinked our plastic glasses together before we knocked them back.

"You've been living with him for more than a year," Marcus noted. "You never noticed any special, secret hiding place… your sister is moving to the blackjack table."

"I see that. And I don't think you find secret hiding places when you're not looking for them. That's what makes them secret," I countered. "He would hide it somewhere I would never check… never even consider going near."

Marcus raised his eyebrows. "The laundry?"

"Oh shut up!" I downed the rest of my drink and started looking around for another cocktail waitress. "We eat the same food, share the same bathroom, listen to the same music, sleep in the same bed. What else…" my voice trailed off as a new idea popped into my head.

"What?"

I squeezed the empty cup in my hand until it made that

plastic scrunching sound. With my free hand, I pulled out my phone. "Mama?" I said when my mother answered my call. "It's me."

"Mommehlah, where are you? Your sister called and said you both were staying through Monday? You're not getting married again, are you? There's only so much an old woman can take before she starts getting ulcers!"

I glanced over at Leah. She was studying her cards with an intensity that implied the stakes were maybe a little higher than they should be. I wondered how much this little rebellion was going to cost her.

"Mama everything's fine... but I need one more favor. In my garage, there is a box of books. The box is marked *Library* and on the top of the pile are a few books on soccer. I need you to look to see if there's anything inside those books."

"Of course there's going to be something inside those books! Pages and pages of something!"

"No, no, something else. Look, if you see any cars parked anywhere near my place or anyone even slightly suspicious hanging around, you just drive on past. But if not, get those soccer books. Please?"

"The things I do for you, mommelah! If we were Catholic, I'd be a saint already!"

I almost pointed out that one would have to die for that honor but decided against it. "Thank you, Mama, I owe you."

I hung up the phone.

"You would never open a soccer book," Marcus noted, approvingly as he finished off his drink.

"No, I wouldn't. Not unless Anatoly's life... and my

manuscript depended on it."

"Found you."

We both looked up to see Dena approaching. She pushed herself between us and leaned lightly on her cane. "Well, you two have had quite the day, haven't you?" She said, irritably. "I can't believe you didn't come right back here after Natasha tried to *kill* you."

"It wasn't my call. Anatoly took us out to Red Rock. Anyway, he promised Natasha wouldn't try to kill us again."

"Oh, gee, really? Was it a pinky promise?" Dena asked. "Too bad he couldn't promise that no one would break into our room. Did you happen to see if this intruder made off with my leather underwear?"

"I don't think so," Marcus said. "I'm not sure the black market value for leather panties is all that high. Of course there are fetishists who have a thing for used panties..."

"Yeah, but those guys are usually into granny panties," Dena acknowledged. Our waitress came back and Dena took one of the drinks for herself. "How 'bout my sex toys? Did he get those?"

The waitress gave her a funny look and took off quickly.

"I did see them." Marcus said, taking a swig of the remaining drink. "I think they're all there. Still, a few of them, like your vibrator, had been thrown on the floor."

Dena made a face. "Looks like I'm going to have to soak that in alcohol before I bring it anywhere near me again."

"You could," Marcus said, "or you could just toss it and try to make do with the remaining twelve you have at home."

Dena eyed the plastic bag in Marcus' hand. "What's that?"

"Hair products."

"Well all right then," Dena flashed us a relieved smile. "We've got leather underwear, sex toys, hair products and a gun. That pretty much covers the necessities, doesn't it? Oh," she reached into her large hobo bag and pulled out her iPad, "we also have this. I can't say I have your manuscript stored on it but at least we do have access to the Internet."

I exhaled in relief. It was a small thing since I still had my smartphone but at this point every little advantage helped.

"Sophie wants to go see Alex again."

Dena hesitated. "That's probably not such a bad idea."

Marcus' mouth dropped open in shock. "But you're always against Sophie taking risks!"

"And she never listens to me," Dena pointed out. "Look, Sophie hasn't been arrested yet so clearly this Alex guy has followed through on at least one promise. Find out from him if there's anything else we need to worry about and if there isn't let's get the hell outta Dodge."

"But—" Marcus began and then stopped short. "Look!" he said in an urgent whisper.

I followed Marcus' gaze to the middle of the crowded casino. And there he was, standing next to the roulette table.

"Oh my God," I hissed. "It's Bo-Bo, the gay mafia thug!"

Dena lifted her eyebrows and took a sip of her cocktail. "Well that's a new one."

"Should we get out of here?" I asked.

"No," Marcus said, thoughtfully. "Go deal with Alex, I'll deal with this guy."

"You can't be serious! Natasha could be around!"

"Maybe… but I doubt it."

"You do?"

"Yeah, I do. He may be a fighter by profession, but he's a lover at heart. He just needs the right guy to bring it out in him."

"Marcus," I stepped in front of him and grabbed both his arms. "This isn't like the time you decided to try out that gay biker bar. This guy really is a violent criminal, no matter what he did for us back in the limo!"

Dena looked at Marcus curiously. "What did Bo-Bo do for you in the back of a limo?"

"Not as much as I would have liked," Marcus admitted with an evil grin before turning back to me. "I'm going to take care of Mary Ann and Leah. I'll protect them like… like they were my own little Bumble & Bumbles. But this time *you* have to trust *me*."

I glanced at Dena who shrugged. "I don't know what the fuck either one of you are talking about so I don't have an opinion. But I do agree that if we're going to confront this Alex guy, we should do it now and do it together."

"We're not going to confront him." I glanced back at Leah and Mary Ann. There seemed to be several stacks of chips in front of Leah. Had she emptied out her savings account or something? That would be very bad.

"What are we going to do then?" Dena asked.

I hesitated. "We're going to play him," I finally said. "We're going to make him believe that he has our trust, get his guard down and get the information we need, even if it means we do a tag-team search of his house."

"And how long is this going to take?" Marcus asked, his eyes still on Bo-Bo.

"I don't know, don't wait up."

That was enough to get Marcus' attention. "Now you're the one who can't be serious."

"I'm not going to do anything bad… but if he offers me a room to stay in, with Dena, then I'm going to take it. He's not going to murder me in the middle of the night. What would be the point? But I need him to trust me enough to let me wander around his place without being watched. It might be easier to do that if we stay the night."

"Now *that's* crazy."

"It is," Dena agreed. "But like I said, I want to get this whole drama in the rearview mirror. I'll be with her," she said to Marcus, although she was looking at me. "I won't let her completely throw caution to the wind."

"I have to do this, Marcus."

"For Anatoly?"

"For my manuscript." *And for Anatoly,* I added, silently.

Dena patted Marcus on the arm. "Try not to sleep with the enemy." She started to pull me away, showing surprising strength for a woman who used a cane.

"Why are you being so accommodating of this?" I asked as she pulled me out of the casino and toward the hotel lobby. "You never go along with my crazy plans."

"Never say never," Dena said dryly. "Come upstairs with me. We'll throw a few things in an overnight bag just in case we do end up sleeping over."

I stared at her. This was *so* unlike her. She sighed, clearly impatient with my lack of response, and pulled me toward the elevator.

We didn't say much as we picked a few things from the mess in our rooms and put them in Anatoly's duffle bag.

And I didn't say a word when she led me out of the hotel and worked with the valet to get us a town car for a decent price. I was paying more for town cars than I had paid for my hotel and plane tickets combined.

I held onto my silence for the first half of the drive to Alex's house. Confusion had knocked some of the anger out of me. It wasn't just the mystery of who was after Anatoly that was nagging at me. It was my friends' behavior. Marcus, I sort of understood. He had been an At-Risk-Youth before he came to terms with his sexual orientation and he had a serious soft spot for dysfunctional, self-destructive closet cases. I thought expanding that soft spot to make room for members of the mafia was taking things a bit far, but that was Marcus.

But this wasn't Dena. Dena restricted her wild behavior to her sexual encounters. When it came to the rest of her life, she was amazingly level headed. And yet here she was, encouraging me to spend the night in the home of a mafia affiliate who might also be planning something akin to murder.

I studied her profile. She was staring straight ahead, twisting her cane around and around in her hand.

"This never-say-never thing," I said, slowly as I watched the movement of her cane, "does it have anything to do with Fawn or... what happened to you?"

Even in the dark, I could see Dena's nostrils flare. "I was shot in the back," she said, quietly. "I had to relearn how to walk, and while you were out there trying to bring my shooter to justice, I was in a hospital bed staring at the ceiling. I wasn't given the opportunity to so much as lift a finger to set things right. I had to let others do that for me while I lay there... I was... helpless."

She said the word *helpless* the way others might say the word vomit or excrement. I bit down on my lip and tried to take her hand but she jerked away.

"Now we have Fawn's brother," Dena said, the sarcasm dripping from her voice, "and he wants to help. He's really, really sorry about almost setting you up for murder, for lying to you about who he is and who he's related to but now, *now* we're supposed to trust him. He wants you to put your fate in his hands. You're right, I could have tried to talk you out of this, and I could have pretended to believe you after making you swear to stay away from him. I could totally turn my back on all of this and let you deal with this mess by yourself because clearly you're *not* walking away. I could put myself in a position where I can't help you... where I'm... helpless. Or," she turned to me and the fire that was coming from within her was almost bright enough to illuminate the whole backseat, "I could help you. I have a choice this time. I'm choosing the latter."

"Well," I breathed, "I guess that's settled then."

"Yeah, I guess it is."

Again we fell into silence, but this time it was a silence I understood.

CHAPTER
TWENTY-ONE

"The thing about betrayal is that it can only come from people you trust completely."
—Death Of The Party

Alex didn't seem surprised to see me, although he was taken off guard by Dena. He listened with sympathy as I told him about the break in and about how Natasha had kidnapped me. "She's a whore," he said smoothly. It was a sweet lie calculated to win my favor. It almost worked, but now I was on my guard. He was the viper in Rome's bosom. I couldn't trust anything he said without proof. Margarita wasn't there which is what I had been counting on. The fewer people in the house, the easier it would be to snoop. Besides, Margarita creeped me out. There was just something very off about her.

He offered both Dena and me our own rooms and Dena insisted on going to bed right away as Alex and I had cocktails in his study. I knew Dena wasn't really in bed. People often harbored the misguided assumption that those who used a cane couldn't be stealthy, but Dena was the queen of stealth when she wanted to be. Late tonight, while Alex slept, I would try to look in the rooms she missed.

"How did you get away from Natasha?" Alex asked as he poured me yet another glass of his sipping vodka.

"It wasn't that hard. She drove me all the way out to some national park in the middle of the desert, but all she wanted was to scare me into leaving Vegas. Now that she has Anatoly—"

"She has Anatoly?" Alex interrupted. "Since when?"

"He called her while I was with her. I could just tell that he's back with her by the way they were talking. I'm done with him." I raised my glass above my head. "Here's to new beginnings."

Alex kept his glass by his side. "Are you leaving Vegas then?"

"Tomorrow."

"Where are the rest of your friends?"

"Back in San Francisco. They all had their tickets to leave tonight. Dena and I originally had tickets for tonight too but she had our flight switched to tomorrow back when I thought there was something to stay for." *A poker player is only as good as his ability to bluff.* Alex didn't need to know how much backup I had here in this city. He certainly didn't need to know that I had seen Anatoly. For once I would be the one with the secrets and he would be the one to show his hand.

But as I watched him stare into the fire I wondered how much he had really kept from me. His lies had all been lies of omission and when I asked more pointed questions, he had answered them and every answer had checked out so far. What was it that made this man less worthy of my respect than Anatoly? Was it that he was currently with the mafia while Anatoly had left? Because really, even if Anatoly did leave the mafia, he was certainly back in the thick of it now.

"You never told me the real reason why they killed your brother," I said, quietly.

For a few seconds Alex just continued to stare into the fire. Then he walked over to the piano in the corner. "This was Kenya's piano." He let his fingers run over the smooth, polished wood. I hadn't noticed before but it shone like no other object in the room. It had been polished and cared for like... well like the memorial it probably was.

"I bought it for him," he continued. "He loved to play but he never had a decent piano."

"He had that one," I noted.

Alex shook his head. "I never got the chance to give it to him." After a moment's thought, he put his glass on top of the instrument. "It'll leave a ring," he said, softly. "I've been taking such good care of it but what's the point? If I had given it to Kenya, he would have treated it as carelessly as he treated everything else in his life... *including* his life."

"He was younger than you, right?"

Alex nodded. "Fawn's my mother's daughter and Kenya was my father's son. Maybe if my father was still around, he could have convinced the family to keep him alive."

"Why did they kill him, Alex?"

Alex picked up his drink and put it back down on another part of the piano. "They thought he helped Anatoly bring the FBI agent into the fold."

I hesitated, momentarily impressed. Once again his story was matching up with what I knew... sort of. Natasha had suggested that the mafia never suspected Anatoly at all, but still it was close enough, right?

He was telling me everything and Anatoly was telling me nothing.

"If you're serious about not wanting to reconcile with Anatoly... well, I respect that," he continued. "But if you know where he is I'd like to talk to him."

"Why?"

"I want to know if the mafia was right,' he said simply. "If Kenya really did help Anatoly bring that agent in then at least I'd know he wasn't killed for nothing."

"That still wouldn't make it okay for them to have killed him!"

"No... but if a soldier starts collaborating with the enemy, you can't exactly blame his battalion for dealing with him."

"You would forgive the mafia for killing your brother." That small flash of respect and trust I had felt flew out the window.

"No, but I would understand it." He turned to me with pleading eyes. "You have a sister, right? Can you imagine if she died and you weren't able to figure out why it had happened? I can't get him back. All I can get is understanding. I won't turn Anatoly in to the others but I deserve the truth. So do you."

And just like that, I was impressed again. "I don't know where he is."

Alex nodded and glanced at a clock hanging near the fireplace. "It's late. Perhaps we should both call it a night and talk more in the morning?"

I got to my feet. "When we talk in the morning, can we talk about Margarita?"

Alex smirked. "I'm not sleeping with her if that's what

you're wondering."

"Yeah, it wasn't. I was wondering why she was in my hotel lobby this morning and how it is that a housekeeper can afford expensive jewelry and designer apparel."

"Ah," Alex smiled again, this time ruefully. "Well, I said you deserved the truth. We'll talk about Margarita tomorrow. She works for me in several different capacities."

"Sounds kinky," I teased.

He laughed. "It's not, I promise you."

"OK, I'll take your word for it… for now. Thanks again for letting us stay here."

"Not a problem," he said, taking my now empty glass. As he opened the door for me, he chuckled. "I can't believe Natasha drove you all the way out to Red Rock Canyon just to make a point."

I stopped. "Did I tell you that she took me out to Red Rock?"

Alex blinked. "I'm sorry, I just assumed. There aren't too many national parks within driving distance of here."

"Oh, right." That made sense, right? After all, if he had been following me, he would have known that I had been with Anatoly at Red Rock, not Natasha.

We walked up the stairs together. The guest rooms Dena and I were staying in were to the right of the stairs and his room to the left, all the way at the other end of the hall. Again, I marveled at how large this house was.

He pulled me in for a hug and kissed me on the cheek. "You don't have to stay in the guestroom, you know," he said, teasingly.

I pulled away and stared up into those perfect green eyes. No, I didn't trust him. I wasn't sure if I even liked him.

But disliking him was getting harder. "I'm going to stick with the guestroom."

"Can't blame a guy for trying."

"Mmm," I said, noncommittally. I thought of Tanya in that closet, a bullet hole in her forehead. He had once planned to pin that murder on me... but he didn't. Did that count for anything?

"Goodnight Alex."

He stood at the top of the stairs and watched as I went into my room.

As I closed the door I got a text from Dena:

I'm back in my room and just got off the phone with Leah. Your mom found the USB stick.

CHAPTER
TWENTY-TWO

"I can rarely find the things I'm looking for but I fre-
quently stumble across things I forgot I lost."
—Death Of The Party

It was everything I could do not to rush back into the hall
and pound on Dena's door but I had to wait until I was sure
Alex was in his room. I sat down on the deep red area rug
and dialed her. "Tell me!" I whispered as she picked up.

"Did they really bug your house?" Dena asked cryptical-
ly. "Do you think they do that often?"

I looked around the room as if I was going to actually be
able to spot a recording device. "Um, who knows? I was just
calling to say goodnight."

"Night-night then," Dena said, cheerfully before hanging
up.

As soon as we were disconnected I sent her a text:

TELL ME!!!

Dena sent me a response so long it came in the form of
three consecutive texts. Basically Anatoly had cut out a
small section of a soccer book and put a USB stick in it.

Leah was now slowly walking my mother through the process of sending all the files on it as an attachment to Leah's email—with both my computers gone it was likely that my email account was compromised. Leah was working from the computers in Encore's business center and would send Dena the information for her to read from her iPad. Still, I shouldn't expect anything concrete until the morning.

The next series of texts explained that Dena had checked the rooms on our side of the staircase and found nothing of interest. Tomorrow she thought she might check everything on the other side if I could distract Alex again.

I was still dying to hightail it to her room but it seemed imprudent. After all, Alex thought Dena had been asleep for over an hour now. How would it look if he caught me rushing to her for a late night chat?

Reluctantly I sent her a text telling her to get some sleep. We set our alarms for five a.m. so we could talk and maybe do some more investigating before Alex woke up.

I glanced around my temporary bedroom. It was beautifully appointed with lots of dark leather and mahogany, just like everywhere else in the house. When we had first arrived, he made a point of asking if I needed a toothbrush or a bathrobe. I had already packed the former and didn't need the latter. My room had a bathroom attached to it while Dena was invited to use the bathroom a few doors down. There were a lot of bathrooms in this house. If he ever served bad fish at a dinner party, his guests would have no problem finding a private space to be sick in.

I locked my door and then stood by the window in my nightgown and looked out at the grounds. The sky was that dusky black color that allowed it to hide all its secrets.

Where was Anatoly now?

I opened the window so I could feel the cool air against my face. "Are you okay?" I whispered out into the dark. "Are you coming back to me?"

The wind whispered its reply but I couldn't make sense of it. The air was cold against my cheek. Not at all like a kiss or an assurance. Nothing I could hold onto.

I lay down in the bed. I wanted to feel him next to me. Instead, I squeezed one of the extra pillows to my chest and waited for sleep that I pretty much knew wasn't coming.

An hour passed, then two. A book would have helped. I could have asked Alex for a book. I was sure he was in bed by now, probably asleep. The house had that unnatural quiet that only comes after everyone has retired.

And if everyone was asleep then I should probably be awake looking through his things.

I picked up the gun and stepped out into the hallway. It was pitch black and I didn't know where the light switch was. I considered knocking on Dena's door but again decided not to. I owed her a few hours of uninterrupted sleep. I also needed to assure myself that Alex was asleep. If there was even a flicker of light under his door or any sound coming from his room other than snoring, I would get back to bed immediately.

I kept my hand against the wall to guide me. As I walked my eyes began to adjust. It felt weird, wearing a light, romantic nightgown, holding a gun and feeling my way around a strange house like a blind man.

I knew when I was close to his room, not because I could really see anything, but because I heard the voices. Alex's voice… and… and someone else's. I stood as still as a statue and strained to decipher the words. They were keeping their voices very low so it was hard. I held my breath and tried again.

Oh, now I knew why I wasn't picking up a single word. They were speaking in Spanish, Alex and Margarita.

Well that was hardly a surprise. I knew Margarita was too gorgeous for Alex to resist no matter what he said… except… the tones weren't right. There was nothing romantic or melodic in their murmurs, in fact, if I had to guess, I'd say she was pretty pissed and he was appeasing and… and nervous. This didn't sound like a lover's quarrel. I've had enough of those to recognize them in any language. This lacked the note of hysteria and personal pain that was universal to *those* kinds of arguments. In fact, if this conversation wasn't taking place in a bedroom in the middle of the night I might have thought it was a boss telling off an employee.

And what was *really* interesting was that I would have thought Margarita was the boss. I stepped a little closer to the door. I still couldn't understand the words but the *tones*… Alex wasn't just nervous… he was scared shitless.

If I was wrong and this *was* a lover's quarrel, then I had a lot to learn from Margarita. She *owned* his ass.

Margarita's voice was getting easier to hear… but she wasn't raising her volume. Oh shit, she was getting closer to the door. I jumped into another room and pressed myself up against the wall.

I could hear Margarita's heels click down the hallway. I waited for the sound of Alex following but it didn't come. After a few minutes, I thought I heard the sound of the front door opening and closing, but it was so faint I could have been wrong. A moment later I heard the sound of Alex's door closing. Two possibilities there, he had walked out of his room and closed the door behind him or he had closed himself in, which seemed more likely given the hour. Still, I couldn't afford to take a chance.

I stood there in the black room, stock still, and listened as my eyes once again adjusted to the darkness.

Unfortunately the only light was coming from the charcoal sky. I could see the outline of a desk against the window. That was about it. I took a couple of tentative steps forward, my bare feet felt the hardwood floor give way to a softer area rug and I scrunched up my toes against the fibers.

The house was silent again but I knew Alex was still awake. People didn't just go to sleep after arguments like that.

I could see a little more now. Shapes were coming into focus although the details still belonged to the darkness. When I got to the desk, my fingers brushed against the metal of a picture frame resting on top of it. I lifted it up and held it close to my face but I still couldn't see the people in it... assuming there *were* people in it. But I didn't know a lot of guys who had framed pictures of landscapes on their desks. Did Alex have a significant other? An estranged child? Was it a picture of his brother?

Could it be a picture of Fawn?

Unfortunately I had a gun, not a flashlight.

I felt my way around the desk and tried to open one of the drawers. It was locked. That was interesting. Obviously a lock wasn't going to keep the mafia out so perhaps the person who he was hiding something from was me. I moved my hand to the next drawer. It was shallow and I felt the thin oblong shapes of pens and the cool, metal curves of paper-clips. And then I felt something else... a lighter.

I smiled and carefully pulled it out. It took several flicks of my thumb before I got it to light and in the silence, every little click sounded like the pounding of a drum. But it did light and I held the small flame up to the frame. I could now make out Alex's face. The fire gave his green eyes an unnatural twinkle. And standing next to him was a man who looked like a younger version of Alex. He looked youthful and happy. He was leaning into Alex for the picture. Two brothers.

I couldn't help but notice that Alex's smile looked a little evil in the firelight.

And then I heard something.

I froze in place, my breath caught in my throat. I let the flame of the lighter die.

It was coming from Alex's room. It was soft and muffled and... and... mournful.

It was a sob. Alex was crying.

I put the frame back on the desk and fumbled for a moment as I struggled to find the exact spot where I found the lighter in order to replace it. Again my fingers moved over the paperclips. What could make a man who could speak so casually about murder cry? But it wasn't a question I could ask him. I wasn't supposed to be there, and I had to get back to my room before he wandered out of his bedroom for a just-need-to-dull-the-pain-cocktail. Unlike some psychiatrists, Dr. Vodka's always on call 24/7, ready to medicate.

I found the spot where the lighter belonged and was about to pull my hand away when I felt one more paperclip... this one oddly deformed. If I straightened it out could I unlock the drawer? I picked up the weird shaped paperclip but then thought better of it. Maybe I'd have a chance to try in the morning, but not now.

I don't know why but I held onto that paperclip as I tiptoed out of the room and walked down the dark hallway, the hardwood floor felt almost warm against my feet in comparison to the cool steel in my hand.

And as I crept away Alex's sobs followed me, providing a soundtrack to the night.

It wasn't until I was safely in my room that I was able to look at the oddly shaped paperclip by the light of my bedside lamp.

It was a paperclip shaped like a bone... exactly like the paperclip Dena had put on the strap of my computer case before it had been stolen.

CHAPTER
TWENTY-THREE

"Stalin and Hitler, John Gotti and Paul Castellano, Darth Vader and the Emperor, when are evil people going to learn to stop trusting each other?"
—*Death Of The Party*

This time I didn't hesitate to wake Dena up. I had to call her phone to get her to unlock her door, and when she did, I discovered she was fully dressed. "I can't go anywhere in a hurry," she explained, holding up her cane, "so I figured I'd sleep in my clothes to cut down on my prep time in case of an emergency."

"I've been thinking about it," I said as I breezed past her, "and I don't think Alex would bug his own house."

"Not even his guest rooms?" Dena asked, yawning. "Does this mean you're starting to trust him again?"

"He didn't know we were coming," I pointed out. "He couldn't have planned for it. And no, I don't trust him at all." I held out the bone paperclip for her inspection.

She took it from my hand and held it up to the light. "So?"

"So you put that on the strap of my MacBook case,

remember? I found it in Alex's office."

Dena stared at the paperclip. "Son of a bitch."

"Yeah, exactly."

"Did you look to see if your MacBook was in his office?"

I shook my head. "I had to get out of there. He's awake… and Margarita was here… maybe she still is."

Dena looked up from the paperclip. "Do *we* need to get out of here?"

"Are you kidding? We're so close!"

"To what? Getting your stuff back? Are we just going to find it, grab it, and make a run for it? I think we're going to have to come up with a plan that's a little more subtle."

"No, no, we're close to figuring out what's going on! Alex ordered someone to break into my hotel room. He had my MacBook stolen and I'll tell you something else, he knows I was at Red Rock Canyon." I told her about his little slip of the tongue.

"But he didn't know who you were there with? How is that possible?"

"I don't—"

"And," Dena interrupted, her expression thoughtful, "how is it possible that he knew you were in Mary Ann's room this morning?"

I hadn't thought of that. I sat down on the bed next to her. "He knows where I am but not necessarily who I'm with… he's tracking me."

"With what? You don't have a car here to put a tracking device on and even if you did you didn't drive up to Mary Ann's room."

"No," I said quietly, "the only thing I brought up to that

room was his gun, my purse, and my phone… last time I was here, he insisted that I keep my phone in a different room so it couldn't be used as a recording device."

"You can put tracking devices on phones, Sophie."

"Yes, you can."

Dena and I stared into space for a minute as we mulled this over.

"I think maybe we should leave," Dena said again. "And leave your phone here."

"Check your iPad. Find out if Leah sent you the information yet."

Dena got up and went over to her purse. She seemed a little shaky on her feet but I suspected that was due to nerves rather than any physical disability.

She pulled out the iPad and together we looked over her emails.

There was one from Leah.

She wrote a personal note berating me for not telling her where I was going ahead of time and to tell me that Marcus had a new friend named Bo whom she didn't like the look of. Then there were the files. I don't know what I was expecting. Not records of airline tickets to Mexico, that's for sure. The tickets were all for men with various Russian names and the tickets had been used seven years ago.

"So what?" Dena said aloud, articulating my own thoughts.

"It has to mean something." I stared fixedly at the files. "Where in Mexico is Abraham González International Airport?"

Dena did a quick Google search. "It's in some little city called Ciudad Juarez." she tapped a few more keys and stopped. Carefully she put the iPad down on her lap. "It's known for its drug cartels and extreme violence. It says it's considered the most dangerous city in Mexico."

I stared at Dena. I had asked Anatoly why the Russian Mafia was coming after him again after all these years. His answer had been "*It might not be them… not entirely.*"

"It seems there's been a war between two cartels in the area for years now," Dena went on. "Between a cartel known as *Ángeles de la Muerte* and another cartel known as *Los Tres Seises.*

The pounding of my heart echoed in my ears. "Tres Seises?" I repeated. Margarita's three diamond circles linked together on her pendant… each circle had six stones.

"It says that Los Tres Seises is one of the many cartels these days that's run by a woman."

Anatoly had said that revenge wasn't enough of a motive for Alex. There had to be more.

"Why are they fighting the Ángeles de la Muerte?" I asked.

Dena typed some more words into Google. "That's going to be hard to figure out," she admitted. "It's not like these guys keep public records of their conflicts… but I assume they're fighting over the things drug cartels usually fight about. Drugs and who gets to sell them where and to whom."

"Uh-huh." Natasha had said there would be a war. "This war between the two cartels," I said slowly, "when did it start, approximately."

Dena spent another few minutes searching Google. "Actually I can give you a definitive answer to that. The first truly public and violent battle between the two crime organizations was seven years ago on November 24th . Five innocent people, including a kid, were killed in the crossfire."

"What's the date of the return plane tickets Anatoly has on file?"

Dena pulled up the file again. "Not all of the guys who flew in have return tickets but the ones who did return by plane left seven years ago... November 23rd ."

"Dena, I think that file could spark a war between the Russian Mafia and Los Tres Seises Mexican cartel... and I think the head of Los Tres Seises was just in this house and is working with Alex."

Dena looked down at her iPad. "You know what I think?"

"What?"

"I think we need to get the hell out of here."

I took the iPad out of her hands and put it back in her purse. "Get your things together and I'll be back here in two minutes."

I went back to my room and quickly traded my nightgown for my jeans and a long sleeved tee. I purposely left my phone by the bedside. When I got back to Dena's room, she already had the duffle bag packed back up. I took it from her and held the gun in my free hand. "Come on," I whispered.

As quietly as possible we made our way to the stairs. As soon as we were about to descend, I heard his voice.

"Sneaking out in the middle of the night?" Both Dena and I turned toward him. He looked surprisingly composed for a man who had been sobbing less than twenty minutes ago.

I sucked in a sharp breath. "Look, I don't know why I

came here to begin with." I glanced at Dena and she nodded at me encouragingly. "I don't want to find Anatoly anymore so I don't need your help with that. I can't sleep and we've imposed on you enough."

"It hasn't been an imposition."

"That's sweet but really, we're just gonna head out. We'll find a coffee shop or something to hang out in until we're ready to head to the airport."

"Are you sure you don't want to find Anatoly?"

"I'm sure." I gestured for Dena to start down the stairs.

"Because I just found out where he is."

I froze in place, one foot hovering over the descending step. This time Dena shook her head and mouthed the word *no*. Staying there an extra second would be exceedingly stupid. But...

"Where?" I asked, softly.

"I just got the tip and mapped it out. Here, I'll show you." He started back to his bedroom and held the door open for us but we didn't take a single step toward him.

"Bring it out here to me," I said, warily.

"Come on, I've given you all the information you've asked for. I've 'fessed up to my role in things and I even gave you that gun you're holding."

I looked down at the weapon in my hand. "Is this the gun that killed Tanya?"

Alex laughed. "No, I think that was done with Anatoly's gun... maybe Natasha's. But I swear on my brother's grave that gun was never used in a crime."

"Sophie, we have to go," Dena reminded me.

"You're armed and I'm not, what are you afraid of?" Alex asked, clearly frustrated. Then he sighed and shrugged his shoulders. "You know what? Suit yourself. You said you didn't want to find him anymore so I guess this information is more useful to me than it is to you. Have a safe trip back to San Francisco."

"Wait!" I called out, finally taking a few steps toward his room.

Dena followed me and grabbed my arm. "Please tell me you're not this gullible."

I looked at Alex's hands. They were empty. He was right, I was armed and he wasn't. I didn't think Margarita had come back yet and he was holding open the door to his room... from what I could see there was no one else in it.

And this was Anatoly we were talking about.

"You have two minutes," I said striding into the room. Dena followed at my heels grumbling the whole way.

"Very well." Alex went over to his bedside table.

The same bedside table that I had found the other gun in before. "Stop!" I yelled holding my gun up. I cocked it, ready to shoot.

But he didn't wait. Perhaps he didn't think I would do it? In a second he had that drawer open the other gun was in his hand. But I didn't give him time to turn around.

I pointed the gun at his back and pulled the trigger.

There was a very brief flash that came from the barrel followed by a touch of smoke... but very little sound. Alex turned around, his own gun now pointing at Dena and me.

"It looks real, doesn't it?" he said with a smile. "It even feels real. I got it from a friend who works in Hollywood. Usually you can only rent non-guns that are so realistic, you know, for plays and film production purposes. Now this gun," he aimed to the right of me and shot a picture frame right off his dresser. The sound was deafening. "This one's real."

CHAPTER
TWENTY-FOUR

"I just learned that chaos theory has to do with physics and cosmology. I always assumed it was a metaphor for my life."
—Death Of The Party

I dropped my fake gun on the ground. "But... you let me take that gun before. The real one..."

"And I suspected I could get it back from you. I made a big show of taking the bullets out and proving to you that I didn't mean you any harm. After that display who could blame you for not examining that... prop more carefully."

"So you brought us in here to kill us?" Dena sounded so calm I half wondered if she was in shock. She put both hands on her cane and leaned her weight forward. "You could have done that while we were on the stairs."

"I don't want to shoot you. I want Anatoly."

"Get in line," I snapped. "I really don't know where he is."

"I believe you." His voice was deceptively kind. "I have an idea, why don't you two sit down here," he waved toward the bed, "and I'll tell you a—a bedtime story."

Keeping my eyes firmly on his, I walked over to the bed and sat down putting the duffle bag at my feet. Dena sat next to me.

"Seven years ago the... oh, let's call it the Ignatov *branch* of the Russian Mafia, was doing business with the Mexican Drug Cartel, Los Tres Seises. Los Tres Seises supplied and the Ignatovs sold. But at some point, some of the top members of the Ignatov family got themselves in a personal financial pickle. They had spent some money that wasn't theirs to spend. See, the Ignatovs are only one syndicate of the Russian Mafia. They don't run the whole show and they don't get to do whatever the hell they want. They have to work by the rules of our organization. The Ignatovs conveniently forgot that. They decided to get back the considerable amount of money they had lost by selling the drugs Los Tres Seises was going to supply without paying out the wholesale price."

"Stop being cute and get to the point," Dena growled. I turned toward her, truly impressed. But when I looked at Dena's face I didn't see calm. I saw intense anger.

"The Ignatovs managed to confiscate the drugs from Los Tres Seises," Alex said with a smile, "and they made it look like it was another cartel who stole them. While the cartels were fighting each other, the Ignatovs were selling the drugs without splitting the costs. Los Tres Seises was never the wiser... until I told them about it."

"When and why did you do that?" I asked.

"I did it after my brother was killed."

"So this *is* all about revenge?" I asked and shook my head. *Stupid, stupid, stupid!*

"No," Alex sighed, "it's about power. Los Tres Seises

will kill the top players in the Ignatov family, the ones who orchestrated this whole thing. The rest of the Russian Mafia will quickly become aware of the Ignatov's misuse of funds, and I will step in and engineer a peace between the mafia and Los Tres Seises again. Like I said, the mafia is a business. They want to deal with profits not criminal rivalries, and they're certainly not going to shed a lot of tears over some people who had secretly managed to betray their trust. When I get Los Tres Seises to back down and even reestablish a trade relationship with them, I'll be a hero to the mafia bosses. The Ignatov territory will be given to me to run and Los Tres Seises will work with me because they'll know that I owe my position to them. They'll be able to trust me and count on my business. A lot of drugs are sold through the Ignatov family's networks. We're a good account to have. There are a few people who work with the Ignatovs who I trusted enough to bring into my plan. Unfortunately, thanks to Natasha's interference, two of them are dead."

"Tanya and that guy Anatoly killed."

"Yes. Anatoly came back on Natasha's radar when I tried to convince everyone that he was the one to introduce Daniil to Kenya. She's been tracking his movements ever since, and when she found out he was in Vegas, she went to see him. She screwed everything up when she followed him to that room."

Dena made a face of disgust. "So, just to break this down, you don't give a shit about your brother being killed —"

"Of course I give a shit!" Alex shouted and for the first time, I saw the emotion that had elicited the previous sobs. "When I'm in control no one will ever, *ever* hurt those I care for again! The decision of who gets to live and who gets to die will be mine! I will have the power and the control and if you have that you have *everything*."

"Okay," I held up my hands in a plea for peace. "Why do you need Anatoly for any of this? Just have Los Tres Seises kill those who they need to kill and be done with it."

"Don't you see?" Alex asked, a hint of desperation creeping into his voice. "None of this works if the other people in the mafia aren't convinced the Ignatovs broke the rules. Not many people know about the drug theft in Mexico and only Anatoly has anything that will link them to it! If the mafia leaders believe that the cartel is just indiscriminately killing their members, there *will* be a full on war and no one will get ahead, least of all me."

"Ah." I clasped my hands in my lap. "You told the cartel about this before you realized you would need the proof. And now Los Tres Seises is threatening to kill you just for wasting their time, is that it?"

Alex flinched. "The situation doesn't need to be that dire. If Anatoly thinks I'm going to kill you, he will come forward with the evidence I need."

"And then you'll kill both of us?" I took Dena's hand. "You could have played that card a long time ago."

"I could have," Alex agreed. "But I don't *want* to." He went over to his closet and pulled out my MacBook. "If the information had been on here everything would have been fine. The whole point of this was to make sure those I care for remained safe. I care about you, Sophie. I shouldn't and I do."

"You care about her?" Dena spat. "You have a weird way of showing it. I mean this goes way beyond the whole

I'm-pulling-your-hair-because-I'm-crushing-on-you thing we all had to deal with in grade school. You're holding her and her best friend at gunpoint. You're setting up stupid, desperate traps at your hotel, traps that could have landed Sophie in prison or worse—"

"I didn't want to do this!" he yelled. It was the kind of yell that is so violent it brings an immediate silence.

"I told you," Alex said, this time quietly, "Anatoly is taking my choices away. He has to come forward with the evidence."

"But how is this going to get you Anatoly?" I asked, frantically. "None of us know where he is!"

"True," Alex said. He shifted the gun so it was directly pointing at Dena. "If one of your friends turns up dead it'll get back to him, wherever he is. He'll show up."

"No," I chocked. "Come on, Alex, please... don't do this."

"I know it'll hurt you." He stepped back and the broken glass from the picture frame crunched under his shoes. "Like I said, I'm running out of choices."

Dena put a hand self-consciously on her purse. "So if you had the information you would just let us go on our merry ol' way?"

Alex laughed, ruefully. "Well we'd have to work out an arrangement that would assure me that both of you would remain quiet about all this... but there are ways of doing that which don't involve pain or death."

Dena looked at me questioningly. I knew what she was thinking. Give him the iPad. We wouldn't be out of the woods but maybe we would be buying ourselves time. I don't know why, but I believed Alex when he said he didn't want to hurt me. Maybe that was stupid too, but to use his words, I didn't have a lot of choices.

"Alex," I said slowly, "I have—"

The door to the bedroom was thrown open and in walked Margarita with three men behind her. They all had tattoos on their arms and guns in their hands.

"Well will you look at this," Margarita purred. "The gang's all here!"

Her English was perfect.

"I have this under control," Alex said with gritted teeth.

"Do you?" Margarita asked. She walked up to him. I noticed now that she was the only one who didn't have a gun... she had a knife with a gracefully curved blade. She lifted that blade to his face as the men kept their guns trained on all of us and rubbed it against his cheek without cutting him. "You told me you had it under control when you got Anatoly to Vegas. You told me you had it under control when you lost him. You even told me you had it under control when you suggested I pretend to be your housekeeper. You know what I think?"

"That he doesn't have it under control?" Dena offered but quickly shut up when one of tattooed men took a step closer to her.

"I think," Margarita continued, gently taking Alex's gun from his hand and giving it to one of her companions, "that you should never send a boy to do a woman's job. I'm done playing your games. It's time to start cutting off a few of these ladies body parts and sending them to people who care. Maybe that'll get your Anatoly to step forward," she said, flashing me a smile. "If not, it'll still be fun."

"Margarita, if you would just let me tell you my plan—"

"Alex darling, I think we've all had enough of your plans."

"Hear me out for five minutes. It'll get you the proof you need and everything else that you want. Five minutes, Margarita."

Alex's expression was cool but I could hear the tremor in his voice.

"You want to talk?" She took a step back. "But I'm already bored."

"Just—"

"Five minutes, I heard you the first time." She looked back at the tattooed men and barked out some orders in Spanish.

Two of the men moved toward us, each one of them grabbing one of our arms. Dena struggled to balance herself and keep her injured back straight when one of the guys yanked her to her feet. I wanted to kill them for not being careful with her but I worried that calling more attention to her frailty would just egg on their cruelty. She clung to her cane, and I reached for the duffle bag, but they jerked me away from it causing my purse to fall to the ground.

"Where are you taking us?" I screamed as they pulled us away from our things. But the only answer they gave was to rip Dena's handbag from her arm and throw it toward the rest of our stuff before dragging us down the hall.

I really wished I had taken Spanish in school instead of French.

They pulled us back toward the guestroom I had been staying in and threw us both in before they stepped out and slammed the door closed.

I looked at the bedside table. My phone was gone. They

had thought of everything.

I felt sick. If they found the files on Dena's iPad, Margarita would just kill us. She was in charge now, not Alex... assuming Alex ever held any real authority at all. Margarita would torture Dena and me until she got what she wanted and then we would die.

I looked toward the window. Could we get out that way? Maybe if I tied the sheets together? That's how they always do it in the movies, right?

I struggled to open the window. "Help me!" I said, glancing back at Dena.

"Wait until we're sure they're not coming back in right away!" Dena insisted in a whisper. "We're not going to have a lot of chances here, we can *not* fuck them up!"

"Fine, I need to be patient. I'll just count to twenty and then I'll try the window, okay?" I crossed my arms over my chest. "One, two, three, four... nope, can't do it." I rushed right back to the window and this time I managed to pull it open. "I think we might be able to escape this way." I examined the moldings on the side of the buildings... and that tree, could we reach that tree and climb down it? I leaned out the window from my waist...

... and that's when I saw one of the men who had just thrown us in here walking out. He glanced up at the window I was hanging out of. Even in the darkness, I could clearly see his toothy grin as he waved his gun at me.

I pulled myself back in and closed the window. No doubt the other one was guarding the door.

Dena was standing in the middle of the room, as straight and unmoving as a Swiss soldier. "Dena, I'm so sorry I did this. I don't know how I'm going to protect you but I swear

I'm going to do it."

She didn't turn to look at me. Instead she reached inside the back of her shirt and pulled out her iPad. "Did you really think I was going to leave this in my purse?" She asked. "Obviously it would be the first place anyone would look."

I jumped forward and threw my arms around her before grabbing the iPad from her hand. "Can we email the police? How does that work? Is there any way to send a text from this?"

"It's not a phone, Sophie." Dena glanced at the door as she took her device back. "I kinda doubt the guys over at the 911 phone center have an IM account. But Marcus does."

She sat down and started typing away, faster than I'd ever seen her type.

"Email Leah too," I urged. I started opening drawers as quietly as possible. There had to be something I could use as a weapon. I felt like *such* an idiot. I had thought Alex had given me that gun to set me up for a crime and now I find out it wasn't even a real gun? Did the drugs Anatoly slipped me screw with my brain? How could I have not noticed that!

"I don't think we need to contact Leah," Dena whispered. She held up the iPad to show me Marcus' response:

> *Try to stay in that room for as long as possible,*
> *HELP IS ON THE WAY.*

Now it was my turn to cry. The hot tears burned my eyes and trickled down my cheeks. Maybe there was hope!

Out in the hall, I could hear Margarita's voice. She said something in Spanish and the man outside our door replied. I leaned in and listened to their short conversation that I couldn't understand and then the sound of Margarita's heeled shoes walking away. Dena tucked the iPad into the back of her pants, pulled her shirt over it again and I took several steps back. *Help was on the way. Everything was going to be okay.*

Everything *had* to be okay.

It became a little harder to convince myself of that when the door opened and the man walked in with a hand pruner. Usually a hand pruner is something you use to prune bushes by hand but I had a horrible feeling that today the name would have a double meaning. He clipped the blades together a few times for his own entertainment.

"Looks like we got a lead on where your boyfriend is," he said with a heavy accent. "Do you know which finger you want to send him? Your choice."

His gun was tucked in his waistband. How could I get it from him? Dena was a few feet to my right, her cane in her hand. I knew she was trying to figure out how to best use it as an effective weapon.

"You have a lead on Anatoly?" I asked, taking a step back. Maybe if I dived to the floor and tripped him? Then maybe I could get the gun. "Where is he?"

"Here."

I gasped and looked up at the doorway to see Anatoly. The tattooed man whirled around just in time to see the crowbar coming toward his head. He fell to the ground. Anatoly swiftly stepped inside and closed the door behind him before hitting him in the head again. Blood spurted out of his skull and Dena and I instinctively turned away.

When I turned back the man was either dead or close to it. "Help is on the way," I said, weakly.

In three swift steps Anatoly was in front of me. He pulled me into a brief, fierce embrace. "We have to get out of here, now."

He took the gun from the bloody man on the floor and went back to the doorway where he looked both ways before gesturing for us to follow him out.

"Did you come in the front or the back?" I asked.

"Back." Quietly, he pulled the door closed behind us. "I dragged the body of that guard into the bushes but they'll figure out what's going on soon."

"How many are there?"

Anatoly just shook his head as we crept down the stairs. He didn't know.

"How did Marcus know you were coming?" I whispered once we were almost at the bottom.

"Marcus?" he asked turning around to face me. Alarm registered in his expression as he looked behind me. "Move!" He grabbed both Dena and me and literally hurled us down the last few stairs as bullets flew above our heads. The iPad flew forward but Dena and I were the only ones to notice as Anatoly returned fire on yet another tattooed man. We grabbed the iPad and scrambled to the side of the room.

"Do we really need that anymore?" I asked breathlessly. "I think we may be past the point of IMing."

Dena just gave me a look before glancing toward the front door. It was still a ways away… and we were in serious danger of getting shot if we stayed in the open.

This time we didn't have to wait for Anatoly to tell us what to do. The little hall that led to the library was right next to us and we quickly ducked in there and ran to the room with the vodka. Anatoly was right behind us.

"You're giving up on your gun fight?" Dena yelled.

"He's on top of the stairs, that's sniper position." We got into the library and another man jumped up from one of the leather chairs. The fire raged in the fireplace behind him. He reached for his gun but Dena slammed down on his hand with her cane and before he could turn on her, Anatoly took his shot. The man fell, falling on top of Alex's sipping vodka. I started for his gun but the man who had been shooting at us from the top of the stairs was now in the doorway. Dena and I leaped behind the couch. The bay window was *right there*. We just had to break it and get the hell out of there!

Dena must have been thinking the same thing because she crawled to the widow and pounded on it using the metal jaguar of her cane. I had always assumed that windows were easy to break. People were always accidently crashing through them in movies but the force of Dena's blows seemed to only scratch this thing. I tried to peek around the couch to see Anatoly. He had taken a position behind a chair. He leaned out and took his shot... and he was out of bullets.

The sound of the trigger being pulled to no effect was by far the most horrifying thing I had ever heard... and it seemed to be becoming the night's theme. Dena was so busy pounding on the window she barely registered what was going on until the tattooed man came around the couch and put the gun to my head.

"I think my boss wants to talk to you," he said, looking straight at Anatoly. Dena stopped banging on the window and Anatoly stood with his hands up high enough for us to all see that they were empty.

"Don't hurt her," he said, softly.

The tattooed man laughed. "But the boss only wants to talk to *you*. We don't need the ladies."

I squeezed my eyes closed and tried to block out the feeling of the barrel pressed up so hard against my head. Would there be pain? Or just... nothing? He pulled the trigger...

... and he was out of bullets too. Anatoly dove for the gun by the corpse on top of the vodka bottle just as I elbowed the tattoo man to get free. In one shot Anatoly had him. The bullet sent him flying back into the window... that still didn't break.

He's the third person I've seen die in the last five minutes. I should be horrified, hysterical, throwing up, crying...

I turned to Dena and Anatoly. "I think maybe we should just try our luck with the front door."

I would worry about the possibility that I was a sociopath later. Right now we just had to get out.

Anatoly nodded and checked the chamber of his newly confiscated gun. "Damn it, he's out too." He knelt by the body, ready to search him for bullets.

"This is not how I planned our first meeting," Alex said as he entered the room. And of course he also had a gun... not the handgun he had waved at me before but a semiautomatic weapon.

Anatoly stopped searching the dead man.

"I imagined I would come to you," Alex went on. "I thought you'd be holed up somewhere with Natasha drinking cognac or something..."

"Where's Margarita?" I asked.

Alex turned to me, as if noting my presence of the first time. "She's upstairs. She'll stay there for now... I wouldn't have let her hurt you, Sophie."

I sucked in a sharp breath. "Oh my God, you are just such a typical man."

Alex looked down at his gun, then at the dead people on the floor and finally back up at me. "Excuse me?'"

"You're just telling me what you think I want to hear without any way to back it up! If Margarita wanted to hurt me, you'd be the last person to effectively stand in her way. You're like those guys who tell you they'll support you five minutes after the credit agency has repossessed their car!"

"She's right," Dena said, finally lowering her cane away from the window, "you're pretty typical."

"You have to trust me, Sophie—" Alex started, but I cut him off by breaking into hysterical laughter.

"Do you see these dead people? They work for your partner in crime and they just tried to kill me. It's not the kind of thing that inspires trust."

"Did you think she was stupid?" Anatoly muttered, but I whirled around and glared at him.

"Shut up, I don't trust you either at this point." I turned back to Alex. "Look, you want Anatoly because he has information, well guess what? I've got that information now too. If you want me to think you are anything short of a completely repugnant monster, then you'll take it and let us all go. *Then* you can talk to me about trust!"

"You don't have the information," Alex said, but I could tell he wasn't sure.

"Dena, do you still have your iPad?"

Dena looked around the room. "I dropped it somewhere... oh." She approached the body of the man who had crashed against the window and pulled her iPad out from underneath him. She looked a little sick to her stomach as she handed it to me.

I stared down at the body as I took the iPad from her. Perhaps I didn't feel upset about these men dying because they didn't seem like men to me. They were predators, weapons, nothing more than embodiments of a threat. Seeing their lifeless bodies was a relief. If that's what it meant to be a sociopath, then it was probably a pathology I could live with.

At that moment I wouldn't have minded seeing someone blow Alex's brains out either.

"What's on the iPad?" Alex asked, pulling me out of my thoughts.

"Evidence that the Ignatovs sent people down to Mexico the day those drugs were stolen from Los Tres Seises."

Alex's eyes widened and he took a step toward me but I leaped away from him, toward the fireplace. I held the iPad over the fire. "If you shoot me now, this will fall into the flames. Maybe it'll survive enough for you to retrieve the files or maybe it won't."

"I don't want to shoot you," Alex said quietly.

"That's good because I don't want to die."

"I wouldn't mind shooting him," Alex said moving the gun to point at Anatoly. "Maybe we can do a trade here."

I needed to stay calm. My ability to lie while staying cool was the only weapon I had at my disposal. "I told you, I'm done with him. But if someone was threatening to destroy evidence that I needed, I probably wouldn't shoot the only other person who was able to confirm that the evidence ever existed."

Alex considered that before moving the gun to point at

Dena. "What about your friend here? Seems to me there are three people in this room who can give me the details of what's in that file."

"If you shoot her I'm *definitely* going to destroy this thing and I will never tell Margarita or anyone else what was on that file. Not *ever,* Alex."

"Sophie," Alex said, almost pleadingly, "Margarita will have you tortured for it."

"And I still won't talk," I said, completely serious this time.

"So it seems we're at an impasse."

"It would seem."

I glanced at Anatoly. His back was to me. Dena could see his face and she seemed to be watching him intently. He was being awfully quiet. Maybe he was strategizing an attack? But I couldn't focus on that now. I had to play out my own hand.

"Any suggestions on how we get past this?" Alex asked.

"I know," Dena said. "We could start by letting me pour myself a glass of that cognac."

I blinked in surprise. That was such a me thing to say. Of course I would have asked for the vodka, but someone had died on it.

Alex chuckled, his eyes still on me. "I can see why you like her." He nodded at Dena. "Help yourself."

Carefully, Dena made her way across the room to the bar.

"What *exactly* is in the files?" Alex asked.

"Copies of airline tickets and records," Anatoly answered, even though he wasn't the one being addressed. "It proves that Vadim Ignatov purchased tickets for several of his men to go to Cuidad the day the drug shipment was taken. I can even show evidence that more income was coming into the Ignatov's coffers during the months that followed than there should have been considering that the shipment supposedly didn't arrive."

I hadn't seen that and I wondered if Anatoly was lying. I can't imagine that the drug dealers working for the Ignatovs kept receipts, but what did I know? Maybe the mafia had their own electronic inventory system.

"You want to start a war?" Anatoly continued. "I can give you that war. But I won't until the people I care about are safe."

"You're the only reason the people you care about are in danger," Alex countered. "But I'm not going to hurt Sophie. You however, are a liability."

"I can help you," Anatoly said.

Alex stared at him. For a moment the only sound in the room was the crackling of the fire and that of cognac being poured into a tall glass.

Who the hell pours cognac into a tall glass? How drunk was Dena going to get? I tried to make eye contact with her but she didn't look up from her task.

"You can't help me anymore," Alex said. "And even Sophie doesn't seem to care that much about protecting you. In fact," again Alex pointed the gun at Anatoly.

"Don't be stupid Alex," I hissed, but I knew my facade of cool was thinning. There was something in Alex's eyes. As far as I knew, Alex had never even met Anatoly before but for reasons beyond my understanding, he hated him enough to kill him.

The iPad was getting hot from being so close to the fire.

It was getting harder to hold. I glanced nervously at Dena... was she pouring herself a second glass of cognac?

"Think before you act, Alex," Anatoly said, his voice low, almost menacing. Impressive when you considered his position.

The sound of the front door opening and the urgent Spanish being called out in a male voice got all of our attention.

"Quick," Alex said in a hushed voice as he moved toward me, "give me the iPad now. I can protect you."

"Don't get closer or I drop it!" In a second I was going to have to drop it anyway. The metal was burning my fingers.

Alex hesitated and started to turn toward the door.

It was while he was turning that Dena leaped forward with a guttural cry of determination and pain and threw her two drinks in Alex's face.

He was drenched in alcohol, the right sleeve of his shirt was now dripping with it, but it was the cognac that got into his eyes that made him cry out, and it was the distraction that gave Anatoly the opportunity he needed to dive into him, knocking Alex backward. I saw the glint of a broken piece of glass from the vodka bottle as Anatoly cut Alex's arm with it.

As they both fell in my direction, Alex's gun went off in the air and I jumped out of the way, accidentally dropping the iPad in the fire.

But Alex still had the gun. He pulled the trigger again and I saw Anatoly's blood. I fell helplessly to my knees.

Anatoly tried to continue to fight but he was weakened. Alex twisted away from him and using his sleeve as a kind of oven mitt tried to quickly retrieve the iPad from the fire.

But here's the thing about cognac, it's highly flammable.

By the time Margarita's latest thug entered the room Alex was running around in a panic, screaming as he waved his now flaming arm in the air. He ripped the shirt from his body and threw it off of him... which set the curtains on fire.

In the chaos, Margarita's man didn't even notice that Dena was standing behind him. The silver jaguar on her cane proved to be much more effective on his head than on the window.

Alex was screaming in pain as Anatoly, Dena and I were running out of the room. Blood coated the right side of Anatoly's shirt but he was up and moving as if he was suffering from nothing more than painful cramps. Dena tried to help him, running forward to get the door even though I could tell that her own physical acts of self-defense had caused her to aggravate old injuries. What would be their condition when the adrenaline ran out? But I couldn't think ahead right now because I too was running on that same adrenaline.

And maybe that's why I barely registered the pain when Margarita came out of nowhere and grabbed me by the hair. I stomped on her foot and was able to turn around, but she hit me with the blunt end of the fake gun Alex had given me. In her other hand was the knife. She lifted it and from the corner of my eye, I could see Anatoly rushing toward me.

What I didn't see was Alex coming from the other side. He got there first and tackled her just as the knife was being lowered. I heard her scream. I smelled Alex's burnt flesh.

No one in my party had any interest in hanging out long enough to find out how the fight turned out. The room was already filling with smoke and both Dena and Anatoly were hurt. We rushed out the door into the yard. Anatoly took my hand as we approached the gate. I could hear the fire now as it consumed more of the house.

It was about then that we heard the sirens. Not just of the fire trucks but several police cars, black & whites as well as unmarked vehicles. In fact, there were already police cars all around that must have come in silently earlier on in the evening. It was from one of those unmarked vehicles that Bo-Bo the gay, Russian thug jumped out with a gun and screamed, "FBI, everybody get down!"

If I hadn't been so scared, frenzied, and exhausted, I think I would have laughed.

CHAPTER
TWENTY-FIVE

"I'm not a big fan of happy endings. They're too neat and too final. But I absolutely love happy new beginnings."
—Death Of The Party

The chaos that ensued was almost as harrowing as the chaos that proceeded. The firefighters ran in to try to save the house and the neighborhood and then Anatoly was whisked away to the hospital in an ambulance. They wouldn't let me go with him. That right there was more than enough to make me hysterical and Dena couldn't calm me because she was taken away to be examined by an EMT. It was Bo-Bo—AKA Agent Pearson—who took me aside to question me.

"You got yourself into a real mess, didn't you?" he said.

"Look, if you're going to book me with something then book me," I growled. "Otherwise let me go to Anatoly."

"I could book you with all sorts of things. What were you thinking, not reporting that body you found in The Hotel Noir?"

I bit down on my trembling lower lip. How did he know? Marcus? I would kill him.

"The thing is, the FBI has an arrangement with a friend of yours," he said.

"Who? Marcus?"

Bo-Bo gave me a look.

"Okay, then who?" I snapped right before the obvious dawned on me. "Anatoly?"

"He should have let us put him in protective custody from the get go." He glared at the smoldering house. "Then none of you would have been in this mess, but he was sure he could get the mafia to allow him to walk away from it all. The way he introduced our agent into the family—it *was* subtle. He arranged for what seemed like a chance meeting between our guy and this guy Innokenty Kinsky."

"Kenya."

"That's right. He gave our agent all the information he needed to get close to Kenya and it worked. It made it seem like our agent was actually being brought in by Kenya. Anatoly's hands were clean."

"How did you trick Natasha into hiring you?" I asked. I was cold... colder than I probably should have been based on the weather.

"Can't really get into that."

The smoke had gone from black to light grey as the flames died beneath the power of the firefighters' hoses. Out of the front door, a slightly singed Margarita was being led off in handcuffs.

"Anatoly told us about what happened between the mafia and Los Tres Seises too," he said, following my gaze. "But our goal was not to start a war between the Russians and a major drug cartel. We want to bring both crime organizations down but in a way that doesn't involve so much indiscriminate bloodshed."

"Well, it's all going to come out now," I said ruefully. *So cold.* I hugged myself for warmth.

"Yeah, but now Margarita has had several men attempt murder at her behest, on American soil, while she was on the premises. And we have that all on tape."

"There's no way you were able to bug Alex's house. That place has a crazy security system."

Bo-Bo shifted his weight and examined his nails.

My mind was beginning to work again. "You didn't bug his house... you bugged my purse when Natasha tried to kidnap Marcus and me. Wow, that was smooth—wait, if you could hear what was going on in there, why the hell didn't you come in earlier!"

"Well, we couldn't hear much. You left your purse in the room with Alex and Margarita. All we knew was that we had a hostage situation. We don't just burst in on hostage situations without figuring out what's going on."

"Yeah, well I think you might want to rethink those tactics! My friends and I were almost killed like, two dozen times!"

"You look like you did okay for yourself."

Frustrated, I turned away from him. And there was Margarita again, being forced into a police car. "So she's going to prison?" I asked, putting my frustration momentarily aside. "You won't strike up some kind of plea deal in exchange for information on her cartel?"

"She doesn't have that much to bargain with. It is, as you said, *her* cartel. She's the biggest fish we're gonna get out of this." He shrugged. "Maybe we'll spare her the death sentence for a list of names or somethin'. That's the best offer she'll get."

I nodded and glanced over at the ambulance where Dena was being evaluated. "Is she going to be okay?"

"She looks okay from here."

"I have to get to Anatoly."

"Sophie, you really could be in a lot of trouble here. You've done a lot of things wrong—"

"Under rather extreme circumstances," I pointed out.

"Look, if you cooperate, give a complete testimony and if…" Bo-Bo's voice faded and he leaned down and whispered in my ear, "if you say that you agreed to let me bug your purse, we'll give you a free pass."

I narrowed my eyes. "You didn't get a warrant to place it."

"I got it… but the problem is it didn't actually come through until after I did the placing." He smiled apologetically, but I could see the desperate plea in his eyes. "We really need the conversation we got between you, Alex, and Margarita to be admissible."

"Ah." Tonight I had seen a handful of men die, one set himself on fire, and a house come very close to burning down… and now I was smiling.

"I'll testify, although I don't really have anything on the mafia, just Alex and Margarita."

"That's enough."

Yes, it certainly was. I didn't really need to be the lead witness against an entire mafia. However, I could probably deal with testifying against an individual who had betrayed the mafia and the head of a drug cartel that might now become defunct.

Bo-Bo looked down at my arms. "Goosebumps. You're in shock."

"I want to see Anatoly. Now."

He nodded. "I'll drive you."

"Dena's coming too."

"She probably should go to the hospital anyway. I'll drive both of you unless the EMTs think she needs to go in the ambulance."

He unlocked the passenger side door and I got inside. Before he closed it for me, he leaned in again. "I need to ask you one more question, just between us."

"OK."

He looked around to ensure no one was within hearing distance before leaning in a little further. "Is Marcus single?"

Dena was well enough to ride in Bo-Bo's car with me and by the time we got to the hospital, Anatoly was already stitched up and doped up. The bullet had gone straight through without hitting anything vital. Given time he was going to be okay. When Dena heard this, she allowed a nurse to take her from my side so she could get a more thorough exam. I waited until she was out of sight and then just burst into tears. I sat in the waiting room sobbing like I had just been given the news that someone I loved had died. It had been too much. I was still hazy on what exactly had happened, and I couldn't believe how many times I had come *this close* to death within the last forty-eight hours. And then… when Anatoly was shot I had thought…

Even in my mind, I couldn't complete the sentence. I just cried harder still. The other people in the waiting room looked at me sympathetically at first and eventually they just averted their eyes. I thought about how I had sobbed after kicking Anatoly out. How could I have thought that was a catastrophe? I had been forced to deal with a million bigger catastrophes since then!

I was sobbing for at least ten minutes before I ran out of breath and energy. I gulped in some air and went to the bathroom to throw some water on my face before going to see Anatoly.

Lying in a white hospital bed in a white paper hospital gown, he looked more vulnerable than I had ever seen him. I sat by his side and stared into his glassy eyes.

"You and Dena… you saved me," I said softly, taking his hand.

"Are you going to forgive me now?" he asked in a slightly slurred speech.

"I'm sorry, I'm having a hard time understanding you. It's hard to talk when someone's drugged you, huh?"

"I take that as a no."

"Take it as a warning," I said with a little smile. "The way you handled this was seriously fucked up. One more strike and you're out for real."

"I wasn't supposed to tell you," he muttered. "They said not to tell anybody."

I repressed a giggle. I had never seen Anatoly stoned before. "I'm not going to ask if *they* represent the mafia or our government, because as far as I can tell they're both do-as-I-say-not-as-I-do kind of organizations. I, on the other hand, promise you that I will put you and the friends, family, and cat I love most before everyone else. I need you to promise me you'll do the same. If someone asks you not to tell me something you have to tell me anyway. That's what love and loyalty are all about. No secrets."

"Ok."

I wasn't sure if I believed him but decided it would be more effective to push the issue when he wasn't high. However, there was one thing that couldn't wait.

"Anatoly, I also need you to divorce your wife."

Through the fog of pain medicine, I could see a spark of cognizance. He understood the importance of what I was saying and when he squeezed my hand I knew he was aware of how much he had hurt me.

"As soon as I'm out of here we can go to the courthouse to file the papers."

I tilted my head and studied his complexion under the fluorescent light. Even here in this sterilized room in that stupid gown, he had a certain—radiance. Maybe he had started to use the Aveeno after all. We had such a unique relationship. Here he was asking me to go to city hall with him, not to get married but to witness him file for divorce.

"Will Natasha try to drag this out?"

Anatoly sighed. "I think Natasha's going to disappear."

"What makes you say that?"

"She made a major mistake and the mafia's going to find out about it. They're not going to cut her any breaks on this no matter whose daughter she is. She'll have to go on the lam."

"What kind of mistake?"

"I told you I needed to be with her in order to make this whole thing go away. What I didn't tell you is that one of the men working with her is an FBI agent. He's the one I was trying to stay close to. I knew he was our only chance of getting out of this. Either I would help him make the arrests necessary to get the pressure taken off of both of us or I would tell Natasha that she had hired an FBI agent into her protection service and would expose her mistake to the higher ups in the family if *she* didn't find a way to ensure your safety."

"That would have put Bo-Bo's life in danger."

"It would have, but he's a professional, capable of taking care of himself. My first and last concern was to keep you safe." He paused for a moment before adding, "Bo-Bo... that's what you and Marcus are calling him?"

"Yeah, turns out his real name is Agent Pearson. But to me, he'll always be Bo-Bo, the gay Russian thug."

Anatoly's mouth twitched at the corners and I giggled. Then he started to chuckle and soon we were both in hysterics. Perhaps the drugs were making him silly and I knew that I was at that point where almost anything could be silly, but hearing Anatoly laugh like that, here, safe, holding my hand... it just made me want to laugh more. Because it was funny and wonderful and everything I wanted...

Everything I wanted was right here, holding my hand.

When I left Anatoly's room, Dena was sitting in the waiting room. For the first time, I really saw the pain she was trying to hide. "How badly did you hurt yourself?" I asked, taking a seat beside her.

"It set me back a bit," she said casually, but you could hear the effort she was making to keep her voice from revealing the full extent of the truth. "They gave me some Vicodin, but I'm not gonna take it. I'll be relying on my cane a little more for the next few months."

"Dena, I'm so sorry I got you into this."

Dena toyed with her cane, letting it roll back and forth over the diamond pattern on the carpet. "You know, when it comes to their take on things like ethics and morality, I don't think there's a lot of daylight between Fawn and her brother."

"No, there isn't."

"In fact," Dena continued, "it's almost like he's the male version of Fawn. Alex *is* Fawn."

"Um, okay."

Dena's eyes had taken on a bit of a glaze as well, but I could tell this wasn't drug induced. She was reliving something, whether it was what had happened with Fawn or what had happened with Alex was unclear, but whatever it was, it wasn't exactly pleasant.

"When I threw that cognac on him, the cognac that temporarily blinded him, it was like I threw it on both of them. When it set on fire..." she faltered for a moment. There weren't many people in the waiting room now. A drunk in the corner had a magazine lying limply on his lap as he snored; a teenager by the wall bit her cuticles while watching some video on her phone. Dena's eyes drifted over them as she considered her next sentence. "I'm not some kind of medieval monster. It's not like I want to burn people at the stake."

"I know that."

"But—I'm glad I was there to fight him and—and what *they* represent. And I'm glad that *we* won. He was evil and I'm not sorry about what happened to him."

I nodded. Dena hadn't been helpless this time. That cane

that was supposed to represent her disability had disarmed one man and knocked another unconscious. As brutal as the night had been I could see that this was a multilayered victory. I had meant it when I told Anatoly that he *and* Dena had saved me. I owed my life to them.

But the thing is, I also sort of owed my life to Alex. He had tackled Margarita even when his skin was burned and the pain must have been unbearable. Dena and Anatoly had saved me out of love and maybe even virtue. But Alex? I suspected he had saved me due to something that resembled obsession. So I couldn't exactly be grateful to him for that… and I didn't really feel sorry about his pain.

But I wasn't exactly happy about it either.

And there had been another loss too. I raised my fingers to my temples as I thought about my lost manuscript. Maybe my MacBook had survived the fire. Maybe it would be retrieved by the authorities…

And maybe they would hold it as evidence for months on end. That would take me way past my deadline. I squeezed my eyes closed and silently cursed at myself. Anatoly was back with me and he was safe. All my friends were safe.

If someone gives you the moon, you can't complain because they didn't think to throw in the stars.

It was at that moment that Leah and Mary Ann burst in. "Oh my gosh, you're okay!" Mary Ann squealed and threw her arms around Dena who yelped in pain.

"Wait, you *are* okay, aren't you?" Mary Ann asked quickly stepping back.

"A little bruised and battered. Nothing that won't heal with time," Dena said with a dismissive wave that was completely contradicted by her wince.

"I thought you were going to call me when you needed my help!" Leah snapped.

"You did help. You sent me the information mama sent you. Why did she call you and not me, anyway?"

"Because she wanted *me* to tell her what was really going on!" Leah put both her hands on her hips, perfectly channeling the disapproving principle from any number of cartoons. Even the snoring drunk woke up and sat up a little straighter. "She trusts *me.* She knows that when things get a little crazy, *I'm* the one who's going to stay sane!"

That wasn't quite true. Leah was never exactly sane. She just didn't take the same over the top risks that I did... but there were extreme sports enthusiasts who wouldn't take the same kind of risks that I did, so that wasn't saying a lot.

"She called me because she expected me to be rational with an eye toward propriety, caution, and prudence and you know what I was doing when she called me, Sophie?"

I shook my head.

"I was gambling! While you were burning down a house full of people, I was playing blackjack!"

I repressed a smile and tried to give her a solemn stare. "Leah, I'm shocked."

Leah blinked and then immediately fell into the seat beside me and buried her face in her hands. "I have a problem."

"How much did you lose?" I asked.

"I won $39,000."

"*What?*"

Dena leaned forward, with effort, so she could see past me to Leah. "Did you say $39,000?"

"I kept thinking, *this is it*! I'm going to do something totally irresponsible and reckless! I'm going to lose a whole bunch of money and I was going to go home and tell everybody how crazy, irresponsible and out of control I was but then I won like, a whole bunch of hands of blackjack! And the worst part is that when the dealer pushed me to keep playing... you know, because the whole idea is to gamble away your winnings, that's what people *do* when they're being irresponsible... I couldn't do it! I cut my losses! I can't even gamble irresponsibly, Sophie! What is wrong with me?"

Dena leaned back in her chair. "Yeah, you've definitely got issues."

"How's Anatoly?" Mary Ann asked taking the seat next to Dena.

"He was shot and he's going to need a bit of healing time, but he's definitely going to be okay," I said.

"Oh wow, well at least he's going to be okay!" She smoothed the fabric of her skirt before adding, "How are *you* and Anatoly?"

I thought about that for a second. "We're going to need a bit of healing time, but we're definitely going to be okay."

Mary Ann clapped her hands together. "I knew you'd get back together! I knew it! True love always prevails! Ask Disney!"

Dena gritted her teeth. "You know, maybe I'll take that Vicodin after all."

I turned to Leah, who still had her head in her hands. "Where's Marcus?"

"On the way in here, we ran into that man... um—"

"Bo-Bo," I supplied.

"I don't think that's his real name."

"I keep telling people, once a Bo-Bo, always a Bo-Bo." I got to my feet. "Come on, let's find him and get Dena back to the hotel."

Everyone got up and filed out, with Leah and me taking up the rear.

"I can't believe I couldn't get myself to gamble at least some of it away," she moaned.

"Well," I said carefully, "at least you got it on with an octopus. Not very many people can say that."

"I don't know what you're talking about," Leah said, her volume a little louder than necessary, "but it sounds absolutely vile." Then she added in a hushed voice, "I wasn't kidding when I said I'll kill you if you tell anyone! Unlike some people here, I have a reputation to maintain!"

I smiled to myself. Yeah, *she* was the sane one.

I went back to the hotel with my friends. The sun was almost up and they had a flight to take them back to San Francisco later in the afternoon, but everyone needed a nap first. Dena took my room and Bo-Bo agreed to hang out with Marcus in his room—just for added security of course. I had booked a flight back the following day when Anatoly would be able to fly. As soon as I had made arrangements with the hotel to stay an extra night, I was ready to go back to the hospital to be with him. But before I was able to leave Bo-Bo pulled me aside in the hall outside my room. "You're still going to testify, right?"

"You just give me the whens and wheres and I'll be there. I want to be sure Margarita and Alex are put away for the rest of their lives… or at least for the rest of mine."

"Yeah," Bo-Bo muttered. I watched him shift his weight

from foot to foot.

"What's going on?" I asked, suddenly feeling a little paranoid.

"Look, Margarita's locked up and she's not going anywhere, ever."

"And Alex?"

Again, Bo-Bo shifted his weight. "We didn't find him."

"What!"

"We will!" Bo-Bo added quickly. "But it was a chaotic scene, you know? There was a fire, there were dead bodies and we didn't know at first how many we were looking for and then, somehow in all that, he managed to slip out."

"He was burnt! His right arm was, like, crispy!"

"That'll just make it easier to find him. Course, guys like that always know unlicensed doctors who will see them in some backroom for cash payments, if you know what I mean. Still, we'll find him."

My heart was beating a little faster again. "I'm going back to Anatoly. Find him soon, okay? Like really soon."

"We got all our best guys on this. We'll get him and you'll put him away."

I nodded and went back to the hospital to see Anatoly.

When I got back to the hospital, I found that they had moved Anatoly out of the emergency room and put him in a room on a higher floor that was marginally less cold and sterile. He was sound asleep when I got there and I took a moment to confer with the nurse in the hall about his condition. She didn't really want to talk to me since I wasn't technically family but she gave me a very basic rundown before briskly walking away. I took a deep breath and turned to go back into Anatoly's room.

"Excuse me, are you Sophie Katz?"

For a second I panicked, thinking about my first meeting with Natasha. Slowly I turned around. But of course it wasn't Natasha at all. This woman had a chestnut bob and obviously fake boobs.

"I'm Sophie," I said, trying to push aside the déjà vu feeling.

"Some guy just paid me $250 bucks to give you this."

And that's when I noticed my MacBook carrying case over her shoulder. I stood stock still as she handed it to me along with an envelope.

"Is he here?" I asked quietly.

"I don't think so. He handed it to me when I came in and told me where I'd find you. He seemed like he was in a hurry to get some place and he kinda looked like he was in pain too. But hey, for $250 I don't ask a lotta questions."

I opened the carrying case. That was my computer all right. I opened the envelope and pulled out a 3x5 note card.

I meant to tell you that I read your unfinished manuscript. It's quite good. Can't wait to see how the story ends.

'til next time.

—A

I stared at the note.

'til next time.

Swiftly I walked back to Anatoly's room. Was he really okay? Had Alex been here too?

I walked right up to his bedside and considered waking him up. But as I watched his chest rise and fall in the even breathing patterns of sleep I found myself becoming almost mesmerized and… calm. Anatoly was fine. As Marcus would say, he was so very, very fine.

How many times had I lost myself in his arms?

How many times would I do it again?

At least once… every day for the rest of my life.

I put my purse, the MacBook, and the note on a chair and carefully crawled into bed with him, choosing the side that wasn't injured. Without opening his eyes, he pulled me to him, allowing me to gently put my head on his shoulder.

"Are you awake?" I whispered.

"If I am, will you get out of bed?"

"Maybe."

"Then I'm asleep."

I smiled as he pulled me closer and kissed my hair.

If I had to, I'd deal with Alex later. But right now…

My smile widened as Anatoly's hand moved down to my butt.

Right now I had the only man I wanted and he was wearing nothing but a thin paper gown that didn't even cover that perfect ass of his.

Yeah, I wasn't going anywhere.

 **ABOUT THE AUTHOR**

Kyra Davis is the New York Times and USA Today best-selling author of the *Sophie Katz Mystery* series and the *Just One Night* series, The *Pure Sin* series, and the stand-alone novel, *So Much For My Happy Ending.* Her books have been translated and published in seventeen different countries. After spending the majority of her life in the Bay Area, Davis now lives in Los Angeles County with her husband, son, fabulous dogs, and an endearing but occasionally moody leopard gecko.

Find out more about Kyra Davis and her books at www.kyradavis.com